Seasonal Southwest Cooking

Seasonal Southwest Cooking

Contemporary Recipes & Menus For Every Occasion

BY BARBARA POOL FENZL

FOREWORD BY JACQUES PÉPIN

FOOD PHOTOGRAPHY BY CHRISTOPHER MARCHETTI

Northland Publishing

www.northlandbooks.com

Composed in the United States of America
Printed in China

Edited by Tammy Gales-Biber
Designed by Katie Jennings
Food Photography by Christopher Marchetti

FIRST IMPRESSION 2005
ISBN 13: 978-0-87358-882-9 (HC)
ISBN 10: 0-87358-882-7 (HC)

09   08   07   06   5   4   3   2

Library of Congress Cataloging-in-Publication Data

Fenzl, Barbara.
Seasonal Southwest Cooking : contemporary recipes and menus for every occasion / by Barbara Pool Fenzl.
p. cm.
1. Cookery, American–Southwestern style. 2. Menus. I. Title.

TX715.2.S69F483 2005
641.5979–dc22
2005040569

FRONTISPIECE: *Monument Valley at sunset, the Mittens and Merrick Butte*

PAGES VI-VII: *Grand Canyon from Mather Point, stormy sunset*

PAGES VIII-IX: *Island in the Sky at sunset with summer storm clouds, Canyonlands National Park*

The following recipes or versions of the following recipes were originally published by Barbara Pool Fenzl in *Bon Appétit*:

Goat Cheese and Shrimp Stuffed Poblanos
    with Red Bell Pepper Sauce
Tomato, Hominy, and Chile Soup
Chilled Tomatillo and Cucumber Soup
Jicama, Orange, and Nopalitos Salad
Achiote Butter-Basted Turkey with Ancho Gravy
Cranberry Relish
Chipotle Glazed Shrimp
Cowboy Beans (Previously printed as Ranch Beans)
Mashed Potatoes with Cheddar Cheese and Poblano Chiles
Chipotle Cornbread
Cornbread Pecan Stuffing
Cumin Rolls
Pecan and Chocolate Pie

A version of the following recipe was originally published by Barbara Pool Fenzl in *Outdoor Style* by Suzanne Pickett Martinson, published by Northland Publishing:

Grilled Portabello Mushroom and
    Roasted Red Bell Pepper Sandwiches

Publisher's Note: The recipes contained in this book are to be followed exactly as written. Neither the publisher nor the author is responsible for your specific health or allergy needs that may require medical supervision, or for any adverse reactions to the recipes contained in this book.

We would like to offer a special thank you to Aunt Maude of Aunt Maude's Antique Mall and to George Averbeck of Fire on the Mountain Gallery for letting us photograph their beautiful wares.

To Julia Child, my friend and mentor.
I miss you very much.

—B. P. F.

CONTENTS

IX   FOREWORD

I   INTRODUCTION

2   Seasonal Menus

15   Appetizers

41   Soups

61   Salads

79   Entrées

121   Vegetables

143   Breads

157   Desserts

184   ACKNOWLEDGEMENTS

185   RESOURCES

186   INDEX

FOREWORD BY *Jacques Pépin*

THERE IS NOTHING BETTER THAN COOKING with friends—unless it is sharing the food after you cook with friends. This is why I always look forward to going to Phoenix to cook and share food with Barbara Fenzl and her family.

I have taught at Barbara's Les Gourmettes Cooking School for more than 20 years, and now, although I have very little time to teach in private cooking schools, I still go to Les Gourmettes because I always have fun sharing food ideas and cooking with Barbara, as well as learning from her.

Seasonal Southwest Cooking is a polished, elegant, and very personal cookbook with spicy accents of the Southwest, where Barbara's expertise is undeniable. In this new, original work, her knowledge as a cooking teacher is apparent; she presents simple, well-explained, and trustworthy recipes in an easy way that entices people to make them in their own kitchens.

I am always surprised to realize how eclectic the cooking of the Southwest can be in expert hands and how important the seasons are in that part of the world and in Barbara's dishes. I can enjoy Poblano Chile and Smoked Salmon Toasts any time of the year, but the Cream of Chayote Soup is perfect for a fall menu, and the Artichoke Quesadillas are an excellent spring dish. I also love the Pulled Pork, a fall dish, and her new,

intriguing Duck Breasts with Hot Orange Sauce for the winter holiday season. I have personally enjoyed many of the appetizers and hors d'oeuvres like the Scallop Seviche, the Hand-Mixed Guacamole, the Tostaditas of Shrimp, which are ideal for a buffet, and the Oyster Shooters along with a lot of tequila and beer.

However, *Seasonal Southwest Cooking* is more than a cookbook full of reliable and flavorful recipes. The culinary and cultural sidebars scattered throughout the book offer great insight into Native American legends and regional food. These are welcome additions that enable you to understand the depth of the recipes, the culture behind them, and the native lore, history, and origins of the ingredients.

Of the plethora of cookbooks that are published each year, not many are as well thought out, original, and reliable as *Seasonal Southwest Cooking*. I know that you will have as much fun cooking from it as I have had and in sharing the food with friends and family.

INTRODUCTION

LIVING IN THE SONORAN DESERT for over 36 years has given me a deep appreciation for the culture and cuisine of the Southwest. I am constantly inspired by the vibrant colors and flavors of our food, the outdoor lifestyle that fosters casual entertaining, our rich Native American heritage, and the breathtaking beauty of our surroundings.

Because I love to entertain, I wrote this book for those who also like to gather family and friends around a table, whether once a year or every night of the week. The recipes are designed to produce vivid flavors in an eye-appealing manner without requiring you to spend all day in the kitchen. And even though they are innovative and contemporary, they honor and preserve the past.

At the same time, many of the recipes are intended to showcase seasonal, locally-grown ingredients, which not only make meals more varied and exciting, but also provide reasons to look forward to each unique time of year. Keeping the seasons in mind, I have put together twelve menus for special gatherings with the hope that you will adapt them to your own preferences, locales, customs, and cherished occasions.

In addition to 150 recipes and twelve seasonal menus, I've included some bits of culture to add perspective to the recipes and provide a few insights into this fascinating part of the world. For instance, there's quite a bit of information on chiles, for which I've developed an insatiable appetite and appreciation. Besides keeping me healthy, I've discovered they can keep my weight under control because they increase metabolism, so I use them, rather than fat, to add flavor to many dishes. And the cultural extras don't stop with chiles–you'll find countless Southwest secrets scattered generously throughout the following pages.

It is a joy to cook and share my recipes with others, so I hope you'll join me in a journey through the seasons, when every day is a reason to celebrate.

DINNER TO START THE *New Year* ON A HEALTHY NOTE

SPICED ALMONDS

A sampling of lightly-spiced almonds seasoned with the bold flavors of cumin and cayenne.

YOU'LL-NEVER-MISS-THE-MEAT CHILI

A hearty, zesty chili filled with roasted Anaheim and serrano chiles, Great Northern beans, garlic, black olives, and corn all infused with fresh cilantro and oregano.

JICAMA, ORANGE, AND NOPALITOS SALAD

A light, refreshing salad of strips of tart cactus pads, crispy jicama and succulent naval oranges.

MARGARITA AND CHILE POACHED PEARS WITH PEAR AND RASPBERRY COULIS

A mouth-watering dessert made with a poaching liquid from rich ancho chiles, tequila, and lime juice.

Sunrise over Grand Canyon from Mather Point

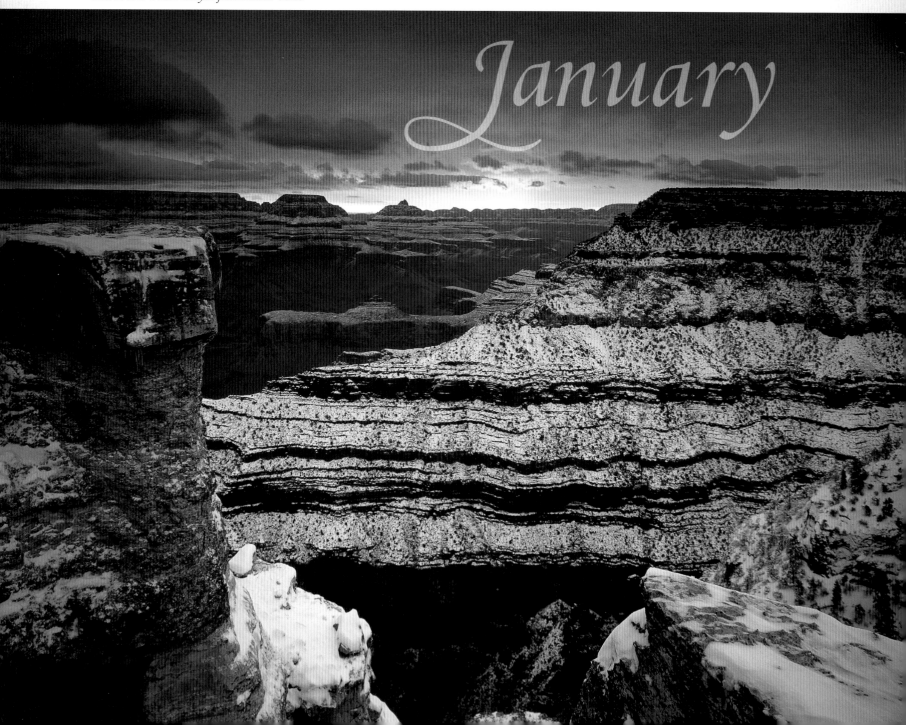

January

A winter storm at dusk over the mesquite-covered grasslands near Madera Canyon, Coronado National Forest

February

ROMANTIC *Valentine* SOIRÉE FOR TWO

❄

POBLANO CHILE AND SMOKED SALMON TOASTS
A delicious appetizer featuring rich poblano chile and smoked salmon, perfectly accentuated by tangy Dijon mustard and a hint of lime.

BLOODY MARY SOUP WITH AVOCADO MOUSSE
A spicy, hearty soup complemented by light and creamy avocado mousse.

DUCK BREASTS WITH HOT ORANGE SAUCE
Succulent breast of duck marinated in an intense habanero chile and tangy orange sauce.

STUFFED CHAYOTE SQUASH
Subtlety-flavored chayote squash brimming with crispy red bell peppers, salty cheese, and sweet corn.

DULCE DE LECHE AND CHOCOLATE MOUSSE
Sumptuous, creamy mousse combining the rich flavors of chocolate and caramel.

Après *Ski* Dinner

❋

Bacon, Avocado, and Raspberry Quesadillas with Chipotle Sauce
Crisp bacon, creamy avocado, smooth cheese, and smoky raspberry sauce encased in a whole wheat flour tortilla.

Beef and Black Bean Chili
Earthy black beans and browned steak cubes slowly simmered with dark beer, spices, mild chiles, and lemony tomatillos.

Greens with Ancho Dressing, Blue Cheese, and Toasted Pecans
Tender young salad greens, buttery pecans, and rich blue cheese tossed with a creamy ancho chile dressing.

Cheddar Cornmeal Biscuits
Slightly crunchy biscuits with a slightly sweet, tangy flavor.

Pecan and Chocolate Pie
Rich, decadent chocolate combined with buttery pecans in a flaky crust.

Owl clover by Stewart Mountain Lake with Four Peaks in background

March

Après *Ski* Dinner

Senita cactus with sand verbena, daisies, and poppies, Viscaino Desert, Baja California, Mexico

CELEBRATION OF *Spring* BUFFET

ARTICHOKE QUESADILLAS
Toasted flour tortillas filled with artichoke hearts, cheese, pungent basil, and piquant poblano chiles.

SHRIMP TORTILLA SOUP
Succulent tomatoes, tart lime, and cubes of avocado in a vegetable broth, all finished with plump shrimp and crisp tortilla strips.

CHICKEN FAJITA SALAD
Lime-marinated and seared chicken strips, roasted red bell peppers and poblano chiles, yellow tomatoes, Cotija cheese, and julienned tortillas over a bed of crisp salad greens tossed with silky avocado dressing.

SONORAN PASTA
Grilled sweet peppers, smoky poblanos, sharp white onion, and corn mixed with smoked chicken breast, cilantro, and tangy cheese served over rich pasta.

CHIPOTLE CORNBREAD
Moist cornbread with a hint of smoky, sweet heat.

CHOCOLATE BANANA BREAD PUDDING WITH BANANA CARAMEL SAUCE
Pieces of moist, dense chocolate banana bread baked in a silky custard and served with a sweet caramel sauce studded with plump bananas.

A carpet of owl clover dot the landscape in the glow of the Red Rocks around Sedona, Arizona

May

Mother's Day BRUNCH

MARINATED SHRIMP WITH RAINBOW VEGETABLES

Crunchy chayote squash, crispy carrots, sweet bell pepper, and avocado over a bed of Romaine lettuce and topped with zesty shrimp.

BLUEBERRY CORNMEAL PANCAKES WITH BLUEBERRY SYRUP

Melt-in-your-mouth pancakes full of blueberries, served with a syrup of sweet blueberries and maple.

GRITS WITH ATTITUDE

Velvety grits flavored with snappy poblano pieces and nutty cumin.

FIESTA FRUIT SALAD

Sweet melons and blueberries combined with lime juice, salty cheese, and tangy cilantro.

FROZEN LIME PIE

Creamy, tart lime filling in a gingerbread crust.

Father's Day BARBECUE

CHICKEN CHIPOTLE NACHOS WITH AVOCADO CREAM

Shredded chicken, smoky chiles, and mild cheese melted on crisp tortilla rounds and drizzled with luscious avocado sauce.

GRILLED SHRIMP SALAD

Plump shrimp, chayote squash, and onion marinated in spicy pickling liquid, grilled, and placed atop lettuce, juicy tomatoes and cooling avocado that have been tossed in a cream chile ranch dressing.

SPICY LAMB CHOPS

Flavorful, meaty lamb chops grilled with a zippy coating of cilantro, garlic, spices, and olive oil.

TOMATOES STUFFED WITH QUESO FRESCO AND CILANTRO

Broiled juicy, ripe tomatoes filled with fresh, tangy cheese, pungent cilantro, and mild red onion.

SKILLET CORNBREAD

Moist and hearty cornbread with crispy bacon, sharp Cheddar cheese, and piquant poblano.

GRILLED BANANAS WITH BUTTER PECAN EL DIABLO ICE CREAM AND MEXICAN CHOCOLATE SAUCE

Warm, honey-coated bananas with buttery, slightly spicy ice cream and cinnamony chocolate sauce.

Saguaro cactus, jumping cholla, sunset, the Bates Mountains in the distance, Organ Pipe National Monument

June

July

Fourth of July Picnic

✸

Chilled Tomatillo and Cucumber Soup

Lemony tomatillos, crunchy cucumbers, piquant chiles, and mild green onions blended to create a light, silky soup with a subtle heat.

Southwest Club Wraps

Succulent turkey, crisp bacon, juicy tomatoes, sumptuous guacamole, smoky chipotle mayonnaise, and tender greens rolled in a flour tortilla.

Tri-Color Potato Salad

Purple potatoes, red potatoes, and waxy creamer potatoes combined with hard-cooked eggs, sweet red bell peppers, blue cheese, and crunchy red onions coated with a slightly smoky, subtly hot, creamy dressing.

Cotija and Cherry Tomato Salad

Sweet, ripe tomatoes, pungent cilantro, tangy cheese, and red onions tossed in a balsamic vinaigrette.

Red, White, and Blue Tart

Buttery tart shell with a hint of lemon filled with plump blueberries in a cinnamony sour cream filling and topped with rings of raspberries.

A rainbow appears as a summer storm moves through the Canyon, Shoshone Point, South Rim of Grand Canyon National Park

Seafood Extravaganza Under the Stars

CREAMY CRAB ON CORN PANCAKES

Light, silver dollar-sized corn pancakes topped with a creamy blend of succulent lump crabmeat, earthy cumin, chipotle chile, and zesty lime.

OYSTER SHOOTERS

Briny oysters served in a shot glass with piquant tomato juice, pepper vodka, and zippy horseradish.

SANGRITA CRAB COCKTAIL

Plump, juicy crabmeat in citrusy, piquant tomato juice, garnished with cilantro.

FISH IN CORNHUSKS WITH ORANGE-TOMATO SALSA

Fish fillets glazed with zesty cilantro and pecan pesto, cooked in corn husks, and accompanied by a sweet-tart orange and tomato salsa.

SANTA FE SLAW WITH CARAMELIZED PECANS

Crispy cabbage, sweet red bell pepper, carrots, radishes, and jicama veiled in a light, lime/chipotle vinaigrette and studded with sweet, crunchy pecans.

PEACH AND CINNAMON CRISP SUNDAES

Vanilla ice cream topped with tender peaches, cinnamon sauce, and cinnamon graham cracker crunch.

August

Prairie sunflowers and San Francisco Peaks, near Flagstaff

September

Ladies *Tennis* Luncheon

❧

Chilled Red Bell Pepper Soup with Basil Cream

Light, vibrant, and velvety sweet, this citrusy soup is drizzled with verdant basil cream.

Individual Serrano Soufflés on Greens with Pears and Piñon Nuts

Tender baby greens in a raspberry walnut dressing, bedecked with an airy, nutty cheese soufflé, lush pear slices, and delicate pine nuts.

Apple Pecan Bread with Cinnamon Butter

Sweet, moist loaf bread studded with pecans and tart apples, served with silky cinnamon butter.

Chocolate Flan with Dulce de Leche

Satiny chocolate custard baked in caramel and dolloped with caramel-flavored whipped cream.

A mature sycamore tree amid brilliant orange canyon maple in Miller Canyon

October

AFTER-A-HIKE-IN-THE-AUTUMN-WOODS *Hearthside* DINNER

CILANTRO AND PECAN PESTO ON GOAT CHEESE TOASTS

Pungent cilantro, peppery parsley, salty Cotija cheese, spices, fruity olive oil, and buttery pecans pureéd and paired with a tangy cheese spread on crispy slices of baguette.

BLACK BEAN SOUP WITH LIME CREAM

Sublime, all vegetable black bean soup drizzled with tart lime cream.

SPICE-RUBBED BUFFALO TENDERLOIN WITH PORCINI BUTTER

Tender, melt-in-your-mouth bison, coated with spices, pan fried and baked to medium, topped with a medallion of earthy mushroom butter.

MASHED POTATOES WITH CHEDDAR CHEESE AND POBLANO CHILES

Creamy mashed potatoes flavored with sharp Cheddar cheese and rich poblano chiles.

SAUTÉ OF TOMATOES, CORN, AND EDAMAME

Vibrant, fresh soybeans, plump corn kernels, and zesty tomatoes tossed with Southwest spices and sautéed until crisp-tender.

PUMPKIN GINGER LAYER CAKE

Moist, tangy pumpkin cake enhanced with fresh ginger and spread with a cream cheese and crystallized ginger frosting.

Southwest-Style *Thanksgiving*

✳

Pumpkin and Ginger Soup with Toasted Pepitas

A peppery, slightly sweet, velvety soup topped with crunchy, delicate pumpkin seeds.

Achiote Butter-Basted Turkey with Ancho Gravy

Succulent turkey basted with butter creamed together with chiles, spices, and achiote seeds; dotted with drippings blended with masa harina, stock, and a purée of fruity ancho chiles and rich poblanos.

Cornbread Pecan Stuffing

Moist cornbread made with spicy chorizo, sweet red bell pepper, savory herbs, and buttery-rich pecans.

Cranberry Relish

Chopped red bell peppers, oranges, and hazelnuts paired with cranberries, cilantro, and diced poblanos.

Green Beans with Shallots and Chile Oil

Fork-tender green beans and sliced shallots glazed with fiery chile oil.

Butternut Squash with Blue Cheese and Walnuts

Salty, creamy blue cheese and plump, meaty walnuts encased in soft, sweet butternut squash.

Gingerbread-Crusted Apple Tart

Juicy apples dotted with savory serranos in a spicy gingerbread crust under a crunchy oatmeal and toasted almond topping.

White Sands National Monument, dusk over yucca and gypsum dunes

November

Winter view of San Francisco Peaks, near Hidden Hollow

Holiday OPEN HOUSE

❄

LAYERED AVOCADO, SOUR CREAM, AND RED BELL PEPPER MOLD

An eye-catching round made of three layers: avocados, sour cream and onions, and sweet red bell peppers.

WHITE BEAN DIP WITH CUMIN TORTILLA CHIPS

Puréed white beans, spices, and chile accompanied by crunchy cumin-flavored tortilla chips.

ROASTED JALAPEÑOS AND SOUTHWEST HUMMUS ON PITA TOASTS

Chipotle-flavored hummus on toasted pita chips, garnished with roasted and diced fiery jalapeños.

PIQUANT PEPITAS

Hulled pumpkin seeds tossed in frothy egg whites and Southwest spices, then baked until crisp.

WILD MUSHROOM TOASTS

Meaty, earthy mushrooms slowly simmered in butter and cream, spread atop slices of toasted baguette.

CREAM OF CHAYOTE SOUP

Delicate and velvety chayote squash soup, freshened with tangy cilantro and mellowed with rich cream.

CHIPOTLE-GLAZED SHRIMP

Marinated plump shrimp, grilled and glazed with a smoky, spicy, citrusy sauce.

PULLED PORK

Pork loin on a bed of onions and dried cherries, braised with a fruity ancho and tart cider sauce until tender, then shredded into its mouth-watering juices.

CHICKEN MOLE

Chicken slow-cooked in a complex sauce of fruity chiles, chocolate, almonds, plump raisins, and spices.

LEMON BIZCOCHITOS

Crisp, buttery-rich, melt-in-you-mouth cookies with a hint of tart lemon.

DOUBLE CHOCOLATE, ANCHO CHILE, AND ALMOND TART

Intense, rich chocolate crust filled with a sumptuous chocolate ganache studded with almonds.

Appetizers

CHICKEN CHIPOTLE *Nachos* WITH AVOCADO CREAM

The smokiness of the chipotle and the creaminess of the avocado come together in a winning combination in this zesty appetizer. This is a great way to use leftover chicken or turkey. ❀ SPRING

WITH AN ELECTRIC MIXER, cream together the cooked chicken, cream cheese, chipotles, onion, garlic, cumin, Monterey Jack, salt, and pepper. Blend well. Cover and refrigerate until ready to use, but bring to room temperature before assembling so the mixture is spreadable.

PREPARE THE AVOCADO CREAM. In a medium bowl, mix together all the ingredients and refrigerate, covered, until ready to use.

Preheat broiler. Evenly spread each chip with a generous amount of the chicken chipotle mixture. Arrange chips on a baking sheet and broil about 3 minutes away from the heat until puffed and golden. Transfer nachos to a platter and top each with a teaspoon of Avocado Cream and a leaf of fresh cilantro. Serve warm.

1 cup shredded cooked chicken breast
8 ounces cream cheese, softened
2 chipotle chiles in adobo sauce, chopped
3 tablespoons finely chopped red onion
2 cloves garlic, finely chopped
1 teaspoon cumin seed, toasted and ground
1 ½ cups grated Monterey Jack cheese
Salt and freshly ground pepper

AVOCADO CREAM
½ cup peeled, pitted, and finely diced avocado
2 tablespoons sour cream
1 tablespoon fresh lime juice
1 tablespoon finely chopped cilantro
1 tablespoon milk
Salt

Approximately 6 dozen flat tortilla chips
   (2 ½-inches wide)
72 fresh cilantro leaves

Makes about 72 Appetizers

PAGES 14-15: *Snow-capped saguaro cactus in Tucson, Arizona, with Windmill and Rincon Mountains in background*

Goat Cheese Crisps with
Smoked Salmon and Roasted Peppers

This is not only a delicious beginning to a southwestern meal, but it is also a lovely luncheon or brunch entrée, especially when complemented by a soup or salad. ❋ SPRING

PREHEAT THE BROILER. Put tortillas on a baking sheet and broil about 3 inches away from the heat until browned on one side. Remove from the oven and turn tortillas over. Spread the untoasted side of each tortilla with ¼ of the goat cheese. Evenly divide the poblano strips, red pepper strips, and the green onions among the tortillas, placing them on top of the goat cheese. Put tortillas back under the broiler and heat just until cheese is melted, about 2 minutes. Remove from the oven and top each tortilla with ¼ of the smoked salmon strips. Cut each into 12 wedges and serve immediately.

4 (8-inch) flour tortillas
1 (11-ounce) log mild goat cheese, at
    room temperature
1 poblano chile, roasted, peeled, and cut into
    strips (see page 47)
1 red bell pepper, roasted, peeled, and cut into
    strips (see page 47)
¼ cup chopped green onions
4 ounces smoked salmon, cut into strips

Makes 8 Servings

Artichoke *Quesadillas*

These little treats are so easy to make and always get rave reviews. Serve them with soup or salad for a light summer dinner. ❋ SPRING

WITH A FOOD PROCESSOR RUNNING, add the garlic clove through the feed tube until it is finely chopped. Add the drained artichoke hearts and the basil; pulse until mixture is finely chopped. (This can be prepared a few days ahead, covered, and chilled).

Spread one half of each tortilla with a few tablespoons of the artichoke mixture. Sprinkle about ⅓ cup of the grated cheese over the artichoke spread. Arrange a few strips of chile over the cheese. Fold tortillas in half over the filling and brush both sides with some of the reserved artichoke marinade. Heat a large non-stick skillet over medium-high heat. Put 2 to 3 quesadillas

into the skillet and cook until one side is lightly browned, about 2 minutes. Turn each quesadilla over and cook until golden, about 2 to 3 minutes more. Remove from skillet and cut into 4 to 6 wedges. Repeat with remaining quesadillas.

1 large clove garlic, peeled
2 (6-ounce) jars marinated artichoke hearts,
    drained and liquid reserved
6 large basil leaves, cut in chiffonade
6 (8- to 10-inch) flour tortillas
2 cups grated Queso Quesadilla (or substitute
    Monterey Jack)
1 poblano chile, roasted, peeled, and cut into thin
    strips (see page 47)

Makes 4 to 6 Servings

OPPOSITE: *Agaves on the South Rim of the Chisos Mountains, with the Sierra Quemada below, and the Rio Grande and Mexico in the distance, Big Bend National Park*

Mexican Cheeses

IN THE SOUTHWEST UNITED STATES most mainstream and specialty grocery stores carry Mexican cheeses, so if you can find them, use them! They make Southwest dishes taste so much more authentic and exciting. However, if they are not available, more familiar cheeses such as Monterey Jack and Cheddar can usually be substituted.

HERE ARE SOME BASIC DESCRIPTIONS of the Mexican cheeses used in this book:

ASADERO: a mild, soft cheese with the flavor of provolone and the texture of mozzarella. It melts well and is a good cooking cheese, especially in quesadillas and enchiladas.

COTIJA: a firm, very salty cheese similar to dry feta. It is used crumbled and sprinkled like a condiment over soups, salads, and beans or in baked dishes.

PANELA: a mild, moist cheese with a sweet, fresh milk flavor. It does not melt easily so it is often used in cooked foods, sandwiches, salads and with fruit.

QUESO FRESCO: a soft, moist cheese with a mild saltiness and slight acidity. It crumbles easily and does not melt so it is often used as a topping or filling in cooked dishes.

QUESO QUESADILLA: a light yellow, mild cheese that melts well but doesn't ooze, making it perfect for quesadillas and other grilled dishes.

BACON, AVOCADO, AND RASPBERRY
Quesadillas WITH CHIPOTLE SAUCE

The sauce that is spread on the tortillas before the filling is added gives these quesadillas a unique and wonderful taste. Happily, this recipe makes more sauce than you'll actually need, and because it's so good, I also use it as a sauce for grilled chicken or pork tenderloin. ❄ WINTER

TO PREPARE THE CHIPOTLE SAUCE, put all sauce ingredients in a blender and purée. Strain into a medium bowl. Cover and refrigerate until ready to use.

Lay the tortillas on a work surface. Over the entire surface of each tortilla, spread about 1 tablespoon of Chipotle Sauce. Over one half of each tortilla sprinkle some onions, cheese, and bacon, dividing evenly. Cover with a few slices of avocado. Fold the unfilled tortilla halves over the filled halves and, if made ahead of time, cover and refrigerate.

Heat a large skillet over medium heat. Add the quesadillas and cook until the bottom side is lightly browned, about 2 minutes. Turn the quesadillas over and continue cooking until cheese is melted and tortillas are golden brown, another 2 to 3 minutes. Cut each quesadilla into 4 wedges and serve immediately.

CHIPOTLE SAUCE
1 (12-ounce) package frozen raspberries, thawed
3 tablespoons raspberry jam
¼ cup port wine
1 chipotle chile in adobo sauce, coarsely chopped

4 (8-inch) wheat tortillas
4 green onions, finely chopped
1 ½ cups coarsely grated Asadero cheese
   (or substitute Monterey Jack)
6 slices bacon, crisply cooked, well-drained,
   and chopped
1 avocado, peeled, pitted, and thinly sliced

Makes 4 to 6 Servings

White Bean Dip with Cumin Tortilla Chips

It's always nice to offer crudités with a flavorful dip for those watching their diets or for vegetarian guests. As a change from the usual celery and carrot sticks, I cut up chayote squash, jicama, and bell peppers into strips for dipping. These cumin tortilla chips go beautifully with this bean dip and are healthier than the store-bought version because they're baked, not fried. ❄ WINTER

TO PREPARE THE DIP, with the machine running, add the garlic through the feed tube of a food processor. Remove top and add the remaining ingredients. Purée until smooth and transfer to a serving bowl. Cover and refrigerate until ready to serve.

TO PREPARE THE CHIPS, preheat oven to 400°F. Stack the tortillas on top of each other and, using a sharp knife, cut the stack into 12 wedges. You should have 60 tortilla pieces. Spread them out on baking sheets and spray with vegetable spray. Bake until light brown, about 6 to 8 minutes.

Meanwhile, put the cumin seeds in a small, dry skillet and toast over medium heat until a shade darker, about 3 minutes. Transfer to a spice grinder and process until finely ground. Set aside. When tortillas are finished baking, remove them from the oven and immediately sprinkle them with the toasted, ground cumin and salt. Cool slightly. Serve dip in a decorative bowl surrounded by warm chips.

1 clove garlic, peeled
1 (15-ounce) can Great Northern beans, rinsed and drained
¼ cup chopped fresh cilantro
1 tablespoon fresh lime juice
1 ½ tablespoons olive oil
½ teaspoon chile powder
½ teaspoon ground cumin
1 teaspoon salt
1 teaspoon chopped serrano chile

CUMIN TORTILLA CHIPS
5 (8-inch) flour tortillas
Vegetable oil cooking spray
1 tablespoon cumin seeds
2 teaspoons kosher salt

Makes about 1 ½ Cups Dip and 60 Chips

HAND-MIXED *Guacamole*

I like my guacamole to have some texture to it so I always mix it by hand, not in a food processor. It's best to use Haas avocados because of their superior flavor and texture. This dip is delicious with tortillas chips or raw vegetables, but in the Southwest, it's also used as a garnish for just about any type of tortilla dish—fajitas, tostadas, tacos, and flautas.
✻ SPRING

IN A MEDIUM GLASS OR CERAMIC BOWL, mash the avocados with the back of a fork. Sprinkle with lime juice and salt and mix again. Add serrano, tomato, garlic, green onions, and sour cream and stir until mixture holds together. If not using right away, place plastic wrap on the surface of the guacamole (air is what causes it to turn brown) and refrigerate. Bring it back to room temperature before serving.

2 ripe Haas avocados, peeled and pitted
2 teaspoons fresh lime juice
1 ½ teaspoons salt
1 serrano chile, seeded and diced
¼ cup seeded and diced tomato
1 teaspoon finely chopped garlic
2 tablespoons diced green onions
¼ cup sour cream

NOTE: *Avocados need to be fairly soft for good guacamole, and grocery stores often have only very hard ones. To ripen them more quickly, put them in a brown paper bag with a ripe banana (bananas give off the same ripening gas as avocados) and store in a dark place until they are soft enough, usually 24 to 48 hours.*

Makes 4 to 6 Servings

YELLOW TOMATO *Salsa*

With juicy, flavorful heirloom tomatoes now available at farmers markets and specialty grocery stores, it's a joy to make homemade salsa. Celebrate summer with this yellow tomato version, which is delicious on its own served with blue corn chips or is a terrific accompaniment to a piece of grilled fish or chicken.
☀ SUMMER

IN A MEDIUM GLASS BOWL, combine all the ingredients, except for the blue corn chips, and allow flavors to blend for at least 30 minutes. Place salsa in a serving bowl on a large platter and surround with blue corn chips.

NOTE: *Salsas are best served within a few hours of being made. The components start to break down and get mushy after that.*

2 ½ cups seeded and diced yellow tomatoes
   (2 large or 3 medium tomatoes)
1 serrano chile, seeded and finely chopped
1 clove garlic, finely chopped
1 tablespoon fresh lime juice
1 teaspoon sugar
¼ cup diced red onion
1 tablespoon chopped cilantro
Salt and freshly ground pepper
Blue corn chips

Makes about 2 ½ Cups

OPPOSITE: *Snow blankets an agave at Maricopa Point on the South Rim of the Grand Canyon with Zoroaster Temple in background*

ROASTED JALAPEÑOS AND SOUTHWEST *Hummus* ON PITA TOASTS

Putting a chipotle chile in this Southwest version of hummus gives it added zing. The flatbread is toasted, spread with the hummus, and topped with roasted jalapeños, the green version of the chipotle. Some people may want a bit less heat, so you may prefer to pass a bowl of jalapeños for individual serving.
✳ WINTER

WITH A FOOD PROCESSOR RUNNING, put the garlic through the feed tube until it is finely chopped. Add the beans, lemon juice, olive and sesame oils, chipotle, cumin, bell pepper, and cilantro. Purée. Gradually add the water through the feed tube until the hummus is the desired consistency. You may need to add more water. Add salt and freshly ground pepper to taste.

Preheat an oven to 350°F. Place the pita rounds on a baking sheet and toast until crisp, about 10 minutes.

Spread about 1 tablespoon of hummus on each toasted round and sprinkle a few pieces of roasted jalapeño over each one.

SOUTHWEST HUMMUS
1 clove garlic, peeled
1 (15-ounce) can garbanzo beans, drained
   and rinsed
2 tablespoons fresh lemon juice
1 tablespoon olive oil
1 teaspoon sesame oil
1 chipotle chile in adobo sauce
1 teaspoon toasted and ground cumin
1 red bell pepper, roasted, peeled, and seeded
   (see page 47)
2 tablespoons chopped cilantro
3 tablespoons water
Salt and freshly ground pepper

12 mini whole wheat pita pockets, cut in
   half horizontally
6 large jalapeños, roasted, peeled, seeded,
   and diced (see page 47)

Makes about 24 Appetizers

Layered Avocado, Sour Cream, and Red Bell Pepper Mold

With its red and green colors, this three-layered mold, which is served with crackers, bread, chips, or crudités, is a beautiful addition to a holiday cocktail buffet. Since they are the same colors that are in the Mexican flag, it could also be part of a fiesta or a Cinco de Mayo celebration. ❋ WINTER

LIGHTLY OIL AN 8-INCH SPRINGFORM PAN. Put cold water and gelatin in a small saucepan; when gelatin is softened, heat the mixture over low heat until the gelatin is liquefied. Set aside; the gelatin will be divided among the three layers.

TO MAKE THE AVOCADO LAYER, put 1 of the avocados, the green onion, lemon juice, mayonnaise, salt, and hot pepper sauce into the bowl of a food processor. Purée. Transfer to a bowl. Cut the second avocado into ¼-inch cubes and stir it, along with 1 tablespoon of the gelatin, into the purée. Spread the mixture evenly over the bottom of the springform pan. Refrigerate while making the next layer.

TO MAKE THE SOUR CREAM LAYER, in a medium bowl, stir together the sour cream, onion, and 2 tablespoons of the gelatin. Spread over the avocado layer and refrigerate.

TO MAKE THE RED BELL PEPPER LAYER, put the bell peppers, red onion, mayonnaise, cumin, salt, and hot pepper sauce into the bowl of a food processor; purée. Transfer to a bowl and stir in the remaining gelatin. Spread the mixture over the sour cream layer; cover and refrigerate until firm, at least 6 hours.

To serve, remove the sides of the springform pan. Place the mold, still on the base of the pan, on a decorative platter and surround with crackers, cocktail rye bread, raw vegetables, or tortilla chips.

¼ cup cold water
1 package unflavored gelatin

AVOCADO LAYER
2 large avocados, peeled and pitted
¼ cup diced green onion
2 tablespoons fresh lemon juice
2 tablespoons mayonnaise
1 teaspoon salt
⅛ teaspoon hot pepper sauce

SOUR CREAM LAYER
1 cup sour cream
¼ cup finely chopped onion

RED BELL PEPPER LAYER
3 red bell peppers, roasted, peeled, and seeded
   (see page 47)
¼ cup finely chopped red onion
2 tablespoons mayonnaise
½ teaspoon toasted, ground cumin seed
½ teaspoon salt
⅛ teaspoon hot pepper sauce

Makes 1 (8-inch) Mold, about 1 quart

CREAMY CRAB ON CORN *Pancakes*

Succulent crabmeat blended with cream cheese and spices makes a yummy topping for these light, silver dollar-size pancakes. It's an elegant appetizer worthy of any cocktail party. ☼ SUMMER

WITH AN ELECTRIC MIXER, beat together cream cheese, mayonnaise, chipotle, and cumin in a medium bowl. Turn mixer to low and mix in crabmeat, green onions, cilantro, and lime zest. Season to taste with salt and pepper.

TO PREPARE THE CORN PANCAKES, in a medium bowl, stir together the cornmeal, flour, salt, baking powder, and sugar. In a glass measuring cup or small bowl, mix together the egg, butter, and buttermilk. Add wet mixture to the dry ingredients and blend well; fold in green onions and jalapeño.

Heat a medium nonstick skillet over medium heat and spray lightly with vegetable oil. Drop batter by teaspoonfuls into the pan, forming circles 1 ½ to 2 inches in diameter. Cook until golden brown, turning once. Remove and cool on a wire rack.

Spread each pancake with some of the crab mixture and garnish with a cilantro leaf. Serve on a decorative platter.

1 (3-ounce) package cream cheese
¼ cup mayonnaise
1 teaspoon finely chopped canned chipotle chile
    in adobo sauce
½ teaspoon ground cumin
½ pound fresh lump crabmeat
¼ cup finely chopped green onions
1 tablespoon chopped cilantro
1 teaspoon grated lime zest
Salt and freshly ground pepper

CORN PANCAKES
¼ cup cornmeal
¼ cup all-purpose flour
½ teaspoon salt
1 teaspoon baking powder
2 teaspoons sugar
1 egg
1 tablespoon melted butter
½ cup buttermilk
2 tablespoons finely chopped green onions
1 teaspoon finely chopped jalapeño chile
Vegetable oil cooking spray

36 cilantro leaves

Makes about 36 Appetizers

SCALLOP *Seviche*

Light and refreshing, seviche is a classic in Mexico and the Southwest region of the United States. This version uses small bay scallops, which don't need to be cut and can be easily eaten with a cocktail fork.
☼ SUMMER

BRING A MEDIUM POT OF WATER TO A BOIL over high heat. Add the scallops and boil for 1 minute. Drain and put in a non-reactive bowl. Pour lime juice over the scallops and add remaining ingredients. Stir, cover, and refrigerate for 2 hours. The action of the acid in the lime juice "cooks" the scallops, firming the flesh and turning it opaque. Spoon equal amounts into 6 martini or margarita glasses and serve immediately.

1 pound small bay scallops
½ cup fresh lime juice
½ cup diced tomato
½ cup diced red onion
1 serrano chile, seeded and finely diced
1 poblano chile, roasted, peeled, seeded, and diced (see page 47)
¼ cup chopped cilantro
Salt and freshly ground pepper

Makes 6 Servings

Sangrita Crab *Cocktail*

Sangrita is often drunk as a chaser to a shot of tequila to temper the fiery liquid. Here, it's used in this recipe as a lovely base for a crab cocktail. Make it a few hours ahead so the flavors can marry, and serve it in martini glasses with a cocktail fork.

☼ SUMMER

HEAT A HEAVY SKILLET OVER MEDIUM HEAT. Stem the ancho chile, slit it open, remove all seeds, and flatten it. Add the ancho to the hot skillet and toast until fragrant, about 1 minute. Turn it over and toast the other side, another minute. Remove from the pan and cool. When cool, tear into small pieces.

Put the juices, onion, Worcestershire sauce, and ancho pieces into a blender. Purée and strain into a medium bowl; season with salt and pepper. Refrigerate for 2 hours or overnight.

Ladle sangrita into 6 martini glasses. Divide crab among the glasses and top each with a sprig of cilantro. Serve immediately.

SANGRITA
1 ancho chile
1 cup tomato juice
1 cup fresh orange juice
¼ cup fresh lime juice
2 tablespoons finely chopped onion
1 teaspoon Worcestershire sauce
Salt and pepper

½ pound lump crabmeat, broken into pieces
6 sprigs fresh cilantro

Makes 6 Servings

Havasu Falls below a blue sky framed by cottonwood trees, Havasupai Indian Reservation

OYSTER *Shooters*

If you have access to fresh oysters, this recipe offers a unique, fun way to serve them. Pepper vodka is available in most grocery and liquor stores, but it's also easy to make your own. Simply put 1 teaspoon crushed red chiles in one cup of vodka, cover, and allow to steep for 1 week (or longer if you want hotter vodka). Strain the mixture and keep the vodka indefinitely. ✦ FALL

LINE UP FOUR SHOT GLASSES or other small glasses. Put a tablespoon of tomato juice in each one and top with a tablespoon of vodka and a dash of hot pepper sauce. Place an oyster in each glass and top with a dab of horseradish and a few chopped green onions. Serve immediately.

¼ cup tomato juice
¼ cup pepper vodka
½ teaspoon hot sauce
4 oysters, shucked
1 teaspoon horseradish
2 teaspoons diced green onions

Makes 4 Servings

Tostaditas OF GUACAMOLE AND SHRIMP

Guacamole is addictive on its own, but if you want to dress it up a bit, make these ambrosial little tostadas to wow your guests. ✿ SPRING

IN A MEDIUM BOWL, mix together the chopped shrimp, tomato, jalapeño, and red onion. Drizzle lime juice and olive oil over the mixture and stir well. Season to taste with salt and pepper.

Spread each tortilla chip with about 1 tablespoon of guacamole. Top each with a spoonful of the shrimp mixture. Put on a serving plate and serve immediately.

1 cup chopped cooked shrimp
⅓ cup seeded and diced plum tomato
1 jalapeño chile, seeded and diced
2 tablespoons diced red onion
2 teaspoons fresh lime juice
2 teaspoons olive oil
Salt and freshly ground pepper
32 (2 ½-inch) round, flat tortilla chips
2 cups Hand-Mixed Guacamole (see page 22)

Makes about 32 Appetizers

GOAT CHEESE AND *Shrimp* STUFFED POBLANOS WITH RED BELL PEPPER SAUCE

Colorful and absolutely scrumptious, these stuffed peppers are a great first course or luncheon entrée. You may get so hooked on them that you'll want to try variations by substituting cooked chicken or crabmeat for the shrimp. 🌿 FALL

PREHEAT OVEN TO 350°F. Carefully slit the poblanos down one side and remove the seeds, leaving the stems attached. In a medium mixing bowl, combine the goat cheese, Panela cheese, shrimp, shallots, bell pepper, cilantro, and basil. Season with salt and pepper to taste; mix well. Stuff the chiles with the mixture, being careful not to overfill. Pulling the slit together, close the poblanos. (These stuffed chiles can be made a day ahead of time and refrigerated). Transfer to a baking sheet and place in the oven for 10 minutes until just slightly warm.

MEANWHILE, PREPARE THE RED BELL PEPPER SAUCE. In a medium skillet, heat the olive oil. Add the garlic, shallots, and serrano and sauté until shallots are tender, about 5 minutes.

Transfer mixture to a blender; add roasted red peppers and chicken stock. Blend until smooth. Season to taste with salt and pepper. (The sauce can be made a day ahead of time and refrigerated). Pour sauce back into the skillet and warm slightly before serving.

Ladle about 3 tablespoons of sauce onto each serving plate, and place a warm stuffed poblano on top of the sauce.

8 poblano chiles with stems left intact, roasted and peeled (see page 47)
4 ounces mild goat cheese
½ cup grated Panela cheese (or substitute Monterey Jack)
½ pound cooked shrimp, peeled, deveined, and chopped
1 tablespoon chopped shallots
¼ cup diced red bell pepper
1 tablespoon chopped fresh cilantro
1 tablespoon chopped fresh basil
Salt and freshly ground black pepper

RED BELL PEPPER SAUCE
1 tablespoon olive oil
2 cloves garlic, finely chopped
¼ cup chopped shallots
1 serrano chile, seeded and finely chopped
2 large red bell peppers, roasted, peeled, and seeded (see page 47)
1 cup chicken stock
Salt and freshly ground black pepper

Makes 8 Servings

MARINATED *Shrimp*
WITH RAINBOW VEGETABLES

This colorful first course is as delicious as it is beautiful. Chayote squash, also known as a vegetable pear, is called a mirliton in the South. Rather bland itself, it is a good vehicle for other flavors and adds a nice texture to dishes. ☼ SUMMER

TO PREPARE THE MARINADE, combine vinegar, lime juice, shallots, garlic, serrano, cayenne, cumin, and salt in a medium bowl; slowly whisk in the olive oil.

Pour half the marinade into a bowl; add the shrimp. Reserve the remaining marinade to use as dressing on the vegetables. Cover and refrigerate the marinated shrimp for 1 to 3 hours.

MEANWHILE, PREPARE THE RAINBOW VEGETABLES. In a large bowl, combine all the vegetable ingredients and add just enough of the reserved marinade to lightly coat. Season to taste with salt and pepper. Set aside.

Just before serving, toss the lettuce with enough of the reserved marinade to make the leaves just glisten. Divide the lettuce among 6 serving plates or stemmed glasses. Evenly distribute the vegetables over the lettuce and top each serving with 5 marinated shrimp. Serve immediately.

MARINADE

¼ cup white wine vinegar

4 tablespoons fresh lime juice

2 tablespoons finely chopped shallots

1 clove garlic, finely chopped

1 serrano chile, seeded and finely chopped

¼ teaspoon cayenne pepper

½ teaspoon cumin seed, toasted and ground in a spice grinder (see page 38)

½ teaspoon salt

½ cup olive oil

30 medium-large, cooked shrimp, about 1 pound

RAINBOW VEGETABLES

1 cup chopped, seeded tomato

1 chayote squash, peeled, cored, and julienned

1 long green Anaheim or New Mexico chile, seeded and finely chopped

½ cup diced red onion

1 cup julienned carrot

1 yellow bell pepper, seeded and julienned

1 avocado, peeled, pitted, and diced

¼ cup chopped fresh cilantro

Salt and freshly ground pepper

1 head Romaine lettuce, washed and finely sliced

Makes 6 Servings

Poblano Chile AND Smoked Salmon Toasts

Simple to make but so good you can hardly stop eating it, this little treat has become a staple at our house. It's delicious on toasts as an appetizer or as the filling for a sandwich or quesadilla. ❄ WINTER

IN A MEDIUM BOWL with an electric mixer, blend together the cream cheese, mayonnaise, lime juice, and mustard. Fold the salmon and poblano chile into the cream cheese mixture with a rubber spatula. Season with salt. Refrigerate; return to room temperature before serving.

Spread each baguette slice with a heaping tablespoon of cream cheese/salmon mixture. Arrange on an attractive platter and serve immediately.

8 ounces cream cheese
½ cup mayonnaise
1 tablespoon fresh lime juice
2 teaspoons Dijon mustard
4 ounces thinly sliced smoked salmon
1 poblano chile, roasted, peeled, seeded, and diced (see page 47)
Salt
36 slices toasted baguette

Makes about 36 Appetizers

Cilantro and Pecan Pesto on Goat Cheese Toasts

This is a perfect appetizer to get your taste buds singing and ready for more. The creaminess of the cheese, the crunch of the toast and the pizzazz of the pesto form a symphony of texture and flavor. 🌿 FALL

TO PREPARE THE PESTO, in a blender or food processor, pulse together the pecans, Cotija cheese, parsley, cilantro, garlic, cayenne, and cumin. Add the olive oil and pulse again until well blended but not completely smooth. Add salt and pepper to taste. If not using immediately, cover and refrigerate for up to 24 hours.

Preheat broiler. Place baguette slices on a baking sheet and broil on one side. Remove from the oven and turn the slices over. Spread about a tablespoon of goat cheese on the untoasted side of each slice. Return to the broiler and cook until the cheese is bubbly and starting to brown. Transfer the toasts to a serving platter and drizzle each one with some of the pesto.

NOTE: *Use any leftover pesto to toss with freshly cooked pasta or to use as a sandwich spread.*

CILANTRO AND PECAN PESTO
½ cup pecans, toasted
½ cup crumbled Cotija cheese (or substitute Parmesan)
½ cup flat-leaf parsley leaves
½ cup cilantro leaves
1 clove garlic, coarsely chopped
¼ teaspoon cayenne pepper
½ teaspoon cumin seed, toasted
½ cup extra virgin olive oil
Salt and freshly ground pepper

1 baguette, cut into ½-inch slices
12 ounces mild goat cheese, such as Montrachet

Makes about 24 Appetizers

WILD *Mushroom* TOASTS

Wild mushrooms are easily found in the forests in Northern Arizona in the fall and winter months, and those who know what they're doing rejoice in the bounty. But those of us who are not experts should rely on the grocery store to find these delectable morsels. The dried porcini add a depth and richness to the mixture. 🍂 FALL

PREHEAT OVEN TO 350°F. Melt 1 tablespoon of the butter and brush on the bread slices. Toast the slices on a baking sheet in the center of the preheated oven until golden, about 10 minutes. Set aside.

Chop the parsley finely and set aside. Cook the shallot in 1 tablespoon of the butter in a skillet over low heat until softened, about 3 minutes. Add the remaining 3 tablespoons butter and the shiitake and portabello mushrooms. Sauté over high heat for 2 minutes. Strain the dried mushrooms through cheesecloth or a very fine sieve to trap any dirt, reserving the liquid, and coarsely chop. Add the dried mushrooms, along with the reserved liquid and the cream, to the shiitake/portabello mixture and cook over low heat, stirring, until thickened, about 20 minutes. Stir in the parsley, salt, and pepper. Spoon 1 heaping teaspoon mushroom mixture on each toast and serve immediately.

NOTE: *Dried mushrooms are available in most grocery stores (usually in the produce department) or by mail order. The mushrooms known as porcini in Italy are called cèpes in France.*

5 tablespoons unsalted butter
1 baguette, cut diagonally into ¼-inch slices
¼ cup parsley leaves
1 medium shallot, peeled and finely minced
4 medium shiitake mushrooms (about 2 ounces), stemmed, cleaned, and cut into fine strips
1 portabello mushroom, stemmed, cleaned, and diced
½ ounce dried cèpe or porcini mushrooms, soaked in water for 30 minutes (*see* NOTE)
½ cup heavy cream
Salt and freshly ground pepper

Makes 20 to 24 Appetizers

Toasting Nuts and Seeds

TOASTING BRINGS OUT THE ESSENTIAL OILS in nuts and seeds and makes them much more flavorful. It is an easy process, and you will definitely notice the difference in taste.

To toast nuts, place them on a baking sheet in a 350°F. oven until they are fragrant and slightly brown, about 5 to 10 minutes.

Seeds such as cumin, coriander, pepitas, or peppercorns are best toasted in a dry skillet over medium-high heat until aromatic and slightly brown, about 3 to 5 minutes. To grind the toasted seeds, place them in a spice or coffee grinder.

SPICED *Almonds*

Medical research has shown that adding a moderate amount of almonds to a healthy diet can lower cholesterol and help prevent heart disease. Adding a little spice to them makes them even more appetizing. These spiced nuts are a tasty between-meal snack or a delightful accompaniment to cocktails. ❄ WINTER

PREHEAT OVEN TO 350°F. Line a baking sheet with a silicon liner or a piece of parchment paper.

Toast the cumin seeds in a small skillet over medium heat until lightly browned and aromatic, about 3 minutes. Transfer to a spice grinder; mix to a powder. Add cayenne and salt to the grinder and mix again.

Whisk the egg white in a medium bowl; add the spice mixture and beat until well incorporated.

Add the almonds and stir to coat well. Turn the coated almonds out onto the lined baking sheet and cook until egg white is dry and nuts are lightly browned, about 15 minutes. Remove from the oven and lift the silicon liner off the baking sheet onto a cooling rack. Cool completely and serve immediately, or store in an airtight container.

1 ½ teaspoons cumin seed
1 teaspoon cayenne pepper
1 teaspoon salt
1 large egg white
2 cups whole almonds

Makes 2 Cups

Piquant PEPITAS

These spicy seeds are addictive so be sure to use self restraint when you're making them. Wrap them in attractive packages to give away as hostess gifts. 🌿 FALL

PREHEAT OVEN TO 350°F. Spray a baking sheet with nonstick spray. Mix all the ingredients in a medium bowl and spread the coated pepitas in a single layer on the baking sheet. Bake until the pepitas are golden and dry, stirring occasionally, about 15 minutes. Remove from the oven; separate with a fork while warm and cool to room temperature. Store in a tightly covered container.

NOTE: *Pepitas are hulled, roasted pumpkin seeds that are found in specialty grocery stores or Latino markets. They come raw or toasted and salted and make a great snack on their own. In Mexico, they are often used as a thickener for sauces.*

2 cups shelled unsalted pepitas
⅓ cup sugar
1 large egg white, beaten until frothy
1 tablespoon chili powder
1 teaspoon ground cinnamon
½ teaspoon salt
¼ teaspoon ground cumin
½ teaspoon cayenne

Makes 2 Cups

Soups

Bloody Mary Soup
with Avocado Mousse

The light, creamy mousse adds a nice contrast to the flavorful, zesty soup. This soup is delicious anytime, but it is particularly appealing at brunch.

❋ SPRING

TO PREPARE THE SOUP, in a small skillet, toast the caraway and celery seeds until lightly browned and fragrant, about 1 minute (see page 38). Set aside.

In a large saucepan, melt the butter over medium heat. Add the celery, red bell pepper, and jalapeño. Cover the pan, lower the heat, and sweat the vegetables until very soft, about 30 minutes. Stir in the tomatoes, tomato juice, water, lime zest, horseradish, toasted seeds, salt, and pepper. Raise heat to medium and cook another 5 minutes. Put the soup in a blender, in batches if necessary, and purée until smooth. Return soup to the saucepan and stir in the lime juice, Worcestershire sauce, and vodka. Heat until hot.

TO PREPARE THE MOUSSE, put the avocado and lemon juice in a mini processor or blender and purée until smooth. Transfer to a medium bowl and stir in the tomatoes; add salt to taste.

In a medium bowl, beat the cream until stiff peaks form, either by hand or with an electric mixer. Fold into the avocado mixture. This can be covered and refrigerated for up to 2 hours.

To serve, ladle soup into bowls or mugs and top with a scoop of avocado mousse.

BLOODY MARY SOUP
1 teaspoon caraway seeds
½ teaspoon celery seeds
2 tablespoons butter
½ cup diced celery
1 cup diced red bell pepper
1 jalapeño chile, seeded and chopped
1 (14 ½-ounce) can diced tomatoes with their liquid
2 cups tomato juice
½ cup water
Zest of 1 lime
2 tablespoons prepared horseradish
Salt and freshly ground pepper to taste
¼ cup fresh lime juice
1 tablespoon Worcestershire sauce
½ cup vodka

AVOCADO MOUSSE
1 ripe avocado, peeled and pitted
1 tablespoon lemon juice
¼ cup diced tomatoes, well-drained
Salt
⅓ cup heavy cream

Makes 6 Servings

PAGES 40-41: *Early morning light on the rock formations of Fairyland Point, with Thor's Hammer in background, Bryce Canyon National Park*

Black Bean Soup with Lime Cream

The lime juice and the lime cream round out the sublime bean flavor of this hearty soup, but for a vegetarian version, you can eliminate the cream garnish and simply sprinkle some chopped cilantro on top of the soup before serving. 🍂 FALL

IN A SMALL SKILLET over medium heat, toast the cumin seeds until they are lightly browned and give off their aroma, about 3 to 5 minutes. Transfer to a spice grinder and grind to a powder (see page 38); set aside.

In a large, heavy saucepan, heat the oil over medium heat. Add the onion, celery, carrots, garlic, cumin, salt, and pepper. Sauté until onions are tender, about 10 minutes. Add one can black beans and all of the stock, bring to a boil; lower heat to simmer and cook until carrots are tender, another 10 minutes. Add cilantro and lime juice and transfer to a blender. Purée, in batches if necessary, until smooth. Return the soup to the saucepan and add the remaining black beans; heat through.

IN A SMALL BOWL, mix together the sour cream and the lime juice and zest. Transfer the cream to a squeeze bottle. Put the soup into six bowls and drizzle with the lime cream.

1 teaspoon cumin seeds
2 tablespoons vegetable oil
1 cup diced onion
¼ cup diced celery
½ cup diced carrot
2 cloves garlic, finely chopped
Salt and freshly ground pepper to taste
2 (15-ounce) cans black beans, drained and rinsed
4 cups vegetable stock
¼ cup chopped cilantro
1 tablespoon lime juice

LIME CREAM
¼ cup sour cream
Juice and zest of 1 lime

Makes 6 Servings

Bigtooth maple trees in Oak Creek Canyon

Pumpkin AND Ginger Soup
WITH Toasted Pepitas

The ginger adds a peppery, slightly sweet flavor to this silky, satisfying soup, and the pepitas add just the right amount of texture. 🌿 FALL

IN A MEDIUM SAUCEPAN, heat butter over medium-high heat. Add ginger, carrots, celery, and onion and sauté until vegetables begin to soften, stirring frequently, about 3 to 5 minutes. Add pumpkin and stir well. Add vegetable stock and bring to a boil. Add salt, pepper, cinnamon, and cayenne. Reduce heat and simmer, uncovered, until vegetables are soft, about 20 minutes.

Transfer to a blender or food processor and purée the mixture until smooth. Strain the soup back into the saucepan and add the cream. Keep warm.

Put the raw pepitas in a medium nonstick skillet and toast over medium-high heat, stirring, until the seeds are fragrant, light brown, and begin to pop, about 3 minutes.

To serve, ladle the warm soup into serving bowls and garnish with toasted pepitas.

1 tablespoon butter
1 tablespoon peeled and diced fresh ginger
¼ cup diced carrots
¼ cup diced celery
½ cup diced onion
1 ½ cups pumpkin purée, either fresh or canned
3 ½ cups vegetable stock
Salt and freshly ground pepper to taste
¼ teaspoon ground cinnamon
⅛ teaspoon cayenne pepper
½ cup heavy cream
¼ cup raw, hulled pepitas (pumpkin seeds)

Makes 6 Servings

YOU'LL-NEVER-MISS-
THE-MEAT *Chili*

*There are so many zesty and satisfying flavors in
this hearty chili that meat would only be superfluous.
I always like to have vegetarian dishes on hand for
guests who'd rather not eat meat, and this is one they
all clamor for.* ❄ WINTER

PLACE BEANS IN A LARGE, heavy pot and cover
with plenty of water. Let soak for 1 hour. Drain
the beans, rinse, and set aside. Using the same
pot, heat the oil over medium heat. Add the
onions and cook, stirring, until translucent,
about 10 minutes. Add the garlic, chiles, cumin,
oregano, and cayenne and cook a few minutes
longer. Add the tomatoes with their juice and
cook another minute or so. Add the beans and
stock and bring to a boil. Cover, reduce heat, and
simmer, stirring occasionally, until the beans are
tender, about 2 hours. Add corn, olives, and
cilantro and cook until warmed through, about
5 minutes more. Add salt and adjust the seasoning.

Spoon chili into individual bowls and garnish,
if desired, with chopped green onions, diced
tomatoes, and chopped cilantro.

2 cups dried Great Northern beans
2 tablespoons olive oil
2 cups finely chopped white onion
4 cloves garlic, finely chopped
5 Anaheim chiles, roasted, peeled, seeded, and
   diced (see page 47)
2 serrano chiles, seeded and diced
2 teaspoons ground cumin
1 teaspoon dried oregano
¼ teaspoon cayenne pepper
1 (28-ounce) can diced tomatoes
7 cups vegetable stock
2 cups corn kernels
½ cup sliced black olives
¼ cup chopped fresh cilantro
Salt to taste

Chopped green onions
Diced tomatoes
Chopped fresh cilantro

Makes 6 to 8 Servings

Handling and Roasting Chiles

CHILES HAVE A CHEMICAL CALLED CAPSAICIN in them that can burn your hands or mouth if you get too much of it. Most of the capsaicin is in the membranes and seeds of the chile, so its best to avoid handling them. When working with more than a few chiles, wear disposal rubber gloves to avoid burning your hands, and be sure to wash your hands thoroughly with soap and water when you are finished, especially before touching any sensitive part of your body. If your hands still tingle, rub some aloe gel or lotion on them.

If you eat something that is too spicy, don't reach for an alcoholic beverage or even water. The alcohol intensifies the heat and the liquid just spreads the capsaicin throughout the rest of your mouth. Cheese, yogurt, sour cream, or ice cream—anything that contains casein—will break the bond of the capsaicin and cool the burn. Other remedies are to eat sweets, because the sugar interferes with the capsaicin's ability to bind to the nerve cells; to take a swig of oil, because fats strip the oily capsaicin out of the nerve receptors; and to eat bread, which absorbs the capsaicin.

When buying dried chiles, look for ones that are flexible and without blemishes. Store them in the freezer if you're not using them immediately or they will dry out. To reconstitute them, soak them in hot water for about 30 minutes, and then remove the stems and seeds. Or, you can remove the stems and seeds before soaking, if desired.

Roasting fresh chiles helps remove their sometimes bitter skin and brings out the chile's earthy, smoky flavor. There are a number of ways to roast chiles, the easiest being with a chile grill* that fits over any burner, either gas or electric. You can also use a barbecue grill, a broiler, or a butane torch, but the object is to blister and blacken the skin without damaging the flesh of the chile. When the skin is blackened all over, place the chile in a plastic or paper bag or in a covered bowl. The steam created by the hot, enclosed chile loosens the skin so that you can easily remove it with your hands or a knife. It's best not to run the chile under running water, though, because you will remove the essential oils and the smoky taste by doing so. After skinning, cut the chile open and remove the ribs, seeds, and core. Store in the refrigerator for up to 2 days or freeze for up to 6 months.

*Chile grills are available from the Santa Fe School of Cooking: (800) 982-4688

A familiar scene at Santa Fe's farmers' market is the fire-roasting of fresh peppers

Corn Soup with Poblano Chiles

The base for this soup is a broth made from the cobs of the corn and the ancho, a dried poblano chile with a mild fruit flavor. Adding reserved corn kernels and chopped poblano after the soup has mellowed adds texture and additional flavor. ☼ SUMMER

CUT THE KERNELS OFF THE COBS, and divide kernels evenly into 2 bowls. Put the cobs in a large saucepan and cover with 2 quarts of water. Add ancho chile pieces. Bring the mixture to a boil over medium-high heat; lower the heat to simmer and cook for 45 minutes. Strain mixture into a bowl; discard cobs and chile pieces.

In the same saucepan, heat the corn oil; add onion and garlic and sauté until soft, about 5 minutes. Add one portion of the corn kernels to the onion/garlic mixture and cook until corn is tender, about 8 to 10 minutes. Transfer to a blender and add 2 cups of the corn broth. Purée the mixture and strain back into the saucepan.

Add the remaining broth, corn, and the chiles to the saucepan and cook until corn is tender, another 10 to 15 minutes. Salt and pepper to taste. Gently stir in the cream, and serve immediately.

6 ears corn
1 ancho chile, stemmed, seeded, and torn
    into pieces
2 tablespoons corn oil
1 ½ cups chopped onion
1 tablespoon chopped garlic
2 poblano chiles, roasted, peeled, seeded, and
    chopped (see page 47)
Salt and freshly ground pepper to taste
½ cup cream

Makes 6 to 8 Servings

Cathedral Rock and Oak Creek at sunset, Coconino National Forest

CHILLED *Red Bell Pepper* SOUP WITH BASIL CREAM

This soup is delightfully refreshing on a summer evening or at a mid-day lunch, but it can also be served warm to take the chill off a winter night. Either way, it's beautiful to the eye and appealing to the palate. If you're short on time, purchase a good quality brand of jarred roasted red bell peppers.
☼ SUMMER

TO PREPARE THE SOUP, in a small skillet over high heat, toast the coriander and cumin seeds, shaking the pan, until lightly browned and fragrant. Transfer to a spice grinder and process until ground to a powder (see page 38). Set aside.

In a large saucepan, heat the olive oil over medium heat. Add the onions, carrots, and garlic and sauté until the onions are soft and translucent, about 5 minutes. Add the ground toasted seeds, cayenne, and salt and pepper. Stir and continue cooking over low heat until the spices are well incorporated, another minute. Add the red bell peppers and the stock; bring to a boil, lower the heat, and simmer for 30 minutes. Transfer to a blender and purée until smooth. Cool to room temperature. Stir in orange juice, cover, and refrigerate until chilled, about 2 hours.

TO PREPARE THE CREAM, bring the water to a boil over high heat in a medium saucepan. Add spinach leaves and boil until spinach is limp, about 1 minute. With a slotted spoon, remove the spinach from the pan and plunge it into ice water; allow to sit about 1 minute. Drain the spinach and squeeze it dry. Put the spinach in a blender, add basil and milk, and purée thoroughly. Strain the mixture through a fine sieve into a small bowl. Whisk in the sour cream and transfer the mixture to a squeeze bottle. Refrigerate until ready to use.

To assemble, ladle a portion of soup into each of 6 bowls. Drizzle the basil cream in a decorative pattern on top of each bowl.

CHILLED RED BELL PEPPER SOUP
1 teaspoon coriander seeds
1 teaspoon cumin seeds
1 tablespoon olive oil
1 cup diced yellow onion
½ cup diced carrots
1 tablespoon finely chopped garlic
¼ teaspoon cayenne
Salt and freshly ground black pepper to taste
6 medium red bell peppers, roasted, peeled, seeded, and coarsely chopped (see page 47)
4 cups vegetable or chicken stock
½ cup fresh orange juice

BASIL CREAM
2 cups water
8 fresh large spinach leaves
1 cup loosely packed fresh basil
¼ cup whole milk
¼ cup sour cream

Makes 6 to 8 Servings

Yellow *Gazpacho* with Red Gazpacho *Sorbet*

This refreshing summer soup is stunning served in a shallow bowl with a scoop of frozen gazpacho in the center. Besides being visually appealing, your taste buds will sit up and take notice, too! ☀ SUMMER

TO PREPARE THE YELLOW GAZPACHO, add the tomatoes to a food processor and pulse until they are puréed. Strain them into a medium bowl and set aside. With the machine running, add the garlic through the feed tube until finely chopped. Add the remaining ingredients and pulse until they are well mixed but not puréed. Stir vegetable mixture into the tomatoes; cover and refrigerate for at least 2 hours or overnight.

TO PREPARE THE SORBET, in a small saucepan let the gelatin soften in the wine for 5 minutes. Heat the mixture over low heat, stirring until the gelatin is dissolved. In a food processor, with the machine running, add the garlic. When minced, add the remaining ingredients, including the dissolved gelatin. Transfer the mixture to an ice cream freezer and freeze according to the manufacturer's directions, about 1 hour. With an ice cream scoop, form the sorbet into rounds and arrange them on a small baking pan lined with plastic wrap. Freeze, covered, for at least 1 hour or overnight.

To assemble, let the sorbet stand at room temperature for 5 minutes before serving. Place a scoop in the center of each of six shallow bowls. Ladle the yellow gazpacho around the sorbet and serve immediately.

NOTE: *If you're using garlic in a recipe that calls for using the food processor, there is a trick to making sure the garlic gets finely minced. Before adding any of the other ingredients, turn the machine on and drop the garlic through the feed tube of the processor. That way, it gets finely chopped instead of getting caught under the blade.*

YELLOW GAZPACHO

2 pounds ripe yellow tomatoes, cored and cut into quarters
2 cloves garlic, peeled
¼ cup diced red onion
1 yellow bell pepper, stemmed, seeded, and coarsely chopped
½ cup peeled, seeded, and diced cucumber
3 tablespoons chopped cilantro
2 tablespoons fresh lime juice
2 tablespoons white wine vinegar
¼ teaspoon cayenne pepper
1 tablespoon olive oil
Salt and freshly ground pepper to taste

RED GAZPACHO SORBET

2 teaspoons unflavored gelatin
3 tablespoons dry white wine
1 clove garlic, peeled
¾ pound ripe red tomatoes, cored and cut into quarters
½ cup chopped red bell pepper
½ cup peeled, seeded, and diced cucumber
¼ cup diced red onion
1 teaspoon salt
⅛ teaspoon cayenne pepper
1 tablespoon olive oil

Makes 6 Servings

CREAM OF *Chayote* SOUP

Chayote squash has a very delicate flavor and tends to showcase the ingredients with which it is combined. So this soup has a hint of heat, the tangy, fresh flavor of cilantro, and the richness of the cream. ✒ FALL

HEAT BUTTER IN A MEDIUM SAUCEPAN over medium heat; add onion, garlic, and chile and cook until softened, about 5 minutes. Add chopped chayote squash, salt, and pepper and continue cooking, stirring, another 2 to 3 minutes. Add vegetable stock and bring to a boil.

Lower heat, cover, and cook until squash is tender, about 20 minutes. Cool slightly and put mixture into a blender. Purée; add cilantro and purée again. Return mixture to the saucepan and add ½ cup of the cream. Heat to the desired temperature. Ladle the soup into bowls. Put the remaining cream in a squeeze bottle; drizzle a little cream and some of the chives over each serving. Serve immediately.

1 tablespoon unsalted butter
½ cup diced onion
1 tablespoon finely chopped garlic
1 serrano chile, seeded and finely chopped
2 chayote squash (about 1 ½ pounds), peeled, cored, and cut into ½-inch cubes
Salt and freshly ground pepper to taste
2 cups vegetable stock
¼ cup fresh cilantro leaves
1 cup heavy cream
¼ cup chopped chives

Makes 6 Servings

TOMATO, *Hominy,* AND CHILE SOUP

Hominy is a staple of the Southwest and adds a toothsome flavor and texture to its dishes, the most common one being posole. Hominy is available in many forms, but the canned white or yellow varieties are the most prevalent and convenient. ❁ SPRING

IN A LARGE SAUCEPAN, heat the olive oil over medium-high heat. Add the onion, garlic, and green chile and sauté until soft and onion is translucent, about 10 minutes. Stir in oregano, dried chile, and cumin and cook 2 minutes longer. Add hominy, tomatoes, and chicken stock. Bring to a boil, lower the heat, and simmer gently until dried chile is softened and flavors are well blended, at least 1 hour. Add lime juice and season to taste with salt and pepper. Serve immediately.

2 tablespoons olive oil
1 cup finely chopped white onion
2 cloves garlic, finely chopped
1 green New Mexico chile, stemmed, seeded, and diced
1 teaspoon finely chopped fresh oregano
1 dried New Mexico chile, stemmed, seeded, and torn into small pieces
1 teaspoon cumin seed, toasted and ground (see page 38)
1 (14 ½-ounce) can hominy, drained and rinsed
1 (14 ½-ounce) can diced tomatoes
4 cups chicken stock
1 tablespoon fresh lime juice
Salt and freshly ground pepper

Makes 6 Servings

CHILLED TOMATILLO AND *Cucumber* SOUP

This light and silky soup is refreshing and filling and is a great starter for a summer luncheon or dinner party. For an informal gathering, serve it in glass mugs so your guests can walk around with it while they visit. ☼ SUMMER

IN A LARGE SAUCEPAN, heat the olive oil over medium heat. Add the onions and garlic; sauté until softened, about 4 to 5 minutes. Add tomatillos and cucumber and cook for 5 minutes more. Add the poblano chiles and chicken stock. Bring to a boil, lower the heat, and simmer until tomatillos and cucumbers are tender, about 10 minutes. Add jalapeño, lime juice, cilantro, salt, and pepper; let cool. Purée the soup in batches in a blender or food processor. Transfer to a bowl and stir in the cream. Refrigerate for 2 hours or up to 2 days so that the flavors can mellow. Divide among 6 bowls and sprinkle green onions over each serving. Serve cold or at room temperature.

1 tablespoon olive oil
1 cup white onion, coarsely chopped
2 cloves garlic, finely chopped
½ pound tomatillos (about 10), husked and diced (*see* NOTE)
1 hothouse cucumber, peeled, seeded, and coarsely chopped
2 poblano chiles, roasted, peeled, seeded, and diced (see page 47)
4 cups chicken stock
1 jalapeño chile, seeded and finely chopped
2 tablespoons fresh lime juice
2 tablespoons finely chopped cilantro
Salt and freshly ground pepper to taste
½ cup heavy cream
¼ cup diced green onions

Makes 6 Servings

NOTE: *When buying tomatillos, which are sometimes referred to as Mexican green tomatoes, look for those that are firm and have their papery husk intact.*

Green Chile SOUP

The heat of this soup obviously depends on the type of chile you use. If you use a canned version, the soup will be quite mild. Instead, treat yourself to freshly roasted green chiles from Hatch, New Mexico, where the most flavorful chiles are cultivated. You usually even have a choice between mild, medium, hot, and extra hot, so you'll remember the soup long after you've licked the bowl. ✿ FALL

IN A MEDIUM SAUCEPAN, heat the oil over medium-high heat. Add the onion, garlic, and serrano and sauté until they are softened, about 5 minutes. Add the tomatillos and the chicken stock and bring to a boil; lower the heat and simmer until tomatillos are tender, about 10 minutes. Purée the mixture, in batches if necessary, in a blender with the cilantro. Pour back into the saucepan and add the lime juice, green chiles, and cream. Salt and pepper to taste. Ladle into soup bowls and sprinkle chives over each serving.

1 tablespoon vegetable oil
½ cup diced white onion
1 tablespoon finely chopped garlic
1 serrano chile, seeded and diced
4 medium tomatillos, husked and cut
    into quarters (*see* NOTE *page* 54)
3 cups chicken stock
½ cup cilantro leaves
1 tablespoon lime juice
2 large New Mexico green chiles, roasted, peeled,
    seeded, and diced (see page 47)
½ cup heavy cream
Salt and freshly ground pepper
¼ cup chopped chives

Makes 6 Servings

*Bigtooth maple, south fork of Cave Creek,
Chiracahua Wilderness*

Posole with Chicken and Tomatillos

Posole is a family favorite at our house because it's so satisfying and everyone can garnish it with the toppings of their choice. I often make a double batch and freeze part of it for another time. We usually serve it with cheese crisps or quesadillas. If you have leftover chicken or turkey, this is a great way to use it. Simply substitute chicken stock for the water.
❄ WINTER

IN A LARGE SAUCEPAN, place the chicken breasts and the tomatillos. Add water and salt and bring to a boil. Turn heat to simmer and cook until chicken is cooked through and tomatillos are tender, about 15 minutes. Transfer tomatillos to a blender, add chipotle chiles, and purée. Set aside. Remove chicken from the water and allow to cool; shred into bite-sized pieces. Pour poaching liquid into another container and reserve.

In the same saucepan, heat the corn oil; sauté onion until slightly softened, about 5 minutes. Add garlic, cumin, oregano, salt, and pepper and continue cooking, stirring, until onions are tender, about 5 minutes more. Add hominy, tomatillo mixture, and reserved poaching liquid; bring to a boil, reduce heat and simmer for 20 minutes. Add chicken and lime juice and heat through. Taste for seasoning and add salt and/or lime juice to balance the flavors. Ladle into bowls to serve and pass garnishes at the table.

2 large chicken breast halves, bone in, skin cut off
1 pound tomatillos, husked and rinsed
7 cups water
1 teaspoon salt
2 chipotle chiles in adobo sauce
1 tablespoon corn oil
2 cups diced onion
1 tablespoon finely chopped garlic
2 teaspoons ground cumin
1 teaspoon dried oregano
Salt and freshly ground pepper to taste
1 (28-ounce) can white hominy, drained
   and rinsed
1 tablespoon lime juice

GARNISHES
2 cups shredded cabbage
1 avocado, peeled, pitted, and diced
1 fresh lime, sliced into wedges
1 cup grated Cotija cheese

Makes 4 to 6 Servings

Corn

CORN, ONE OF THE NEW WORLD'S GREATEST GIFTS to the Old, is considered sacred by many Native Americans. It is the traditional food of most Pueblo people, and to them, the colors of corn represent the different directions: white is east, blue is west, yellow is north, and red is south. In the Navajo culture, tiny grains of corn pollen are placed in sand paintings to cure the sick and are also used as body paint in ceremonial dances.

As soon as fresh, sweet corn is picked, the natural sugar in it begins to turn to starch, so it is best to eat it as soon as possible for maximum sweetness. Look for ears with tightly fitting husks that are light brown and moist. Corn that is not eaten immediately is typically dried, creating hominy, masa harina, or cornmeal.

The process of creating hominy transforms the corn's flavor and its ability to nourish. The corn kernels are first soaked in powdered lime to remove their tough outer hulls in order to make the kernels digestible, to release niacin for absorption into the body, and to give them a unique rich and nutty flavor. Hominy is the main ingredient in a traditional Mexican stew called posole, or pozole in Spanish. Hominy is sold dried (soak in water overnight to reconstitute), canned as either yellow or white hominy, and in plastic bags in the refrigerated section of Latino markets.

Masa Harina is a kind of flour made from dried corn kernels that have been heated, soaked overnight in lime water, and then ground. It is combined with water and salt to make masa, the Spanish word for dough, which is used to make tortillas and tamales.

Cornmeal is ground from dried, processed corn kernels and most often used in baked goods. The color of the cornmeal depends on the type of corn used, yellow and white being more common than blue.

Corn husks, the outer wrappings, are used fresh or dried to make wrappings for dishes to be steamed. Dried corn husks, available in most grocery stores, need to be soaked in hot water for at least 30 minutes to make them soft and pliable. They are the traditional wrappers for tamales, infusing them with a fresh corn flavor.

Beef AND BLACK BEAN CHILI

Nothing satisfies like a good bowl of chili on a cold winter's evening. It's our family's favorite after skiing, and this version, with beef, tomatillos, green chiles, and black beans is particularly flavorful and filling. ❄ WINTER

IN A LARGE SAUCEPAN or Dutch oven, heat the oil over high heat. Season the beef cubes with salt and pepper; add them to the hot pan, in batches if necessary, and sear them until brown, about 5 minutes. (They will not brown if the pan is too crowded.) Remove the browned meat from the pan, lower the heat slightly, and add the onions and garlic; sauté until onions are soft, about 5 minutes. Add the diced chiles, cumin, and chile powder and cook, stirring, for about 1 minute.

Add the meat and any accumulated juices back to the pan along with the beer, beef stock, tomatillos, and black beans. Bring to a boil; lower the heat, cover pan, and simmer until meat is tender and chili has thickened somewhat, about 1 ½ to 2 hours. Just before serving, season with salt and stir in cilantro. Ladle into bowls and serve with warmed tortillas.

1 tablespoon canola oil
1 ½ pounds beef round steak, cut into ½-inch cubes
Salt and pepper to taste
2 cups diced onions (about 1 large onion)
2 cloves garlic, finely chopped
2 Anaheim or New Mexico green chiles, roasted, peeled, seeded, and diced (see page 47)
2 poblano chiles, roasted, peeled, seeded, and diced (see page 47)
1 teaspoon ground cumin
1 teaspoon chile powder
1 (12-ounce) bottle amber ale or other dark beer
2 cups beef stock
4 large tomatillos, cut into ½-inch cubes
1 (15-ounce) can black beans, drained and rinsed
¼ cup chopped cilantro

Makes 6 Servings

Shrimp | TORTILLA SOUP

Most tortilla soups get mushy if you don't eat them right away, but the tortillas in this recipe are added at the end so you can make the base a few days ahead, cover and refrigerate it, and then reheat just before serving. ✽ SPRING

IN A MEDIUM SKILLET, heat 2 tablespoons of the oil over medium heat; when hot, add the tortillas and cook, in batches if necessary, until they are crisp and golden, about 5 minutes. Remove from the pan and drain on paper towels; set aside.

In a medium saucepan, heat the remaining tablespoon of corn oil; when hot, add the onion, cook about 2 minutes, and add the garlic and chiles; cook until onion is softened, about 5 more minutes. Add tomatoes, cumin, cayenne, salt, and pepper and cook until flavors are well blended, about 15 minutes. Stir in the vegetable stock, lower the heat, and simmer until slightly reduced, about 20 minutes. Add the lime juice, taste, and adjust seasonings.

Divide tortilla strips, avocado, and shrimp among 6 soup bowls. Ladle hot soup into bowls and serve immediately.

3 tablespoons corn oil
4 (6-inch) corn tortillas, cut into
    3 x ½-inch strips
1 cup finely chopped white onion
2 cloves garlic, finely chopped
2 Anaheim or New Mexico green chiles, roasted,
    peeled, seeded, and finely chopped (see page 47)
1 (16-ounce) can peeled, chopped plum tomatoes
1 teaspoon cumin seed, toasted and ground
    (see page 38)
⅛ teaspoon cayenne
Salt and freshly ground pepper to taste
4 cups vegetable stock
1 tablespoon fresh lime juice
1 ripe avocado, diced
1 pound cooked medium shrimp, split
    horizontally (*see* NOTE)

Makes 4 to 6 Servings

NOTE: *The shrimp are cut in half horizontally for two reasons: it makes it look like there are more shrimp and the shrimp are easier to eat because they are not in such large pieces.*

Small grouping of wildflowers nestled in agave, Sedona, Arizona

Salads

61

Black Bean SALAD WITH VINAIGRETTE DRESSING

If you have the time, this salad will be better if you cook the beans yourself; however, if you are in a hurry, you can use 2 (15-ounce) cans of black beans, rinsed and drained. ❄ WINTER

PUT BEANS IN A LARGE SAUCEPAN and cover them with water; allow to soak for an hour. Drain the beans and put them back into the pot. Cover them generously with water, add the bay leaf, thyme, and oregano, and bring to a boil over high heat. Add salt, reduce heat to a simmer, and cook until beans are tender but still hold their shape, about 1 to 1 ½ hours. Drain.

WHILE THE BEANS ARE COOKING MAKE THE DRESSING. In a small, dry skillet, toast the cumin and coriander seeds until lightly browned and aromatic, about 3 minutes. Transfer to a spice grinder and purée (see page 38). Put spices in a medium bowl and combine with the remaining dressing ingredients. Taste and add more oil if necessary.

While the beans are still warm put them into a large bowl; add the vinaigrette dressing. Toss in the bell pepper, red onion, and celery. Just before serving, add the diced avocado, salt, and pepper.

NOTE: *Lime olive oil can be found in specialty food stores like William Sonoma, or, if you would prefer to make your own, double the amount of lime zest and juice listed above and mix with extra virgin olive oil.*

1 (12-ounce) bag dried black beans
1 bay leaf
½ teaspoon dried thyme
½ teaspoon dried oregano
1 teaspoon salt

VINAIGRETTE DRESSING
½ teaspoon cumin seeds
½ teaspoon coriander seeds
1 tablespoon lime juice
1 teaspoon grated lime zest
1 clove garlic, finely chopped
¼ teaspoon chipotle chile powder
1 tablespoon lime olive oil (*see* NOTE)
1 tablespoon chopped fresh cilantro
Salt and pepper to taste

1 cup diced red or yellow bell pepper
½ cup diced red onion
½ cup diced celery
1 avocado, peeled, pitted, and diced
Salt and pepper to taste

Makes 8 Servings

PAGES 60–61: *Spring bloom with Mexican gold poppies, organ pipe cactus, and saguaro cactus, Organ Pipe National Monument*

GREENS WITH *Ancho* DRESSING, BLUE CHEESE, AND TOASTED PECANS

The complex taste of the ancho chile pairs beautifully with the rich blue cheese and the buttery pecans. The dressing has very little heat–just a lot of flavor.
❄ WINTER

TO PREPARE THE DRESSING, lay the seeded ancho chile out flat; heat a small skillet over medium-high heat and toast the chile on both sides until it becomes flexible and gives off an aroma, about 1 minute per side. Put the chile in a small bowl and cover it with very hot water; allow to soak for 30 minutes. Remove the chile from the water and add it to a blender with the remaining dressing ingredients; purée. Refrigerate, covered, if not using immediately.

In a large bowl, toss the greens with just enough dressing to coat them. Divide evenly among 6 plates; arrange the blue cheese and toasted pecans on top. Serve immediately.

ANCHO DRESSING
1 ancho chile, stemmed and seeded
¼ cup buttermilk
¼ cup mayonnaise
1 tablespoon chopped green onion
1 clove garlic, chopped
1 teaspoon freshly squeezed lime juice
Salt and freshly ground black pepper to taste

8 to 10 cups Mesclun mix
½ cup crumbled blue cheese
½ cup toasted pecans (see page 38)

Makes 6 Servings

Delicate Arch and the La Sal Mountains with snow, Arches National Park

Individual Serrano *Soufflés* on Greens with Pears and Piñon Nuts

Piñon nuts, or pine nuts, are the seeds from the cones of the piñon, the state tree of New Mexico. Gathered during the fall by the Navajo and Hopi peoples, they are prized for their smooth texture and delicate flavor. Native Americans often grind the raw nuts into a meal for making bread, but in this elegant salad, they are toasted to add flavor and texture. ✿ FALL

TO PREPARE THE SOUFFLÉS, preheat oven to 400°F. Butter 8 individual ½-cup ramekins. Mix bread crumbs and finely chopped piñon nuts together and coat inside of buttered ramekins with the mixture; put in a baking dish and chill until ready to fill.

Melt 2 tablespoons butter in a saucepan. Add shallots, chiles, and flour and cook, stirring constantly, for 3 minutes. Add milk and cook, whisking constantly, until thick. Remove from heat and add egg yolks; mix thoroughly. Stir in cheese and season with salt and pepper.

In a separate bowl, whip egg whites until soft peaks form. Fold into the cheese mixture and divide among the chilled ramekins. Fill the baking dish with enough hot water to go half way up the sides of the ramekins. Bake until the soufflés are puffed and golden, about 15 to 20 minutes.

TO PREPARE THE DRESSING, put raspberry vinegar in a bowl and season with salt and pepper. Slowly whisk in the oil. Set aside.

Place lettuce on the bottom of 8 plates and top with julienned pears and piñon nuts. Drizzle dressing over the top. Unmold soufflés, and with the top side up, place 1 on each plate.

NOTE: *Panko is a Japanese-style bread crumb that is available in the Oriental section of your local grocery store.*

SERRANO SOUFFLÉS

1 tablespoon butter
2 tablespoons dry panko crumbs (*see* NOTE)
2 tablespoons finely chopped toasted piñon nuts
2 tablespoons butter
1 tablespoon finely chopped shallots
2 serrano chiles, seeded and finely chopped
2 tablespoons flour
½ cup milk
2 egg yolks
1 cup grated Gruyère cheese
Salt and pepper to taste
6 egg whites

DRESSING

2 tablespoons raspberry vinegar
Salt and pepper to taste
½ cup hazelnut or walnut oil

9 cups washed mesclun mix or European spring lettuce mix
2 pears, julienned
½ cup toasted piñon nuts

Makes 8 Servings

SANTA FE *Slaw* WITH CARAMELIZED PECANS

This colorful salad with its contrasting textures and flavors is a favorite for summer entertaining. Besides holding up well in the sweltering outdoor heat, it's refreshing and light. ☀ SUMMER

TO PREPARE THE DRESSING, in a medium bowl, whisk together the garlic, chile powder, lime juice, vinegar, sugar, and salt. Slowly whisk in the olive oil. Set aside and allow the flavors to blend.

TO PREPARE THE PECANS, heat a heavy-bottomed skillet over medium-high heat. Put the pecans in the pan and toast, stirring constantly, until lightly browned and fragrant. Add the butter and stir until melted. Add the sugar and cook until it is melted and beginning to caramelize. Remove the pan from the heat, stir in cayenne pepper, and then turn pecans out onto a non-stick pad or a piece of waxed paper. When cool, break into pieces. Set aside.

TO PREPARE THE SLAW, in a large bowl, stir together the cabbage, bell pepper, onion, carrots, radishes, and jicama. Toss with the dressing. Just before serving, stir in the cilantro and caramelized pecan pieces. Serve immediately.

DRESSING

1 teaspoon finely chopped garlic
½ teaspoon chipotle chile powder
2 tablespoons lime juice
2 tablespoons white balsamic vinegar
2 tablespoons sugar
Salt to taste
⅓ cup olive oil

CARAMELIZED PECANS

1 cup pecan pieces
2 tablespoons butter
¼ cup sugar
⅛ teaspoon cayenne pepper

SANTA FE SLAW

4 cups shredded green cabbage
1 yellow bell pepper, seeded and diced
½ cup diced red onion
2 carrots, grated
¼ cup julienned radishes
1 small jicama, peeled and julienned
¼ cup chopped cilantro

Makes 8 to 10 Servings

Jícama, Orange, and *Nopalitos* Salad

Nopales are the dark green, fleshy pads of the prickly pear cactus and taste like tart green beans. Nopalitos are the diced or sliced nopales that are sold either fresh in the produce department or pickled in jars in larger supermarkets and Latino grocery stores.
 SPRING

TO PREPARE THE DRESSING, in a medium bowl, whisk together the vinegar, orange juice, honey, anise seeds, and cayenne pepper. Slowly whisk in the olive oil until well incorporated. Season to taste with salt and pepper. Refrigerate until ready to serve.

TO PREPARE THE SALAD, in a large mixing bowl, mix together the nopales, jicama, pimentos, oranges, cilantro, salt, and pepper. Add dressing and toss well. Divide the watercress among 8 salad plates. Spoon salad on top of watercress and serve immediately.

DRESSING
1 tablespoon red wine vinegar
2 tablespoons fresh orange juice
1 tablespoon honey
½ teaspoon crushed anise seeds
¼ teaspoon cayenne pepper
¼ cup olive oil
Salt and freshly ground black pepper to taste

SALAD
½ (15-ounce) jar nopales, rinsed, drained, and cut into 2-inch pieces
2 cups julienned jicama
1 (4-ounce) jar pimentos, drained
3 navel oranges, peeled and sectioned
2 tablespoons finely chopped cilantro
Salt and freshly ground black pepper to taste

2 bunches watercress, washed and stems removed

Makes 8 Servings

Chicken *Fajita* Salad

This showy main dish salad evokes all the flavors of the southwestern favorite: fajitas. But, unlike traditional fajitas, this salad doesn't have to be served sizzling hot at the last minute, so it makes a refreshing warm weather alternative. ❀ SPRING

TO PREPARE THE DRESSING, with the machine running, add the garlic through the feed tube of a food processor. When the garlic is minced, remove the top and add the avocado, lime juice, chile, salt, sour cream, and cilantro. Pulse until blended. With the machine running, add the olive oil through the feed tube and process until the dressing is smooth and creamy. Set aside.

Put the chicken strips in a shallow glass dish and sprinkle them with the lime juice, corn oil, salt, and pepper. Toss and allow to marinate for at least 10 minutes or up to 1 hour.

Preheat oven to 350°F. Put the tortilla strips on a baking sheet and spray them with vegetable oil; sprinkle with chile powder. Bake in the oven until crisp and toasted, about 10 minutes.

In a large skillet, heat the corn oil over medium-high heat. Add the onion and cook, stirring, until tender and starting to color, about 10 minutes. Add chicken strips and their marinade and continue cooking until the chicken is no longer pink in the center, about 5 to 10 minutes. Remove from the heat.

TO PREPARE THE SALAD, put the greens in a large bowl and toss with some of the dressing, just until the leaves are lightly coated. Divide the greens evenly among four large dinner plates. Arrange peppers, chiles, and tomatoes over the salad greens and top each with some of the chicken/onion mixture. Sprinkle cheese and baked tortilla chips over all and serve with the remaining dressing.

AVOCADO DRESSING
1 clove garlic, peeled
1 ripe avocado, peeled and pitted
3 tablespoons fresh lime juice
1 serrano chile, stemmed, seeded, and chopped
1 teaspoon salt
2 tablespoons sour cream
¼ cup chopped fresh cilantro
½ cup olive oil

2 chicken breasts, cut into ½ x 2-inch strips
2 tablespoons fresh lime juice
1 tablespoon corn oil
Salt and freshly ground black pepper to taste
2 corn tortillas, julienned
Vegetable oil spray
½ teaspoon green chile powder (or substitute red chile powder)
1 tablespoon corn oil
1 large onion, thinly sliced

SALAD
8 cups salad greens
2 red bell peppers, roasted, peeled, and cut into strips (see page 47)
2 poblano chile, roasted, peeled, and cut into strips (see page 47)
2 large yellow tomatoes, seeded and diced
½ cup Cotija cheese, crumbled

Makes 4 Servings

Cotija AND CHERRY TOMATO SALAD

At the height of the season there is nothing better than a vine-ripe tomato. That incredible taste is still available almost year-round in cherry or grape tomatoes, so I prefer to use them in this colorful, toothsome salad. ☼ SUMMER

PLACE TOMATOES, CILANTRO, CHILE, COTIJA, onion, salt, and pepper together in a large bowl. In a small bowl, whisk together the vinegar and oil; drizzle over the salad and toss gently. Serve immediately or cover and refrigerate for up to 4 hours.

2 pints cherry or grape tomatoes, halved
2 tablespoons finely chopped cilantro
1 jalapeño chile, seeded and finely chopped
1 cup crumbled Cotija cheese
1 cup finely chopped red onion
Salt and freshly ground pepper to taste

DRESSING
2 teaspoons balsamic vinegar
3 tablespoons extra virgin olive oil

Makes 6 Servings

MARINATED STEAK SALAD WITH *Tomatillo* DRESSING AND COTIJA CHEESE

The marriage of flavors in this main dish salad makes it a memorable meal, and it's beautiful to look at, too. 🌿 FALL

TO PREPARE THE DRESSING, in a medium saucepan, heat the olive oil over medium heat; add the onion and garlic and cook until onion is lightly browned, about 7 to 10 minutes. Add the tomatillos and the water and bring to a boil; lower the heat, cover, and cook until tomatillos are tender, about 10 minutes. Cool. Put cooled mixture into a blender with the chipotle chile and cilantro. Purée and transfer to a bowl. Set aside. Cook the flank steak according to the directions, or, if using leftovers, gently reheat the meat in a skillet.

Put about 2 cups of greens on each of 6 large plates. Distribute tomato halves and green onions over the greens. Arrange sliced flank steak on top and sprinkle with Cotija cheese. Drizzle each salad with some of the chilled dressing and serve immediately. Pass any remaining dressing.

DRESSING
1 tablespoon olive oil
½ cup chopped onion
1 teaspoon finely chopped garlic
6 tomatillos, husks removed and rinsed
¾ cup water
1 teaspoon chopped chipotle chile in adobo sauce
2 tablespoons fresh cilantro leaves

1 Marinated Flank Steak (see page 100)
12 cups salad greens
1 pint cherry or grape tomatoes, cut in half
6 green onions with the green stems, chopped
1 cup crumbled Cotija cheese

Makes 4 to 6 Servings

Cilantro

CILANTRO, one of the world's most widely
known herbs, is common in Mexican,
Southwestern, Indian, and Asian cuisines. Its
distinct, almost musty pungency adds a unique
flavor to salsas and other dishes. And, as with
many other Southwest ingredients, cilantro has
been found to have wonderful health benefits.
The herb contains a natural compound that kills
harmful salmonella bacteria. This new discovery
fits in perfectly with other studies that have
shown that popular spices can keep food from
spoiling—a great reason for eating spicy foods!

When buying cilantro, look for un-wilted,
evenly-colored leaves. To make cilantro last a long
time, wash it well and shake it dry. Cut off the
bottommost stems and put it into a fresh glass of
water. Cover it loosely with a plastic bag and
store in the refrigerator. If you follow this
process, it will stay fresh for up to two weeks. To
cut it, hold the stems in a bunch and slide your
chef knife along the leaves. If you get a few
stems, don't worry, because they are almost as
tender as the leaves.

Grilled *Shrimp* Salad

Brushing vegetables and shrimp with the spicy liquid in which jalapeños are pickled gives them just the right amount of heat in this bright, main dish salad. Serve with a chilled soup and crusty bread, and you'll have the perfect summer meal. ☼ SUMMER

TO PREPARE THE DRESSING, put all the dressing ingredients in a blender and purée. Refrigerate, covered, until ready to use.

In a small bowl, whisk together the pickling liquid, garlic, and olive oil. Put the shrimp in a shallow glass dish and pour all but 2 tablespoons of the garlic marinade over the shrimp; toss well. Cover and refrigerate for at least 30 minutes or up to 2 hours. Brush the remaining garlic marinade on the chayote squash and onion slices; keep covered at room temperature until ready to grill.

Preheat a barbecue grill to medium-high heat. Salt and pepper the chayote and onion slices and put them on the hot grill; cook until lightly browned, about 4 minutes per side. Grill the shrimp until just cooked through, about 1 minute per side.

Put the avocados, tomatoes, and lettuce in a large bowl and toss with just enough dressing to lightly coat the lettuce leaves. Divide among 6 dinner plates. Separate the onions into rings and divide among the plates. Arrange the grilled chayote over the onions and top with the grilled shrimp. Serve with additional salad dressing and chopped pickled jalapeños.

DRESSING

1 Anaheim or New Mexico green chile, roasted, peeled, and seeded (see page 47)
¼ cup mayonnaise
¼ cup buttermilk
1 tablespoon chopped green onion
1 clove garlic, finely chopped
1 teaspoon fresh lime juice
Salt and freshly ground pepper to taste

¼ cup pickling liquid from a jar pickled jalapeños
2 cloves garlic, finely chopped
¼ cup olive oil
2 pounds uncooked large shrimp, peeled and deveined
1 chayote squash, halved lengthwise, pitted, and cut into 24 long strips
1 large red onion, peeled and cut crosswise into ¼-inch slices
Salt and pepper to taste
2 avocados, peeled, pitted, and diced
2 cups cherry or grape tomatoes, cut in half if large
8 to 10 cups washed and torn Romaine leaves
2 tablespoons chopped pickled jalapeño chiles (optional)

Makes 6 Servings

SMOKED *Trout*, APPLE, AND PECAN SALAD

Trout, apples, and pecans are all abundant in the Southwest, and what better way to celebrate the fall than by making a salad with fresh apples and shelled pecans. It's easy to smoke your own fresh-caught trout in a stove-top smoker, but if you weren't lucky at the fishing hole, you may as well buy your trout already smoked. 🍃 FALL

TO PREPARE THE DRESSING, in a medium bowl, whisk together the chipotle, lemon juice, vinegar, and garlic. Slowly drizzle in olive oil. Salt and pepper to taste.

Toss ½ of the dressing with the salad greens and divide among 4 plates. Divide the apple, trout, onions, and pecans over the greens; pass the remaining dressing. Serve immediately.

DRESSING

1 chipotle chile in adobo sauce, finely chopped
2 tablespoons fresh lemon juice
2 tablespoons red wine vinegar
1 teaspoon finely chopped garlic
½ cup olive oil
Salt and freshly ground pepper to taste

6 cups mixed greens
1 apple, cored and thinly sliced
1 smoked trout, skin and bones removed, flesh broken up into pieces
¼ cup thinly sliced red onion
½ cup toasted chopped pecans

Makes 4 Servings

Aspen leaves in autumn along the Bear Lake Trail, Rocky Mountain National Park

SOUTHWEST *Caesar* SALAD

*This twist on a traditional Caesar Salad adds more
zest and exciting new flavors. Because the Panela
cheese doesn't melt easily, it makes a beautiful garnish
that complements the piquant taste of the dressing.
To serve this as a main dish salad, simply add cooked
chicken or shrimp.* ❁ SPRING

TO PREPARE THE DRESSING, put all dressing
ingredients, except the olive oil, in a mini-processor
or a blender and mix until smooth. Slowly add
the olive oil until emulsified. Refrigerate until
ready to use.

Preheat oven to 350°F. Place the corn bread
cubes on a baking sheet and toast until lightly
browned, about 10 to 15 minutes. Set aside.

Raise the oven temperature to 400°F. Line
a baking sheet with parchment paper. Make 8
cheese wafers by spreading 1 tablespoon of the
grated Panela cheese for each wafer into thin 3-
inch diameter circles on the paper. Bake in the
preheated oven until browned and crisp, about 8
minutes. Allow to cool.

To assemble, in a large bowl, toss together
the dressing, toasted corn bread, lettuce, and
Cotija cheese. Divide evenly among 8 salad
plates, garnish each with a cheese wafer, and
serve immediately.

DRESSING
1 canned chipotle chile in adobo sauce
2 cloves garlic
2 tablespoons sour cream
1 tablespoon Dijon mustard
1 tablespoon fresh lime juice
Salt and pepper to taste
½ cup olive oil

2 cups cubed corn bread (cut into ½-inch cubes)
½ cup grated Panela cheese
2 heads Romaine lettuce, washed and torn
    into pieces
½ cup crumbled Cotija cheese

Makes 8 Servings

Tri-Color *Potato* Salad

Potato salad, that perennial favorite at picnics all summer long, is livened up here with a touch of heat and a variety of colors. The red, white, and blue hues make it perfect for the Fourth of July or Flag Day.
☀ SUMMER

CUT ALL THE POTATOES INTO QUARTERS. Bring a large pot of salted water to a boil; add potatoes and cook until tender, about 15 to 20 minutes.

Drain in a colander and put into a large bowl. Sprinkle the vinegar and sugar over the warm potatoes and allow to cool. Add the onion, eggs, bell pepper, and cheese to the bowl.

In a small bowl or measuring cup, stir together the mayonnaise, sour cream, and chipotle. Stir into the potato mixture and season to taste with salt and pepper. Cover and refrigerate until ready to serve.

¾ pound small purple potatoes
¾ pound small red potatoes
¾ pound small new potatoes
1 tablespoon red wine vinegar
1 tablespoon sugar
½ diced red onion
2 hard-cooked eggs, peeled and chopped
½ cup diced red bell pepper
½ cup blue cheese, crumbled
¼ cup mayonnaise
¼ cup sour cream
1 chipotle chile in adobo sauce, finely chopped
Salt and freshly ground black pepper

Makes 6 to 8 Servings

Fiesta Fruit Salad

Fruit salads are usually so sweet that they are best served for dessert, but this one has a unique combination of sweet melons and blueberries, acidic lime juice, salty cheese, and tangy cilantro, which makes it a delicious accompaniment to a summer entrée.
☀ SUMMER

IN A LARGE BOWL, combine the melons and blueberries. Stir in the lime juice, and then stir in the cheese and cilantro. Serve the salad within a few hours of tossing it together.

2 cups diced cantaloupe
2 cups diced honeydew melon
2 cups blueberries
¼ cup fresh lime juice
¼ cup crumbled Cotija cheese
¼ cup coarsely chopped cilantro

Makes 6 to 8 Servings

OPPOSITE: *Organ pipe cactus in bloom at dawn, Organ Pipe Cactus National Monument*

Entrées

Chicken Breasts WITH RED BELL PEPPERS AND POBLANO SAUCE

Colorful and flavorful, this chicken entrée is elegant enough for a dinner party but doesn't require much time in the kitchen. Serve it with corn, yellow squash, or rice. 🍂 FALL

TURN OVEN TO BROIL. Remove fat and sinew from the chicken breasts and lay them out on a board covered with plastic wrap or wax paper; cover with more plastic wrap and pound them until they are about ¼-inch thick; remove plastic wrap.

Heat a medium skillet over medium-high heat; add olive oil and butter. Season chicken with salt and pepper and put into the hot pan. Lower the heat and cook until browned on one side and partially cooked through, about 3 to 4 minutes. Turn the chicken over and cook another 3 to 4 minutes. Transfer to a baking sheet. Put a single layer of bell peppers over each piece of chicken and top each piece evenly with the Cotija cheese.

TO PREPARE THE SAUCE, add the onion and chiles to the hot pan in which the chicken was cooked; sauté until the onion is translucent, about 5 to 7 minutes. Add the chicken stock and cook over medium heat until reduced to ¾ cup. Transfer the mixture to a blender and purée. Add the sauce back to the pan and add the cream; cook until warmed through.

Put the prepared chicken into the oven about 4 inches below the heat and broil until cheese is lightly browned and chicken and bell peppers are warmed through, about 3 to 5 minutes. Remove the chicken from the oven and add any accumulated pan juices to the sauce. Put the chicken on serving plates and spoon poblano sauce over the top. Serve immediately.

4 boneless, skinless chicken breast halves
1 tablespoon olive oil
1 tablespoon butter
Salt and freshly ground pepper to taste
2 red bell peppers, roasted, peeled, and seeded (see page 47)
1 cup grated Cotija cheese

POBLANO SAUCE
½ cup chopped yellow onion
2 poblano chiles, roasted, peeled, seeded, and diced (see page 47)
1 cup chicken stock
¼ cup heavy cream

Makes 4 Servings

PAGES 78-79: *Morning light reflecting in the calm waters of Oak Creek, Sedona, Arizona*

RIGHT: *Last light warms a group of mature aspen with a backdrop of conifer dotted with aspen, Escudilla Mountain Wilderness Area, Apache National Forest*

CHICKEN, GREEN CHILE, AND TORTILLA *Lasagna*

Rich and filling, this savory, layered casserole is perfect for a crowd. Put it together a day ahead and take it to your next pot luck dinner or serve it for brunch. I sometimes use whole wheat flour tortillas for a slightly nuttier flavor. ❄ WINTER

PUT THE CHICKEN BREASTS, water, and salt in a large skillet and bring just to a boil. Cover the skillet tightly, lower the heat to simmer, and poach the chicken until cooked through, about 20 minutes. With a pair of tongs, remove the chicken from the liquid and allow it to cool. Add the tomatillos and serranos to the hot chicken liquid, cover, and cook until tomatillos are tender, about 10 minutes. Cool in the liquid.

In a medium skillet, heat the corn oil over medium-high heat; add the onions and then the garlic and cook until soft, 5 to 10 minutes. Put the cooked onions and garlic in a blender; add the cooled tomatillos, serranos, and the liquid in which they were cooked. Purée. Add the green chiles, cilantro, lime juice, and cumin to the blender and purée again. Adjust seasoning with salt and pepper. Stir in sour cream.

In a medium bowl, mix the cheeses together. Shred cooked chicken from the bone and set aside.

Preheat oven to 350°F. Spray a 13 x 9-inch casserole dish with vegetable oil cooking spray. Arrange ⅓ of the tortilla pieces in the bottom of the pan; top with ⅓ of the tomatillo/sour cream sauce. Arrange ½ of the chicken on top of the sauce and sprinkle ⅓ of the cheese over the chicken. Repeat layers once. Finish with remaining tortillas, sauce, and cheese. Bake until heated through, bubbly, and lightly browned, about 45 minutes. Allow to sit for 10 to 15 minutes before serving.

3 skinless chicken breast halves, bone left in
2 cups water
1 teaspoon salt
8 tomatillos, husked removed
2 serrano chiles, stemmed and seeded
1 tablespoon corn oil
1 cup diced white onion
2 cloves garlic, peeled and coarsely chopped
5 Anaheim or New Mexico green chiles, roasted, peeled, and seeded (see page 47)
½ cup fresh cilantro leaves
1 tablespoon fresh lime juice
1 teaspoon ground cumin
Salt and freshly ground pepper to taste
1 ½ cups sour cream
1 cup grated Monterey Jack cheese
1 cup grated Asadero cheese
9 (8-inch) flour tortillas, cut into 1-inch pieces

Makes 12 Servings

CHICKEN AND GREEN CHILE
Enchiladas

This melt-in-your-mouth dish is perfect for a brunch, a buffet, or part of a family dinner. To make it with leftover chicken or turkey, simply follow the filling directions: cook the onions, cumin, garlic, and chiles together and then add the cooked leftovers to the skillet at the last minute to warm them and blend the flavors. ❄ WINTER

TO PREPARE THE SAUCE, in a medium saucepan, bring the tomatillos, jalapeño, onion, garlic, and chicken stock to a boil; reduce the heat and simmer until liquid is reduced to 1 cup, about 20 minutes. Cool slightly. Put mixture into a blender and add diced green chiles, cilantro, and lime juice. Purée. Season to taste with salt and pepper. (Sauce can be made ahead at this point and refrigerated for 2 days or frozen for up to 1 month.) Pour into a shallow bowl and whisk in sour cream. Set aside until ready to assemble enchiladas.

In a large skillet, heat the oil over medium heat; sauté the onions until softened, about 5 minutes. Season chicken cubes with salt and pepper; add to the skillet and continue cooking until chicken is almost cooked through, about 5 minutes. Stir in cumin, garlic, green chiles, and chicken stock and cook another 5 minutes.

Preheat oven to 350°F. Grease a 9 x 13-inch ovenproof pan. Place 6 tortillas between 2 wet paper towels. Place in the microwave oven for 1 minute on high power. One at a time, dip a warm tortilla into the enchilada sauce and place on a work surface. Place 1 tablespoon of the chicken filling, 1 tablespoon of the grated cheese, and 1 tablespoon of the diced onion in the center of the tortilla. Roll up enchilada style and place in the greased baking dish. Repeat with the remaining 5 warm tortillas. Heat the remaining 6 tortillas in wet paper towels and repeat the process until there are 12 enchiladas in the baking dish. Top the enchiladas with any remaining sauce, onions, and cheese and bake in the preheated oven until warm, about 15 to 20 minutes.

To serve, place 2 enchiladas on each plate and garnish with avocado slices, diced tomato, and a drizzle of sour cream.

ENCHILADA SAUCE
4 tomatillos, husked, rinsed, and cut into quarters
1 jalapeño chile, seeded and coarsely chopped
½ cup chopped white onion
1 clove garlic, peeled and crushed
1 ½ cups chicken stock
2 Anaheim or New Mexico green chiles, roasted, peeled, and coarsely chopped (see page 47)
¼ cup chopped fresh cilantro
1 tablespoon fresh lime juice
Salt and pepper to taste
¼ cup sour cream

2 tablespoons corn oil
1 cup diced white onion
3 boneless chicken breast halves, cut into ½-inch cubes
Salt and pepper to taste
1 teaspoon cumin seed, toasted and ground (see page 38)
1 tablespoon finely chopped garlic
8 Anaheim or New Mexico green chiles, roasted, peeled, cored, seeded, and diced (see page 47)
½ cup chicken stock
12 (6-inch) white corn tortillas
2 cups grated Asadero cheese (or substitute Monterey Jack)
¾ cup diced white onion
1 avocado, thinly sliced
1 tomato, seeded and diced
Sour cream

Makes 6 Servings

Apricot CHICKEN

The dried apricots, apricot jam, and apricot nectar in this recipe all come together to give an intense fruit flavor to this moist chicken. The chipotle adds just the right amount of heat. ✳ SPRING

PREHEAT OVEN TO 250°F. Heat a large skillet over medium-high heat; add the butter and olive oil. Season the chicken breasts with salt and pepper and add to the skillet. Cook until browned on one side, about 4 minutes. Turn over and cook until chicken is done and no longer pink in the center, another 4 to 5 minutes. Transfer to a baking pan and keep warm in the preheated oven.

Add the onion to the hot skillet and cook until tender and translucent, about 3 minutes. Add the garlic and cook for 1 minute more. Add apricot nectar, chicken stock, apricot jam, and dried apricots. Bring to a boil and cook until reduced by half, about 10 minutes. Add chipotle and cook 1 minute more. Reduce the heat and add the butter. Put the chicken breasts and their juices back in the skillet and turn to coat with the sauce. Place a chicken breast on each of 4 plates and spoon a few tablespoons of the sauce over each one. Serve immediately.

1 tablespoon butter
1 tablespoon olive oil
4 boneless, skinless chicken breasts
Salt and freshly ground pepper to taste
1/4 cup finely chopped red onion
2 cloves garlic, finely chopped
1 cup apricot nectar
1 cup chicken stock
2 tablespoons apricot jam
10 dried apricots, cut into quarters
1 chipotle chile in adobo sauce, finely chopped
2 tablespoons unsalted butter

Makes 4 Servings

Mexican gold poppies, owl clover, and decaying jumping cholla branch, springtime, Organ Pipe Cactus National Monument

Sonoran *Pasta*

This colorful pasta is chock full of vegetables and could easily be made into a vegetarian dish by eliminating the chicken. Or, substitute cooked shrimp for the chicken and have a delicious variation. If there are any leftovers, this dish makes a great salad served at room temperature. ✳ SPRING

PREHEAT A BARBECUE GRILL. When it is very hot, place the red bell peppers, poblanos, and the onion slices directly on the grill. When they are blackened on one side, turn them over and cook until charred on all sides. Remove peppers and chiles and put them in a plastic bag. Allow them to cool. Remove the onions, coarsely chop, and place in a large bowl. Lower the heat on the grill to medium. Put the ears of corn on the grill and cook, turning frequently, until lightly browned on all sides. Remove from the grill and cut kernels off the cobs (*see* NOTE); add them to the bowl with the onions.

When the peppers and chiles are cool enough to handle, peel, seed, and coarsely chop; add to the bowl. Stir tomatoes, cumin, garlic, chicken, cilantro, and cheese into the onion mixture. Season to taste with salt and pepper.

Bring a large pot of water to a boil over high heat. Add 1 tablespoon salt and the pasta. Cook until pasta is just tender, about 15 minutes. Drain, but do not rinse; toss pasta into the onion mixture and serve immediately.

NOTE: *To cut the corn off the cob without making a mess, stand an ear in the tube of a bundt or angel food cake pan. With a sharp knife, cut the kernels off the cob, which will fall into the pan rather than splatter all over the work surface.*

2 red bell peppers
2 poblano chiles
1 large white onion, cut into ½-inch-thick rounds
4 ears fresh corn, husked
8 medium tomatoes (yellow, if available), coarsely chopped
1 teaspoon ground cumin
2 teaspoons finely chopped garlic
1 ½ cups diced smoked chicken breast
3 tablespoons chopped fresh cilantro
1 cup crumbled Cotija cheese (or substitute goat cheese)
Salt and freshly ground pepper to taste
1 tablespoon salt
12 ounces farfalle pasta

Makes 6 to 8 Servings

CHICKEN *Mole*

Although a bit time-consuming, this recipe is well worth it. Inspired by Rick Bayless' Mole Poblano with Turkey, this dish has complex flavors that will have you begging for more. Serve it with tortillas and rice to take advantage of the earthy sauce. ❄ WINTER

STEM, SEED, AND DEVEIN THE DRIED CHILES. Tear the chiles into flat pieces. Measure 1 tablespoon of the lard into a medium skillet and heat over medium heat. When hot, fry the chile pieces, a few at a time, until they turn nut brown, about 20 seconds per side. Place the fried chile pieces in a bowl and cover them with boiling water, weighting them with a plate to keep them submerged. Soak for an hour, drain, and add the chipotle chile. Purée the chiles in a blender with 1 cup of the chicken stock; strain chile purée through a sieve into a medium bowl. Discard the solid remains and set aside.

Place the tomatoes and chocolate in a large bowl. Put the peppercorns, cloves, and anise seed in a spice or coffee grinder and purée until smooth. Add to the tomato mixture along with the ground cinnamon.

In a small skillet, dry toast the sesame seeds followed by the coriander seeds over medium heat, until lightly browned. Add to the tomato mixture.

Heat 1 tablespoon of the lard in a small skillet; add the almonds and cook until browned, about 4 minutes. Remove with a slotted spoon and add to the tomato mixture. Fry the raisins in the same oil until they puff and brown, about 1 to 2 minutes. Remove with a slotted spoon and add to the tomato mixture.

Add the onion and garlic to the hot skillet and cook until well browned, about 5 minutes. Remove with a slotted spoon and add to the tomato mixture. Add the tortilla pieces to the skillet and cook until browned, adding more lard, if necessary. Add to the tomato mixture. Stir the mixture well and put into a blender with 1 cup of the stock. Blend until smooth, adding more stock, if necessary, to keep the blender from struggling. Strain tomato mixture purée through a medium sieve into a clean bowl. Discard the solid remains and set aside.

In a large kettle or 8-quart saucepan, heat the last 1 tablespoon of lard. Pat the chicken pieces dry with a paper towel and brown them in batches in the hot pan, about 4 minutes per side. Remove to a large roasting pan and set aside.

Pour off any excess fat from the kettle and, over medium heat, add the chile purée. Cook, stirring constantly, until darkened and thick, about 5 minutes. Add the bowl of tomato mixture purée and continue cooking until the mixture thickens slightly, about 5 minutes. Stir in 2 cups of chicken stock, reduce the heat to medium-low, and simmer gently, partially covered, for 45 minutes. Season with salt and sugar.

Preheat oven to 350°F. Pour the sauce over the chicken, cover the pan, and bake until the chicken is tender, about 45 minutes. Remove the chicken from the pan and spoon any fat off the sauce. Let the chicken cool, skin it, and slice the meat from the bones against the grain; put the chicken back into the pan with the sauce, cover, and heat in the preheated oven until warmed through, about 20 minutes. Uncover the pan and sprinkle with extra sesame seeds, if desired, before serving.

5 guajillo chiles
5 ancho chiles
3 tablespoons lard or vegetable oil
1 chipotle chile in adobo sauce, seeded
1 quart chicken stock
1 (14 ½-ounce) can fire roasted tomatoes, drained
1 ounce Mexican chocolate, coarsely chopped
5 black peppercorns
2 whole cloves
¼ teaspoon anise seed
½ teaspoon ground cinnamon
2 tablespoons sesame seeds
¼ teaspoon coriander seeds
¼ cup unskinned almonds
¼ cup raisins
½ cup sliced onion
2 cloves garlic, peeled
1 corn tortilla, torn into pieces
2 (3 ½-pound) chickens, cut into pieces
1 teaspoon salt
2 tablespoons sugar

Makes 6 to 8 Servings

Chocolate

CHOCOLATE, THE FOOD OF THE GODS, is perhaps Mexico's greatest gift to the world. When Montezuma, the ancient Aztec ruler, drank the unsweetened *xocolatl*, it was a much different drink than what we know as cocoa today. It contained seeds, corn, dried flowers, and chiles, and it is said that Montezuma used to consume 50 golden goblets of it a day to increase his sexual prowess. The much-impressed Spanish took it back to Europe where sugar was added, making it a sensation at the Spanish royal court where it was considered an aphrodisiac and a cure to many ills. Chocolate's popularity quickly spread throughout Europe where the English added milk, the Dutch perfected the process of making cocoa powder, and the Swiss eventually developed the chocolate bar. In Mexico today, chocolate is usually blended with almonds and cinnamon and used in drinks and dark, rich mole sauces. Mexican chocolate is gritty because it doesn't go through the conching, or smoothing, process that American and European chocolates do.

Scientists have found that dark chocolate is rich in flavonoids, which act as antioxidants, and it offers protection against LDL cholesterol and has a positive effect on HDL levels, too. Chocolate is known to help lower the risk of heart disease, and chocolate lovers are happier, too, because chocolate releases seratonin, the "happy" chemical in the brain. So, eat chocolate and live a happier, healthier life!

ACHIOTE BUTTER-BASTED *Turkey* WITH ANCHO GRAVY

Basting the turkey with butter and achiote paste yields a moist, flavorful bird, and the slightly piquant sauce is a refreshing change from traditional gravy. Achiote paste is a combination of chiles, spices, and achiote seeds, which have an earthy taste and are often used as a coloring agent, especially in Cheddar-like cheeses. The perfect complement to this complex dish is my tart and colorful cranberry relish offered on page 89. 🌿 FALL

PREHEAT OVEN TO 325°F. Remove stem and seeds from the ancho chiles, cutting them so they lay flat. Heat a heavy skillet over high heat and when hot, toast the chiles just until fragrant, about 1 minute on each side (see page 38). Place chiles in a bowl and cover with hot, but not boiling, water. Soak until softened, about 15 to 20 minutes.

Remove giblets and neck from the turkey and discard. Thoroughly rinse the bird and pat dry; salt and pepper the cavities. Remove one of the softened ancho chiles from the soaking water and cut it into strips. Place the strips and quartered onion in the breast cavity of the turkey.

Cream together the achiote paste and butter. Gently loosen skin on the breast of the turkey and ease half the butter mixture between the flesh and the skin. Rub the remaining mixture over the rest of the turkey.

Truss the turkey and place it on a rack in a roasting pan. Pour 1 cup of the stock into the bottom of the pan. Loosely cover the bird with an aluminum foil tent and put the turkey into the preheated oven. Baste the turkey after 30 minutes and thereafter every 20 minutes or so with the juices from the pan. Cook turkey until it reaches an internal temperature of 170°F. in the breast and 185°F. in the thigh, about 5 to 6 hours. Remove foil for the last hour of cooking to brown the skin. Remove turkey and rack from the roasting pan and allow turkey to rest while preparing the relish and the sauce.

IF DESIRED, PREPARE THE CRANBERRY RELISH (see page 89) as directed and set aside.

TO MAKE THE ANCHO GRAVY, put remaining 2 ancho chiles and ½ cup of their soaking liquid into a blender. Add poblanos and purée. Season to taste with salt and pepper; set aside.

Pour all liquid from the bottom of the roasting pan into a measuring cup. Skim off all the fat; discard all but 4 tablespoons of the fat, reserving the de-fatted juices from the turkey in the measuring cup. Put the 4 tablespoons of skimmed fat back into the roasting pan. Place the roasting pan over medium heat and stir the masa harina into the fat; continue cooking, stirring constantly, for 2 or 3 minutes, until the mixture forms a paste. Gradually add the reserved de-fatted pan juices and remaining 3 cups chicken stock, scraping up any brown bits and stirring until smooth. Stir in ancho chile purée, season to taste with salt and pepper, and strain, if desired. If the gravy is too spicy, add 2 to 3 tablespoons cream or butter to cut the heat. Carve turkey and serve with ancho chile on the side.

NOTE: *Achiote paste can be found at Latino markets and masa harina is usually found in the same department as the flour in grocery stores.*

3 ancho chiles
1 fresh (22 to 24-pound) turkey
Salt and pepper to taste
1 large white onion, cut into quarters
3 tablespoons achiote paste (*see* NOTE)
¾ cup butter
4 cups chicken stock
2 poblano chiles, roasted, peeled, and seeded (see page 47)
¼ cup masa harina

Makes 14 to 16 Servings

Cranberry RELISH

Hazelnuts, also called filberts, add a delicious crunch to this relish. To toast them, place on a baking sheet and bake at 350°F. for 10 to 15 minutes. Remove them from the oven and wrap them in a clean kitchen towel. Roll the towel back and forth until most of the skins have loosened; use immediately or store in the freezer. For delicious leftovers, create tostadas with tortillas, shredded turkey, lettuce, jack cheese, and this tasty relish. ◢ FALL

PUT ORANGE JUICE AND SUGAR in a small heavy saucepan and heat over medium heat, stirring, until sugar is dissolved. Remove from heat and stir in cranberries; allow to cool to room temperature.

Put cooled cranberry mixture in a non-reactive bowl. Stir in remaining ingredients. If making relish ahead of time, do not add cilantro, salt, or pepper until just before serving.

¼ cup fresh orange juice
½ cup sugar
2 cups cranberries, coarsely chopped
¼ cup coarsely chopped, toasted hazelnuts (see page 38)
1 red bell pepper, roasted, peeled, seeded, and diced (see page 47)
1 poblano chile, roasted, peeled, seeded, and diced (see page 47)
2 tablespoons grated orange zest
⅓ cup chopped cilantro leaves
Salt and pepper to taste

Makes about 3 Cups

SOUTHWEST CLUB *Wraps*

In this scrumptious wrap, you'll find all the flavors of a good club sandwich, plus the addition of a little heat and creamy avocado. You may never go back to the original version. ☼ SUMMER

COMBINE THE CHIPOTLE AND MAYONNAISE in a small bowl. Spread 1 tablespoon on the surface of each tortilla. Cover the mayonnaise with thin slices of turkey breast (about 3 per tortilla) and spread about ¼ cup guacamole over the turkey. Sprinkle tomato and bacon pieces over all and top with sprouts and lettuce. Starting from the bottom of each tortilla, roll it in a tight roll. Slice the roll in half diagonally and decoratively place two pieces on each serving plate.

1 teaspoon chopped chipotle chile in adobo sauce
¼ cup mayonnaise
4 (10-inch) flour tortillas
12 thin turkey breast slices
1 cup Hand-Mixed Guacamole (see page 22)
1 cup seeded and diced tomato
8 slices bacon, cooked crisp and chopped
1 cup alfalfa sprouts
2 cups finely chopped lettuce

Makes 4 Servings

SOUTHWEST *Turkey* BURGERS

My Southwest Spice mix adds just the right zing to the ground turkey in this succulent, healthy alternative to hamburgers. Adding the grilled onions, smoky chipotle, creamy avocado, and mellow cheese elevates this burger to the scrumptious category. 🌿 FALL

IN A MEDIUM BOWL, mix together the turkey, green onions, and spice mix. Form the mixture into 4 patties, about 1-inch thick.

Preheat a barbecue grill. Oil both sides of each onion slice; salt and pepper to taste. When the grill is hot put oiled onions and turkey patties on the grill and cook until onions are tender and slightly charred, about 5 minutes per side. Remove from grill and set aside. Continue cooking patties until cooked through, about 1 minute longer per side. During the last minute of cooking, place a slice of cheese on each patty and continue cooking until cheese is melted. Open the buns and place them cut sides down on the grill; cook about 1 minute, until lightly browned.

In a small bowl, mix together the chipotle chile and the mayonnaise. Spread about 1 tablespoon on 1 half of each bun. Place a cooked patty on top of the chile mayonnaise, top with slices of avocado, tomato, and grilled onions, and cover with the other halves of the buns. Serve immediately.

1 ¼ pounds ground turkey
½ cup chopped green onion
1 tablespoon Southwest Spice Mix (see below)
1 tablespoon olive oil
4 large red onion slices, ½-inch thick
Salt and freshly ground pepper to taste
4 slices Asadero cheese
4 hamburger buns, split in half horizontally
1 chipotle chile in adobo sauce
½ cup mayonnaise
1 avocado, peeled, pitted, and thinly sliced
1 tomato, thinly sliced

Makes 4 Servings

BARBARA'S SOUTHWEST *Spice Mix*

I use this seasoning on everything–as a rub for chicken, seafood, and poultry; sprinkled on tortilla chips before they're baked; lightly tossed with vegetables; and as a seasoning in dips and salad dressings.

HEAT A SMALL SKILLET OVER MEDIUM HEAT; add cumin, coriander, and black peppercorns. Cook until cumin is a shade darker and all of the spices give off their aromas, about 5 minutes. Put the toasted seeds in a spice grinder and pulse until finely ground (see page 38). Transfer to a small bowl. Add the chile powder, sugar, salt, and cayenne and stir together well. Put in a glass jar with a tightly fitting lid and store at room temperature for up to 1 month.

NOTE: *Pure chile powder is simply a dried chile ground up with no added spices or preservatives. It is available in specialty stores and through mail order catalogs. The chile powder found in grocery stores usually has a number of other ingredients added, so carefully check the label.*

1 tablespoon cumin seeds
1 tablespoon coriander seeds
1 tablespoon black peppercorns
2 tablespoons pure chile powder (*see* NOTE)
1 teaspoon sugar
1 teaspoon salt
½ teaspoon cayenne pepper

Makes about ½ Cup

Quail Stuffed with Wild Rice on a Creamy Corn Sauce

A lovely way to celebrate the fall, this robust dish can be served as an entrée with two quail per person or as a first course with just one. It works best with whole quail, not partially boned quail. 🌿 FALL

PREHEAT OVEN TO 350°F. Stuff each quail with about ⅓ cup of the rice pilaf; tie the quail's legs together with kitchen string so the bird keeps its shape and the rice does not spill out. Rub the quail all over with the olive oil.

In a small bowl, mix together the cumin, sage, salt, and pepper and rub each quail with some of the mixture.

Heat a large skillet over medium-high heat; add corn oil. Add quail, in batches, if necessary, and brown on all sides, about 8 minutes total. Transfer browned quail to a baking sheet and place in the preheated oven. Cook until juices run clear when a thigh is pierced with a knife, about 30 minutes.

TO PREPARE THE CREAMY CORN SAUCE, in the same skillet, add the corn, garlic, shallots, and jalapeño and cook over medium heat until the corn begins to lightly brown around the edges, about 4 minutes. Season with salt and pepper and add the chicken stock. Cook about 2 more minutes, scraping up any brown bits on the bottom of the pan. Transfer the mixture to a blender; purée until very smooth. Force the purée through a strainer into a small saucepan and discard any solid remains. Add the cream and heat to the desired temperature.

Spoon the sauce equally onto 4 serving plates and top each plate with 2 cooked quail. Serve immediately.

8 quail
1 recipe Wild Rice and Porcini Pilaf (see page 140), cooled
1 tablespoon olive oil
¼ teaspoon toasted and ground cumin seed (see page 38)
¼ teaspoon dried sage
1 teaspoon salt
¼ teaspoon freshly ground black pepper
2 tablespoons corn oil

CREAMY CORN SAUCE
¾ cup corn kernels
1 clove garlic, finely chopped
¼ cup diced shallots
1 jalapeño chile, seeded and diced
Salt and freshly ground pepper to taste
1 cup chicken stock
¼ cup heavy cream

Makes 4 Servings

Old log watering trough west of Alpine, Arizona

Duck Breasts with Hot Orange Sauce

I rarely use habanero chiles because they are so hot, but adding just a hint to these succulent duck breasts intensifies the orange flavor and adds just enough heat to make your taste buds sit up and take notice.

🌿 FALL

SCORE THE BREASTS by making a series of thin slashes diagonally across the skin of each breast, cutting as deep into the skin as you can without cutting all the way down to the meat. Give each breast a 90° turn and make a new series of slashes that cross over the other ones. Season the breasts with salt and pepper.

Using a sharp vegetable peeler, take the zest off two of the oranges; coarsely chop the zest and place in a bowl or shallow dish large enough to hold the breasts. Squeeze the juice out of the oranges into the bowl with the zest. Stir in 2 teaspoons of the sugar and ½ teaspoon of the diced chile; add the breasts, cover, and let them marinate in the refrigerator overnight.

Take the zest off the other 2 oranges and cut into strips about 3-inches long and ⅛-inch wide. In a small saucepan bring 2 cups of water to a boil and add the strips; cook about 30 seconds, strain, and rinse with cold water. Wipe out the saucepan. Juice the 2 oranges and strain into the dry saucepan. Add the cooked orange strips and the remaining sugar and diced chile. Bring the mixture to a boil and remove it from the heat. Let the zest steep in the hot juice for at least 5 minutes. Spoon or strain the zest out of the juice and reserve the zest and juice separately.

About 20 minutes before serving, take the breasts out of the marinade, pat them dry, and wipe off any pieces of zest clinging to the surface. Heat a large sauté pan over medium-high heat; sauté the breasts, skin side down, until the breasts barely begin to feel firm to the touch and the skin is well browned and crispy, about 8 minutes. Turn the breasts over and cook them for 1 minute more. At this point, the breasts should be slightly underdone. Remove the breasts from the pan and prepare the glaze.

Pour the fat out of the pan into a gravy separator. Pour the reserved boiled orange juice and the vinegar into the pan in which the duck was cooked. Boil the mixture over high heat until it looks syrupy, about 2 minutes. Pouring from the gravy separator, add any duck juices into the pan; add the butter and stir until sauce is smooth. Put the breasts, skin side down, back in the pan. Move them around in the boiling orange juice mixture until they are well coated, about 2 minutes. Turn them over and glaze them on the meat side for another minute.

Slice the breasts diagonally into ¼-inch slices and arrange on hot plates. Drizzle with any remaining orange mixture and sprinkle the slices with the cooked orange zest. Serve immediately.

8 boneless single duck breasts (about 4 pounds)
Salt and freshly ground pepper to taste
4 juicing oranges, washed
3 tablespoons sugar
1 teaspoon diced habanero chile
½ cup sherry vinegar
1 tablespoon butter

Makes 8 Servings

Ostrich Kebabs with Chile-Honey Glaze

Ostrich meat is even lower in fat than turkey and tastes very much like beef. It's available through butcher shops, specialty grocery stores, or mail-order, but because of its rarity, it can be relatively pricey. Try it for a unique experience, or you can substitute beef for the ostrich in this recipe for a less expensive option.

☼ SUMMER

PUT THE OSTRICH MEAT IN a shallow glass baking dish or heavy plastic bag. Mix all the marinade ingredients together and pour over the meat. Cover and refrigerate overnight.

TO PREPARE THE CHILE-HONEY GLAZE, in a small bowl, stir together the honey, orange juice, and chile powder until smooth. Set aside.

Remove the ostrich from the marinade and thread on skewers, alternating meat with bell peppers, onions, and tomatoes. Put skewers on a baking sheet and brush with the Chile-Honey Glaze.

Preheat a barbecue grill to medium heat. Lightly oil the grill surface. Put the skewers on the grill and cook about 4 minutes; turn over and cook until meat is browned (do not overcook) and vegetables are slightly charred, another 4 to 5 minutes. Serve warm.

1 ½ pounds ostrich meat from the inside and outside leg cuts, cut into 1-inch cubes

MARINADE
½ cup Merlot
¼ cup olive oil
1 onion, thinly sliced
1 teaspoon freshly ground black pepper
4 cloves garlic, peeled and crushed
2 serrano chiles, seeded and coarsely chopped
1 bay leaf

CHILE-HONEY GLAZE
2 tablespoons honey
1 tablespoon fresh orange juice
½ teaspoon ancho chile powder

1 yellow bell pepper, cut into 1-inch squares
1 onion, cut into 1-inch pieces
18 cherry or grape tomatoes

Makes 4 to 6 Servings

Ostrich Farming

IN THE YEARS BEFORE WORLD WAR I, ostrich plumes were so popular in women's hats that daring Arizona entrepreneurs tried their hand at ostrich farming. Unfortunately, world fashions changed and plumes went out of style by 1914, and those who had made fortunes in ostrich ranching soon lost them. Today, though, you can still see a working ostrich ranch right along Interstate 10 in the shadow of Picacho Peak between Phoenix and Tucson. "Rooster" Cogburn's Ostrich Ranch raises these flightless birds mainly for their healthy meat, but also for their feathers, which are once again in high demand by car manufacturers who use them to dust their vehicles before painting.

Ostrich meat is popular in many upscale restaurants, because it is unique, delicious, high in iron, and has the lowest fat content of all meats, only 1.2 percent. Its taste is similar to beef and the texture is similar to venison. Most of the meat derived from the ostrich is taken from the leg, thigh, and back. Because it is so low in fat, it is important not to overcook it, as it will become tough if it is cooked past medium-rare. With its increasing popularity, it is now available in butcher shops and specialty stores.

SPICY *Lamb* CHOPS

This is one of my favorite things to cook for a week-day dinner for a small number of people. Keep it informal because the best part is picking up the chops with your hands and chewing on the bones.

☼ SUMMER

MIX ALL MARINADE INGREDIENTS TOGETHER and spread mixture over both sides of each lamb chop. Allow to sit at room temperature for about 1 hour.

Preheat a barbecue grill or a broiler. If using a grill, cook the chops over medium heat for 2 to 4 minutes per side, depending on how thick they are. If using the broiler, put marinated lamb chops on a broiler pan or baking sheet and cook about 4 inches under the heating element for 2 minutes; turn over and cook other side until cooked to the desired amount of doneness. Serve immediately with plenty of napkins.

MARINADE

¼ cup olive oil

¼ cup chopped cilantro

4 cloves garlic, finely chopped

2 teaspoons salt

2 teaspoons ground cumin

1 teaspoon ground coriander

1 teaspoon cayenne pepper

1 teaspoon freshly ground black pepper

8 loin lamb chops, trimmed of fat

Makes 4 Servings

OPPOSITE: *Next to Picacho Peak, between Phoenix and Tucson, Rooster Cogburn's ostrich farm is quite the roadside attraction*

MARINATED AND STUFFED *Filet Mignons* WITH *Merlot* HABANERO SAUCE

These tender filets are marinated in wine and balsamic vinegar, stuffed with pine nuts and cheese, and served with a sauce made simply by reducing the marinade. The habanero, a very hot chile, is used sparingly to add a touch of heat and to complement the fruitiness of the wine. ✳ WINTER

CUT A SLIT HORIZONTALLY through each filet to form a pocket. Rub the salt onto the outer surfaces of the filets and place them in a shallow glass dish. Refrigerate, uncovered, for 1 hour.

Put the wine, vinegar, thyme leaves, and habanero into a blender and purée. Pour the marinade over the filets, rubbing the salt off into the marinade. Cover and refrigerate for another hour.

Preheat oven to 300°F. Take the meat out of the marinade and drain on paper towels. Reserve the marinade. Stuff about ¼ cup cheese and 1 tablespoon pine nuts into the pocket of each filet. Press together to keep filling in.

Heat a large skillet over medium-high heat. Add 1 tablespoon of the butter and the olive oil. When hot, add the filets; sear until brown, about 2 minutes. Turn over and cook the other side until brown, another 2 minutes. Remove filets to a baking sheet fitted with a rack. Pour reserved marinade into the hot skillet and cook over high heat, scraping the bottom of the pan to pick up any bits, until the marinade is reduced to about ¾ cup. Strain into a saucepan and add the remaining tablespoon of butter. Keep warm.

Bake the filets until their internal temperature reaches 135°F. for medium rare. Allow filets to rest for 5 minutes before serving. Put each filet on a serving plate and spoon a few tablespoons of the sauce over it. Serve immediately.

6 (4 to 5-ounce) beef tenderloin filets (filet mignons)
1 tablespoon Kosher or sea salt
½ cup Merlot
½ cup balsamic vinegar
2 teaspoons fresh thyme leaves
¼ teaspoon finely chopped habanero chile
1 ½ cups grated Monterey Jack cheese
6 tablespoons toasted pine nuts (see page 38)
2 tablespoons butter
1 tablespoon olive oil

Makes 6 Servings

MARINATED *Flank Steak* WITH ANCHO CHILE SAUCE

Flank steak is a delicious cut of meat, especially if it is marinated, grilled, and then cut across the grain. Good on its own, it's even more delectable when served with this earthy ancho sauce. If you have leftovers, see the Marinated Steak Salad recipe on page 72. ☼ SUMMER

TO PREPARE THE MARINADE, combine all marinade ingredients in a 9 x 13-inch glass pan. Add the flank steak and turn it to coat both sides. Cover with plastic wrap and refrigerate for at least 1 hour or overnight.

TO PREPARE THE ANCHO CHILE SAUCE, remove the stems and seeds from the ancho chiles and soak them in very hot water until soft, about 30 minutes. Place chiles and ½ cup of the soaking water in a blender with the poblano chiles; purée until smooth and then strain into a small saucepan. Add cream, salt, and pepper and heat over medium heat. Keep warm.

Preheat a barbecue grill to medium-high heat. Remove the steak from the marinade and place on the preheated grill. Cook until browned on both sides and medium rare with an internal temperature of 130°F., about 4 minutes per side. Slice diagonally against the grain and divide the slices among 4 to 6 plates. Serve warm with Ancho Chile Sauce.

NOTE: *Ancho chiles are simply poblano chiles that are ripened until red and then dried, so it makes perfect sense to combine their separately unique tastes in this complex sauce.*

MARINADE
¼ cup vegetable oil
¼ cup soy sauce
1 tablespoon sliced ginger
1 clove garlic, crushed

1 flank steak, about 1 ½ pounds

ANCHO CHILE SAUCE
3 ancho chiles (*see* NOTE)
3 poblano chiles, roasted, peeled, and seeded (see page 47)
½ cup cream
Salt and freshly ground pepper to taste

Makes 4 to 6 Servings

First light below a turbulent sky reddens formations of cross-bedded sandstone, Coyote Buttes, Paria Plateau

Spice-Rubbed Buffalo Tenderloin with Porcini Butter

Buffalo, or more correctly, bison, is a flavorful meat that tastes similar to beef. Bison meat does not marble like beef, though, so it's important to cook it rare to medium for the most tender results. 🌿 FALL

TO PREPARE THE PORCINI BUTTER, put dried mushrooms into a small bowl and cover with ¼ cup very hot water. Allow to sit until soft, about 30 minutes. Line a strainer with a piece of cheesecloth or a paper towel and put it over another bowl; pour the mushrooms and their liquid through it. Reserve the liquid. Put the strained mushrooms, garlic, butter, and 1 tablespoon of the reserved liquid into a food processor or blender; purée until well incorporated. Put the mushroom butter onto a piece of wax paper or plastic wrap and form into a 4-inch log. Refrigerate until firm. The butter will keep, refrigerated, for at least 3 days and up to 1 month frozen (*see* NOTE).

PREHEAT OVEN TO 250°F. In a small bowl, combine the cumin, chile powder, salt, and pepper. Rub all sides of each filet with some of the spice mixture. Heat a large ovenproof skillet over medium-high heat; add the olive oil. When hot, sear the filets until brown, about 1 minute per side. Put the entire pan into the oven and cook until the filets reach an internal temperature of 130°F. for rare, about 8 to 10 minutes. Remove the pan from the oven and allow the filets to rest for 5 minutes. Transfer filets to serving plates. Slice 4 individual ½-inch-thick rounds from the log of porcini butter and place a round on top of each filet. Serve immediately.

NOTE: *If you have any leftover Porcini Butter, it is absolutely fabulous on cooked vegetables.*

PORCINI BUTTER
¼ cup dried porcini mushrooms
1 teaspoon finely chopped garlic
½ cup (1 stick) unsalted butter, at
    room temperature

SPICE RUB
1 teaspoon cumin, toasted and ground
    (see page 38)
1 teaspoon ancho chile powder
1 teaspoon salt
½ teaspoon freshly ground black pepper

4 buffalo tenderloin filets, about 1 ¼-inch thick
1 tablespoon olive oil

Makes 4 Servings

BONELESS LEG OF *Lamb* WITH POTATOES AND JALAPEÑOS

Using the liquid from the pickled jalapeños in the marinade adds flavor but not too much heat and the potatoes pick up flavor from the lamb. ❋ SPRING

PUT THE LAMB IN A NON-REACTIVE DISH or a large zip-lock plastic bag. Combine pickling liquid and oil in a small bowl and coat all sides of the lamb; allow to marinate for 1 hour at room temperature. Preheat oven to 400°F. Remove the lamb from the marinade and sprinkle liberally with salt and pepper.

In a large bowl, toss together the potatoes, onions, jalapeños, and salt. Turn out onto the bottom of a roasting pan large enough to hold the lamb. Place the lamb on top of the potato mixture. Roast until the internal temperature of the lamb is 145°F., about 1 hour to 1 hour 15 minutes. Remove from the oven and allow the lamb to rest for 15 minutes. Slice the lamb, removing any string, and serve it on top of a bed of the potato mixture.

1 (3 to 4-pound) boneless leg of lamb, trimmed of fat and tied
¼ cup liquid from 10-ounce jar of pickled jalapeño chiles
2 tablespoons olive oil
Salt and freshly ground black pepper to taste
4 medium Russet or Idaho potatoes (about 4 cups), cut into ½-inch cubes
2 red onions, thinly sliced
¼ cup diced pickled jalapeño chiles
1 teaspoon salt

Makes 8 Servings

PULLED *Pork*

Cooking the meat in an ancho chile and apple cider mixture yields melt-in-your mouth pork that is absolutely scrumptious wrapped in tortillas, stuffed into roasted poblanos, or tucked into toasted rolls. 🍃 FALL

OPEN ANCHO CHILES, remove stems and seeds. Heat a small skillet over medium heat and add anchos; toast just until they begin to soften and give off their aroma, about 1 minute per side. Put them into a medium bowl and cover with very hot water. Allow to sit until softened, about 30 minutes. Place the softened anchos, cider, vinegar, garlic, serranos, and spices into a blender. Purée until smooth.

Preheat oven to 350°F. Cover the bottom of a heavy roasting pan with half of the onions. Sprinkle half the cherries over the onions. Lay the pork loin on the bed of onions and cherries; cover with the remaining onions and cherries. Pour the ancho mixture over all; cover tightly with aluminum foil or a lid and bake until the pork is tender enough to shred with a fork, about 4 hours. Remove the cover, and with 2 forks, shred the pork into the juices, mixing with the onions and cherries. Serve with warm tortillas or use as a stuffing for roasted poblanos.

3 ancho chiles
3 cups apple cider
¼ cup cider vinegar
4 cloves garlic, coarsely chopped
2 serrano chiles, seeded and coarsely chopped
2 teaspoons ground cumin
¼ teaspoon ground cinnamon
2 teaspoons dried oregano
2 teaspoons salt
2 large onions, thinly sliced
½ cup dried cherries
3 pounds boneless pork loin

Makes 8 to 10 Servings

Grilled *Pork Chops* with Corn and Avocado Salsa

People tend to overcook pork, making it tough and dry, but it's only necessary to cook it to an internal temperature of 150°F. These zingy pork chops are complemented by a soothing, eye-appealing salsa.

☀ SUMMER

COMBINE ALL MARINADE INGREDIENTS together in a shallow glass baking dish. Add pork chops and turn to coat. Marinate at least 30 minutes or as long as 4 hours.

TO PREPARE THE CORN AND AVOCADO SALSA, preheat a barbecue grill to medium heat; coat grill rack with vegetable oil cooking spray and grill the corn, turning occasionally, until lightly browned, about 15 minutes. Cut the kernels off the cob and transfer to a medium bowl (*see* NOTE). Add tomato, jalapeño, onion, cilantro, and lime juice. Just before serving, add the avocado and salt to taste.

Remove the pork chops from the marinade; sprinkle with salt. With the barbecue grill still on medium heat, place chops on oiled grill rack, cover, and cook until browned, about 8 to 10 minutes; turn the chops over, cover, and cook until done, about 8 to 10 minutes more. Place a pork chop on each of 4 serving plates and spoon some of the salsa alongside. Serve immediately.

NOTE: *The best way to cut the corn off the cob without creating a mess is to stand the cob in the tube of an angel food cake or bundt pan, and, with a sharp knife, cut down the sides of the corn cob. The kernels will fall into the pan rather than spray all over the kitchen.*

MARINADE
¼ cup tequila
¼ cup Dijon mustard
1 tablespoon finely chopped garlic
1 jalapeño chile, seeded and finely chopped
1 tablespoon chopped fresh cilantro
½ teaspoon freshly ground black pepper

4 pork loin chops, trimmed of fat
Salt to taste

CORN AND AVOCADO SALSA
1 ear corn, shucked
⅓ cup seeded and diced tomato
1 jalapeño chile, seeded and finely chopped
⅓ cup finely chopped red onion
1 tablespoon chopped cilantro
1 tablespoon lime juice
½ cup diced avocado
Salt to taste

Makes 4 Servings

Havasu Creek, Havasu Canyon, Grand Canyon National Park

Marinated Pork *Tenderloin* with Avocado Sauce

This flavorful pork is delicious on its own but the avocado sauce is a terrific addition. Its cool, silky texture is a perfect contrast to the spicy meat. The sauce was inspired by a soup I learned to make from the late James Beard. If you want to try the soup yourself, simply add another cup of stock to the sauce recipe below and serve the soup chilled. ❀ SPRING

TO PREPARE THE MARINADE, slit open the chiles with a knife and remove the stems and seeds; flatten the chiles. Heat a medium, heavy skillet over medium-high heat; toast the chiles until soft and they begin to give off their aromas, being careful not to scorch them, about 1 minute per side. Place the toasted chiles in a saucepan with the vinegar and ½ cup of water. Bring to a boil, reduce the heat, and simmer until the chiles are tender, about 10 to 15 minutes. Transfer the contents of the saucepan to a blender.

In the same skillet in which the chiles were toasted, toast the cumin seed and black pepper-corns, stirring constantly, until cumin is lightly browned and aromatic (see page 38). Add the cumin and peppercorns to the blender along with the oregano, cloves, cinnamon, garlic, and salt. Blend until smooth. Transfer chile paste to a medium bowl and allow to cool.

Spread a thin layer of chile paste over all sides of the pork tenderloins. Put them in a glass shallow dish or plastic bag, refrigerate, and allow to marinate for 2 to 4 hours or overnight.

TO PREPARE THE AVOCADO SAUCE, in a blender or food processor put the avocado, lime juice, Tabasco, and stock; purée until smooth. Add the cream, salt, and pepper; pulse until blended. If not using immediately, cover and refrigerate. Before serving, bring the sauce to room temperature and stir in the chives, if desired.

Preheat oven to 350°F. Place the tenderloins on a rack on a baking sheet and cook until the internal temperature reaches 150°F., about 30 to 35 minutes. The pork should still be a bit pink inside. Allow the meat to rest for 5 minutes. Slice on the diagonal into ½-inch slices and place approximately 3 slices on each serving plate. Spoon Avocado Sauce alongside the meat and serve immediately.

MARINADE
1 ancho chile
3 dried red New Mexico chiles
¼ cup white vinegar
1 teaspoon cumin seed
½ teaspoon dried black peppercorns
½ teaspoon dried Mexican oregano
⅛ teaspoon ground cloves
¼ teaspoon ground cinnamon
1 clove garlic, coarsely chopped
½ teaspoon salt

2 pork tenderloins, fat and skin removed

AVOCADO SAUCE
1 large ripe avocado, peeled, pitted, and diced
1 tablespoon fresh lime juice
¼ teaspoon Tabasco Jalapeño Sauce
½ cup chicken stock
¼ cup heavy cream
Salt and freshly ground pepper to taste
1 tablespoon chopped chives (optional)

Makes 6 to 8 Servings

OPPOSITE: *A snowstorm clears at first light over snow-blanketed Steamboat Rock with piñon pine foreground viewed from Schnebly Hill Road*

Medallions OF PORK TENDERLOIN WITH CREAMY *Guajillo* SAUCE

A simple, yet elegant dish, this pork tenderloin can be served buffet-style and kept warm in its sauce. The sweet heat in the sauce comes from the guajillo chiles, which are thin-fleshed, shiny, and a deep orange-red color. ❄ WINTER

STEM AND SEED THE GUAJILLO CHILES so they are flat. Heat a small skillet over medium heat; when hot, add the chiles. Toast on each side until they are pliable and give off an aroma, about 1 minute per side. Transfer the chiles to a bowl and cover with hot water. Allow to soak until soft, about 30 minutes. Transfer chiles to a mini-processor or food grinder with 1 tablespoon of the soaking liquid; purée. Strain purée into a small bowl and discard the solid remains.

In a large skillet, heat the clarified butter or butter and olive oil. Salt and pepper the pork medallions. When butter stops foaming, add the pork medallions, in batches if necessary. Sear and cook them about 5 minutes per side, or until the internal temperature is about 150°F. Remove the meat from the pan to a warm plate. Deglaze the skillet with the wine. Add the cream and chile purée and cook until reduced to the desired consistency. Stir in chives. Put the pork medallions back in the pan and cook until heated through. Place two medallions on each plate and spoon sauce over them. Serve immediately.

2 guajillo chiles
2 tablespoons clarified butter (or 1 tablespoon
    butter and 1 tablespoon olive oil)
Salt and freshly ground pepper to taste
1 ½ pounds pork tenderloin, cut into
    12 medallions
2 tablespoons red wine
1 cup heavy cream
2 teaspoons chopped fresh chives

Makes 6 Servings

COTIJA-CRUSTED *Halibut* WITH *Tomatillo* SALSA

Even a non-fish lover will adore this flavorful halibut. The crunchy cheese topping and the zesty green sauce make it a real winner. 🍃 FALL

TO PREPARE THE TOMATILLO SALSA, combine all the ingredients in a non-reactive bowl. Let stand at least 1 hour and not more than 3 hours before serving to allow flavors to blend.

TO PREPARE HALIBUT, set up 3 separate, shallow bowls. Place the flour in the first bowl. In the second, beat the eggs and water. In the third, combine the bread crumbs, Cotija, and lemon zest. Dredge the flesh side of the fillets in the flour first, shaking off the excess. Next, dip the flesh side in the egg. Third, dredge the flesh side in the bread crumb mixture to coat. Pat gently to press mixture into the egg.

Preheat oven to 400°F. Heat the olive oil in an ovenproof nonstick pan on medium-high heat. Carefully place the fillets crust side down in the pan. Sear until a golden-brown crust forms, about 4 minutes. Turn fillets over and place the pan in the preheated oven. Roast until the centers are pearly white and opaque, about 3 to 5 minutes.

Spoon about 3 tablespoons of salsa on each of 8 plates. Place fillets on top of the salsa and garnish each with a sprig of fresh cilantro.

TOMATILLO SALSA

2 jalapeño chiles, seeded and diced
3 cloves garlic, finely chopped
½ cup finely chopped red onion
8 tomatillos, husked and diced
1 cup diced red, yellow, or orange bell pepper
¼ cup chopped cilantro
2 tablespoons fresh lime juice
Salt and freshly ground pepper to taste

½ cup flour
2 large eggs
2 tablespoons water
1 ½ cups panko bread crumbs
¾ cup grated Cotija cheese
2 teaspoons grated lemon zest
8 (4 to 6-ounce) halibut or other firm white fish fillets, skin removed
3 tablespoons olive oil
8 sprigs cilantro

Makes 8 Servings

FISH IN *Cornhusks* WITH ORANGE-TOMATO SALSA

Cooking food in cornhusks keeps it moist and imparts a hint of corn flavor in the food. Dried cornhusks are available in most supermarkets and in many specialty stores. Before using them, it's necessary to soften them in water for about 30 minutes so they are pliable. ☀ SUMMER

FILL A LARGE BOWL OR LOAF PAN with warm water and add the dried cornhusks. Put a weight on top of them to keep them submerged; allow to sit until softened and pliable, at least 30 minutes.

TO PREPARE THE ORANGE-TOMATO SALSA, put the diced tomatoes in a medium, non-reactive bowl. Holding the oranges over the bowl, peel and section them so that any juice drips into the bowl. Cut orange segments into pieces the same size as the diced tomatoes and add to the bowl. Add remaining salsa ingredients. Allow to sit at room temperature for at least 30 minutes so flavors can blend.

Preheat a barbecue grill. Remove the cornhusks from the water, dry with paper towels, and arrange on a work surface. Rub each piece of fish with the Cilantro and Pecan Pesto, and then place one piece of flavored fish on the wide end of each husk. Fold sides over fish, followed by ends. Invert packets over a second husk and repeat the process. Tie packets twice with "strings" pulled from the soaked cornhusks. Place packets on a medium-hot grill and cook, turning once, until husks start to dry and color, about 10 minutes. Test for doneness.

To serve, cut ties and unwrap the outer layer. For a lovely presentation, serve the fish with the bottom cornhusk, but caution your guests that the wrapping is not edible. Place each on a plate with about ½ cup of the Orange-Tomato Salsa.

Moss garden waterfall into Pine Creek a short distance from Tonto Natural Bridge, Tonto Natural Bridge State Park

¼ package dried cornhusks

ORANGE-TOMATO SALSA
2 ripe tomatoes, seeded and diced
3 navel oranges
¼ cup finely chopped red onion
¼ cup chopped fresh cilantro
2 cloves garlic, finely chopped
1 tablespoon red wine vinegar
⅛ teaspoon cayenne pepper
½ teaspoon salt

½ cup Cilantro and Pecan Pesto (see page 36)
4 (1 to 1 ½-pound) firm fish fillets

Makes 4 Servings

CORNMEAL CRUSTED *Orange Roughy* WITH MANGO SALSA

A salsa should have different colors, textures, and tastes, and this one is the ultimate example. It pairs beautifully with this mild, crunchy fish, but it is also delicious on chips, quesadillas, or grilled chicken.
❀ SPRING

TO PREPARE THE MANGO SALSA, combine all salsa ingredients in a non-reactive bowl. Let stand for 1 hour to allow the flavors to mellow.

TO PREPARE THE ROUGHY OR TALAPÍA, salt and pepper the fillets. Put the flour, buttermilk, and cornmeal into 3 separate, shallow bowls. Dip the fish into the flour, then the buttermilk, and then the cornmeal. Heat the corn oil in a large skillet over medium-high heat. Sauté the coated fish fillets in the hot oil until lightly browned, about 3 to 4 minutes per side. Transfer to warm plates and serve with salsa on the side.

MANGO SALSA
1 mango, peeled, seeded, and diced
½ cup diced red bell pepper
1 jalapeño chile, seeded and diced
¼ cup finely chopped red onion
1 tablespoon finely chopped fresh cilantro
1 tablespoon freshly squeezed lime juice
1 teaspoon grated lime zest
Salt and freshly ground black pepper to taste

6 (4-ounce) fillets of orange roughy or talapia
    (about ½-inch thick)
Salt and freshly ground pepper to taste
½ cup flour
½ cup buttermilk
¾ cup cornmeal
2 tablespoons corn oil

Makes 6 Servings

PECAN CRUSTED *Salmon* WITH SUN-DRIED TOMATO AND ANCHO CHILE SAUCE

The mustard and pecan coating adds texture and pizzazz to these salmon fillets. Since both the fillets and the sauce can be prepared ahead of time, this is a terrific do-ahead dish. ✿ FALL

TO PREPARE THE SALMON, preheat oven to 450°F. Line a baking sheet with parchment paper. Combine mustard and milk in a shallow bowl; set aside. Put ground pecans on a flat plate. Dip each salmon fillet in the mustard mixture and then dip in the pecans. Put coated salmon on the prepared baking sheet; set aside and refrigerate if not cooking within the hour.

TO PREPARE THE SUN-DRIED TOMATO AND ANCHO CHILE SAUCE, place chiles and tomatoes in a medium bowl and cover with ¾ cup boiling water. Let soften for 20 minutes. Transfer chiles, tomatoes, soaking liquid, red bell pepper, orange juice, and brown sugar to a blender.

In a medium skillet, heat 1 tablespoon of the oil over medium heat. Add the onion and garlic and cook, stirring, until softened, about 5 minutes. Add sautéed onion mixture to the blender. Blend ingredients until smooth. Heat the remaining tablespoon of olive oil in the same medium skillet. Add blended mixture and cook, stirring, until flavors are well blended and mixture thickens slightly, about 5 minutes. Add fish or chicken stock and continue to cook until sauce is the desired consistency, about 10 to 15 minutes. Season to taste with salt and pepper. Set aside until ready to serve.

Bake salmon fillets in the hot oven until opaque in the center, about 10 minutes. Put one salmon fillet on each plate and top generously with the sauce.

½ cup Dijon mustard
⅓ cup milk
2 cups toasted pecans, finely ground (see page 38)
8 (4 to 6-ounce) salmon fillets, skin removed

SUN-DRIED TOMATO AND ANCHO CHILE SAUCE
4 ancho chiles, stemmed, seeded, and torn into pieces
4 sun-dried tomatoes, chopped
1 red bell pepper, roasted, seeded, and peeled (see page 47)
¼ cup fresh orange juice
1 tablespoon brown sugar
2 tablespoons olive oil
1 cup diced onion
4 cloves garlic, chopped
2 cups fish or chicken stock
Salt and freshly ground black pepper to taste

Makes 8 Servings

Fish | TACOS

Fish tacos have been popular in California for decades, but they are now catching on across the country as fresh fish becomes more readily available and people are more health conscious. These tacos are easy to prepare and absolutely delicious. ❋ SPRING

IN A NON-REACTIVE BOWL, mix together the olive oil, ¾ cup lime juice, chili powder, and garlic. Add the fish and allow to marinate for at least 30 minutes but not more than 2 hours.

IN A MEDIUM BOWL, combine all salsa ingredients. Set aside for at least 30 minutes to allow flavors to blend.

Strain the chipotle into a small bowl to remove the seeds. Discard the seeds; stir the cream or crème fraiche and the 1 tablespoon of lime juice into the bowl with the chipotle. Set aside.

Preheat a barbecue grill. Drain the fish from the marinade, sprinkle with salt and pepper, and cook on the hot grill until cooked through, about 2 minutes per side. Cut into strips and transfer to a warm plate.

Wrap the tortillas in a clean, wet dishtowel. Put the wrapped tortillas in a microwave oven and heat on high until hot and soft, 1 to 2 minutes.

To serve, put the warm fish, corn tortillas, salsa fresca, chipotle cream, and cabbage in separate dishes in the center of the table. Have each person make their own tacos, adding the ingredients of their choice.

½ cup olive oil
¾ cup fresh lime juice
¼ teaspoon chili powder
1 tablespoon finely chopped garlic
3 to 4 (½-pound) talapia, red snapper, or orange roughy fillets

SALSA FRESCA

3 ripe tomatoes, seeded and chopped
½ cup diced red onion
1 serrano chile, seeded and diced
2 tablespoons finely chopped cilantro
1 tablespoon fresh lime juice
1 tablespoon olive oil
Salt and freshly ground pepper to taste

2 chipotle chiles in adobo sauce, finely chopped
½ cup heavy cream or crème fraiche
1 tablespoon lime juice
Salt and freshly ground pepper to taste
12 (6-inch) corn tortillas
2 cups shredded cabbage

Makes 4 to 6 Servings

A rim-lit paddle of prickly pear cactus encircles a brilliant orange blossom, Saguaro National Park

CHIPOTLE-GLAZED *Shrimp*

Succulent, smoky, spicy shrimp are the result of marinating and then glazing with a chipotle-based sauce. Whether grilled or broiled, they're delicious on their own, in pasta, on pizza, or in a salad.
❀ SPRING

HEAT THE OLIVE OIL IN A MEDIUM SKILLET over medium-high heat; add the onions and sauté until golden brown, about 10 minutes. Add the garlic, cumin, oregano, salt, and pepper and cook another minute. Put into a blender; add chipotle chiles, vinegar, and water; purée. Pour half of the purée into a non-corrosive bowl and allow to cool. Add shrimp to the cooled mixture and allow to marinate for 1 to 2 hours in the refrigerator.

TO PREPARE THE GLAZE, pour the remaining purée into a medium saucepan; add brown sugar, orange juice, and adobo sauce. Over medium-high heat, bring to a boil; reduce heat and simmer until slightly thickened, about 10 minutes. Remove from heat and set aside.

Preheat a broiler or barbecue grill. Remove the shrimp from the marinade and pat dry. Thread shrimp on skewers. Brush with glaze and grill or broil until shrimp turn pink, about 2 minutes per side, frequently brushing with additional glaze. Remove from heat and serve immediately.

2 tablespoons olive oil
1 cup finely chopped white onion
4 cloves garlic, finely chopped
2 teaspoons ground cumin
1 teaspoon dried oregano
Salt and freshly ground pepper to taste
2 chipotle chiles in adobo sauce
¼ cup cider vinegar
1 cup water
1 ½ pounds extra-large shrimp, peeled and deveined
1 tablespoon brown sugar
¼ cup freshly squeezed orange juice
2 tablespoons adobo sauce (from the canned chiles)

Makes 4 to 6 Servings

Shrimp *Fajitas*

Fajitas are a favorite in the Southwest and, in restaurants, they are dramatically sizzling and steaming when they arrive at your table. They can be served on their own or embellished with any of the following: guacamole, sour cream, shredded lettuce, tomatoes, or fresh salsa. We serve them family-style at our house, where everyone helps themselves to tortillas, the shrimp mixture, and all the fixings.

❋ SPRING

PREHEAT OVEN TO 350°F. Wrap tortillas in aluminum foil and bake until hot, about 15 minutes. Or, wrap tortillas in a clean, wet dishtowel and put in the microwave oven for 2 minutes. Keep warm.

Put the shrimp in a medium bowl with the pickling liquid, lime juice, and oil. Allow to sit for at least 30 minutes but not more than 1 hour.

Heat a heavy, large skillet over high heat. When it's very hot, add the shrimp mixture, onion, bell pepper, and green chile. Cook, stirring constantly, until shrimp is pink and vegetables are tender, about 3 to 5 minutes. Place the skillet on a trivet on the table with a serving spoon. Put the guacamole, sour cream, lettuce, tomato, and salsa in individual bowls and place on the table. To serve, pass the warm tortillas, the shrimp mixture, and all the condiments. Allow your family and guests to custom create their own fajitas.

12 (8 to 10-inch) flour tortillas
1 ½ pounds shelled, uncooked large shrimp
2 tablespoons pickling liquid from a jar of
    pickled jalapeño chiles
2 tablespoons fresh lime juice
2 tablespoons canola oil
1 white onion, thinly sliced
1 cup chopped red or yellow bell pepper
1 Anaheim or New Mexico green chile, stemmed,
    seeded, and chopped

1 ½ cups Hand-Mixed Guacamole (see page 22)
1 cup sour cream
2 cups shredded lettuce
1 cup diced tomato
1 ½ cups fresh salsa of choice

Makes 4 to 6 Servings

A rare winter bloom of Mexican gold poppy carpets the sloping lowland below the Superstition Mountains, Lost Dutchman State Park

Jalapeño-Orange Glazed Scallops with Beurre Blanc

Using jalapeño jelly adds flavor and ease to this remarkable dish. The beurre blanc adds a silky foil to the scallops. ☼ SUMMER

TO PREPARE THE BEURRE BLANC, put the shallots, orange zest, jalapeño, orange juice, and wine in a small saucepan over medium-high heat; cook until liquid is reduced to about 2 tablespoons. Whisk in the cold butter, one tablespoon at a time, adding the next piece just as the previous one has melted. If sauce gets too hot, remove it from the heat so that it does not separate; season with salt and pepper and keep warm over very low heat.

TO PREPARE THE JALAPEÑO-ORANGE GLAZE, in a small saucepan, combine the jelly and orange juice and cook over low heat, stirring, until smooth. Cool.

Salt and pepper both sides of the scallops. Heat a large skillet over medium-high heat and add the olive oil. When oil is hot, add scallops. Brush the top of the scallops with the Jalapeño-Orange Glaze. When the bottom side is lightly browned, about 4 minutes, turn the scallops over and brush the cooked side with the glaze; sauté until just cooked through, another 4 to 5 minutes. Put 4 scallops on each of 4 warm plates. Spoon Beurre Blanc around the scallops and serve.

BEURRE BLANC

2 tablespoons finely chopped shallots
1 teaspoon orange zest
1 teaspoon finely chopped jalapeño chile
3 tablespoons fresh orange juice
¼ cup dry white wine
8 tablespoons (1 stick) unsalted butter, cut into
   pieces and kept cold
Salt and freshly ground pepper to taste

JALAPEÑO-ORANGE GLAZE

2 tablespoons jalapeño jelly
¼ cup fresh orange juice

Salt and freshly ground pepper to taste
16 sea scallops, patted dry
1 tablespoon olive oil

Makes 4 Servings

Grilled Portabello Mushroom and Roasted Red Bell Pepper *Sandwiches*

Whenever we have guests over for hamburgers on the grill we always have these on hand for the non-meat eaters. They're so good, though, that almost everyone professes to be a vegetarian! ☀ SUMMER

PREHEAT A BARBECUE GRILL to medium-high heat. Brush mushroom caps and onion slices on both sides with the olive oil and sprinkle with salt and pepper. Put mushrooms and onions on grill and cover. Cook about 6 minutes and turn over. Slide mushrooms to the coolest part of the grill and continue to cook onions until slightly charred and soft, about another 6 minutes.

Remove the onions from the grill and arrange cheese slices on top of the mushrooms. Return mushrooms to the heat, cover, and grill until the cheese is melted. Toast the bread or rolls for a few minutes on the grill.

TO PREPARE THE CHIPOTLE SAUCE, in a small bowl, combine all the sauce ingredients. Stir until smooth.

Spread the Chipotle Sauce on the bread or rolls. Set the mushroom caps on one piece of bread or the bottom of the roll. Top each mushroom with a piece of bell pepper. Separate the onions into rings and divide them over the peppers. Put the tops on the sandwiches and serve immediately.

4 large portobello mushrooms, stems removed
2 (¼-inch-thick) slices red onion
3 tablespoons olive oil
Salt and freshly ground pepper to taste
4 slices Asadero cheese (or substitute
   Monterey Jack)
8 slices crusty wheat bread or 4 sandwich rolls
2 large red bell peppers, roasted, peeled, seeded,
   and cut in half lengthwise (see page 47)

CHIPOTLE SAUCE
½ cup mayonnaise
2 teaspoons fresh lime juice
1 chipotle chile in adobo sauce, finely chopped
½ teaspoon ground cumin
Salt and freshly ground black pepper to taste

Makes 4 Servings

The Health Benefits of Chiles

IN THE 16TH CENTURY, the Spanish, who came to the Southwest looking for the Seven Cities of Gold, brought chiles from Mexico. The Spanish explorers never found their golden cities, but they gave us something just as valuable. After salt, chiles are the most frequently used seasoning and condiment in the world, and, besides being enjoyed for their flavor and heat, they have remarkable health benefits. Not only do they have incredible healing powers, but they are also a great preventative medicine, warding off colds and the flu and protecting against cancer, diabetes, heart disease, and stroke.

High in fiber and low in calories, chiles increase metabolism and are used in diets to control weight gain. Furthermore, the capsaicin in chiles appears to suppress appetite, and harmful fats can be eliminated in the diet by using chiles instead of oil to add flavor to bland foods. Fresh chiles are high in Vitamin C with almost twice the amount found in citrus fruits. And when the fresh peppers are dried, the vitamin C content is replaced by another healthful nutrient–Vitamin A.

Chiles also help the heart. Capsaicin is a natural blood thinner and so reduces the risk of blood clots. Capsaicin lowers both blood pressure and levels of LDL, the harmful form of cholesterol that clings to blood vessel walls. At the same time, it amazingly raises the levels of beneficial HDL, thereby reducing the risk of heart disease.

The bottom line? Eat your chiles and stay healthy!

Huevos Rancheros Verdes
with Black Beans

Huevos Rancheros, a favorite breakfast in the Southwest, are typically topped with a red sauce or salsa, but this version features a spicier green one. The tomatillos, chiles, beans, eggs, and cheese come together in a flavor combination that would wake up anyone's taste buds. Our family has adopted it as the perfect Sunday dinner. ❋ WINTER

TO PREPARE THE TOMATILLO SAUCE, put the tomatillos in a medium saucepan, cover with water, and bring to a boil over medium heat. Lower the heat and simmer until tomatillos are soft, about 20 minutes. Drain off water and put tomatillos in a blender with the garlic, onion, lime juice, salt, cumin, cilantro, and serranos. Purée until smooth. Transfer to a bowl and stir in avocado. Set aside.

In a medium skillet, heat the oil over medium heat; add the black beans, undrained, and mash them with a fork while stirring them over the heat. Cook until warm and slightly thickened, about 10 minutes. Keep warm.

To poach the eggs, place water in a skillet or shallow pan to a depth of 2 to 3 inches. Add vinegar and heat until water is at a low boil. Carefully break eggs into the pan and cook until the whites become opaque, about 2 ½ minutes. Remove from the pan with a slotted spoon and gently place on paper towels.

Preheat broiler. Wrap tortillas in a damp, clean kitchen towel. Cook for 1 minute on high power in a microwave oven. Place warm tortillas on a baking sheet and spread black beans over each one; top each with two eggs, about 3 tablespoons of Tomatillo Sauce, and ¼ cup grated cheese. Place under the broiler just to melt the cheese; garnish with chopped cilantro and serve.

TOMATILLO SAUCE

½ pound (about 10) medium tomatillos, husked and stems removed (*see* NOTE *page 54*)
2 cloves garlic, peeled
½ cup coarsely chopped onion
2 tablespoons lime juice
1 teaspoon salt
1 teaspoon ground cumin
1 cup cilantro leaves
2 serrano chiles, stemmed and seeded
1 ripe avocado, peeled and diced

1 tablespoon canola or corn oil
1 (15-ounce) can black beans
2 tablespoons white vinegar
8 large eggs
4 (6-inch) corn tortillas
1 ½ cups grated Cotija cheese (or substitute Monterey Jack)
½ cup finely chopped cilantro

Makes 4 Servings

Vegetables

Grits with Attitude

On their own, grits are pretty bland, so I jazzed them up for those who like a little more flavor in them. Having grits for breakfast is a great way to get your heart pumping, or you can serve them as a side dish with meat, fish, or poultry. ❋ SPRING

PUT WATER, CREAM, AND CUMIN in a medium saucepan and bring to a boil. Slowly stir in the grits; add salt, diced chile, and butter. Reduce heat, cover, and simmer until almost all of the liquid is absorbed, about 5 minutes. The grits will thicken slightly as they sit. Serve immediately.

2 cups water
½ cup heavy cream
½ teaspoon ground cumin
½ cup yellow corn grits
1 teaspoon salt
1 poblano chile, roasted, seeded, peeled, and
    diced (see page 47)
1 tablespoon butter

Makes 4 Servings

Stuffed *Chayote* Squash

Also known as a vegetable pear or a mirliton, the chayote squash has a mild flavor that is reminiscent of watermelon and cucumber. It combines well with other flavors, so with the filling of red bell pepper, salty cheese, and sweet corn, this is a colorful and succulent side dish. ❄ WINTER

PREHEAT OVEN TO 400°F. Peel the chayote squash and cut them in half lengthwise. With a melon baller or sharp spoon, remove the core and make a hole large enough in the center for 2 tablespoons of filling. Sprinkle the squash with salt and pepper. Put ½ tablespoon of the butter into the hole of each squash and wrap them in aluminum foil. Bake until squash are tender, about 1 hour. Remove from the oven and set temperature to broil. Remove the squash from the aluminum foil and place on a baking sheet cut side up.

In a medium bowl, stir together the corn, bell pepper, and cheese. Put 2 tablespoons of filling into the center of each squash. Broil about 4 inches from the heat until cheese turns light brown, about 3 to 4 minutes. Serve immediately.

3 chayote squash
Salt and freshly ground pepper to taste
3 tablespoons butter
¼ cup corn kernels
¼ cup diced red bell pepper
¼ cup crumbled Cotija cheese

Makes 6 Servings

PAGES 120-121: *Grand Falls, Little Colorado River*

SOUTHWEST *Corn* PUDDING

This flavorful side dish is easy to prepare and makes a great addition to the Thanksgiving table or any hearty meal. It's also very versatile–add cooked sausage or bacon, mushrooms, a variety of cheeses, or more chiles to suit your taste. 🌿 FALL

PREHEAT OVEN TO 350°F. Butter an 8-inch, square baking pan.

In a small bowl, mix together the cornmeal, baking soda, and salt. Set aside.

In a large bowl, combing the corn, onions, bell peppers, chiles, and cheeses. Stir in the dry mixture. Add the butter, buttermilk, and eggs; mix well. Spoon into the prepared pan and bake until set; about 45 minutes. Let rest for 10 minutes before serving.

¾ cup yellow cornmeal
½ teaspoon baking soda
½ teaspoon salt
1 (15-ounce) can creamed corn
½ cup finely chopped green onions
½ cup diced red bell peppers
2 Anaheim or New Mexico green chiles, roasted, seeded, peeled, and diced (see page 47)
1 cup grated Cotija cheese
1 cup grated Monterey Jack cheese
1 stick (½ cup) butter, melted and cooled
1 cup buttermilk
2 eggs, slightly beaten

Makes 6 to 8 Servings

BAKED CHILES *Rellenos*

Chile relleno simply means "stuffed chile," but most people think of this dish as the cheese-filled chile that's battered and fried and offered in many Mexican restaurants. This healthier version, filled with a bean and cheese mixture, is baked. ❄ WINTER

PREHEAT OVEN TO 350°F. Carefully cut a slit lengthwise in the poblanos, leaving the stem intact, and scrape out the seeds. Set aside.

Heat a large skillet over medium-high heat; add oil. Add the onion, serrano, and garlic and sauté until onion is soft, about 5 minutes. Add the cumin and oregano and cook another minute. Stir in pinto beans, and with the back of a fork, mash them while cooking, until mixture is warmed through and well combined, about 3 more minutes. Remove the pan from the heat and stir in cheese. Fill each poblano with ¼ of the bean mixture. The chiles should just be able to close. Placing the seam side down, transfer the filled chiles to a baking sheet and heat them in the oven until warmed through, about 15 minutes.

Put a chile on each serving plate and drizzle with Mexican crema.

4 medium-sized poblano chiles, roasted and peeled (see page 47)
1 tablespoon vegetable oil
1 cup finely chopped onion
1 serrano chile, seeded and finely chopped
1 tablespoon finely chopped garlic
1 teaspoon toasted and ground cumin seed (see page 38)
1 teaspoon dried Mexican oregano
1 (16-ounce) can pinto beans, drained and rinsed
1 cup grated Cheddar cheese
Mexican crema (*see* NOTE)

Makes 4 Servings

NOTE: *Mexican crema is available in Latino markets and some supermarkets. Sour cream thinned to desired consistency with milk is a good substitute.*

Pickled *Ancho* Chiles Stuffed with Vegetable Medley

I tried my first pickled ancho chile when Allen Smith, of the Santa Fe School of Cooking, taught a class at my school, Les Gourmettes. Although skeptical before biting into it, I was delighted to discover a whole new taste sensation—sweet, hot, and earthy all at the same time. Allen filled his with refried beans, but in this version, the stuffing is a variation on calabacitas, which simply translates as "little squashes" in Spanish. ❄ WINTER

WITH A SHARP KNIFE, make a slit along the sides of each ancho chile and carefully remove the seeds and veins, trying to keep the stem intact. Set aside.

IN A MEDIUM SAUCEPAN, combine the pickling ingredients and bring to a boil, stirring, over medium-high heat. Turn off the heat and add the ancho chiles. Weigh the chiles down with a plate or bowl so that they are submerged. Soak the chiles until they are soft, about 30 minutes to 1 hour.

In medium sauté pan, heat the oil over medium heat; add the onions, garlic, and red bell pepper. Cook, stirring, until onion is softened, about 5 minutes. Add the corn, zucchini, and spice mix and cook until zucchini is tender, about 5 minutes more. Stir in the cheese and stir until cheese is melted. Remove from heat.

Preheat oven to 350°F. Remove the chiles from their liquid and drain them well. Discard the soaking liquid. Stuff the chiles with the zucchini mixture and place them in a shallow ovenproof dish. Bake in the oven until heated through, about 15 minutes. Drizzle with Mexican crema and serve immediately.

6 dried ancho chiles

PICKLING LIQUID
2 cups fresh orange juice
½ cup cider vinegar
⅓ cup packed brown sugar
4 large cloves garlic, peeled and crushed
2 teaspoons dried Mexican oregano
1 teaspoon dried thyme
1 teaspoon salt

1 tablespoon corn oil
¼ cup diced red onion
2 teaspoons finely chopped garlic
⅓ cup diced red bell pepper
1 cup corn kernels
1 cup diced zucchini
1 teaspoon Southwest Spice Mix (see page 91)
½ cup crumbled or grated Cotija cheese
¼ cup Mexican crema (*see* NOTE *page 123*)

Makes 6 Servings

Gratin OF THE THREE SISTERS

*Corn, beans, and squash are layered in this flavorful
vegetable casserole in tribute to the holy trinity of
Native American food. It's a great side dish for any
meat entrée or a main dish for non-meat eaters.*

🌿 FALL

BUTTER AN 8-INCH SQUARE BAKING PAN. Preheat
the broiler.

TO PREPARE THE BEAN LAYER, in a large
skillet, heat the corn oil over medium heat; add
the black beans and their liquid, garlic, and
chipotle. Cook, mashing the beans with the back
of a fork, until mixture has thickened slightly and
the garlic is tender, about 10 minutes. Spread the
beans evenly in the bottom of the prepared pan.

TO PREPARE THE ZUCCHINI LAYER, melt the
butter in a large skillet over medium heat. Add
the onion and zucchini; season with salt and
pepper. Cook, stirring, until zucchini is golden
and onion is tender, about 10 minutes. Spoon
cooked mixture over the black beans.

TO PREPARE THE CORN LAYER, melt the butter
in a medium saucepan over medium heat. Add
the corn, cornmeal, milk, salt, and chile. Simmer
until thickened, about 10 minutes. Remove from
the heat and add cilantro. Pour the mixture over
the zucchini.

Spread the grated cheese over the corn mixture. Put pan under the broiler and cook until
cheese is golden brown, about 2 to 3 minutes.

NOTE: *If making ahead of time, complete the recipe
through the corn layer and refrigerate, covered. Preheat
oven to 350°F. Reheat the casserole until warmed through,
about 15 minutes. Preheat the broiler. Spread the cheese
over the corn mixture and broil until golden brown.*

BEAN LAYER

1 tablespoon corn oil
1 (15-ounce) can black beans, undrained
2 cloves garlic, finely chopped
1 chipotle chile in adobo sauce, finely chopped

ZUCCHINI LAYER

1 tablespoon unsalted butter
½ cup finely chopped white or yellow onion
4 zucchini (about 1 ½ pounds), diced into
    ½-inch pieces
Salt and freshly ground pepper to taste

CORN LAYER

1 tablespoon unsalted butter
1 ½ cups corn kernels
1 tablespoon yellow cornmeal
½ cup milk
1 teaspoon salt
1 serrano chile, stemmed, seeded, and finely diced
2 tablespoons chopped cilantro

1 cup grated Queso Fresco or Asadero cheese

Makes 6 Servings

The Legend of the Three Sisters

THE THREE MAIN INDIGENOUS FOODS of the Americas are squash, corn, and beans, and most Native American nations have some version of the legend of these "three sisters." One version of the legend is that three young girls from different clans spent the summer together and became inseparable. When it came time to split them up to go to each clan's different winter hunting grounds, they were desolate and plotted a way to stay together. When the people awoke the morning of their departure, they looked out into the field and saw that the ring leader, the strong healthy girl, had become a tall corn stalk. The one that needed support had become a bean vine and was growing up the corn stalk. And the happy, jovial little girl turned herself into a squash plant, smothering the weeds and holding moisture for all three of them. In this manner, they knew that they would always help each other grow, and that they would always be together.

Another version tells of three sisters who did not get along with each other. In order to teach them a lesson, their grandmother took them out into the garden. "Tell me what you see," the grandmother said to the girls. One of the girls said, "There's tall corn, Grandmother." Another said, "And there are beans." The third girl pointed out the squash. "You are right," replied the grandmother. "All three of you have told part of the truth, and only when each of you had spoken was the whole story told. Like the three sisters growing in the garden—the corn, beans, and squash—each of you has a gift for the people. Your gifts will not ripen unto their fullness, though, unless you do as the plants do—help each other and grow together."

BROCCOLINI WITH *Chile-Honey* CARAMEL SAUCE

A cross between broccoli and Chinese kale, broccolini has a milder and sweeter taste than broccoli. Broccolini can usually be found in the specialty produce section of your local grocery store or, if unavailable, you can substitute small broccoli florets. ❁ SPRING

TO PREPARE THE SAUCE, heat a small saucepan over medium heat; add oil and garlic and cook over low heat, stirring constantly, until garlic is soft and starting to lightly brown, about 3 to 4 minutes. Add the honey and chile powder and cook until lightly browned, about 2 minutes. Add the stock and cook until slightly thickened, about 5 minutes. Stir in the lemon juice, season with salt and pepper, and keep warm.

   TO PREPARE THE BROCCOLINI, heat a large skillet over medium-high heat and add the canola oil. Add the broccolini, stir, and cover the pan; lower the heat and cook until broccolini is tender, about 3 to 5 minutes. Remove cover and stir in sauce. When warmed through, serve immediately.

CHILE-HONEY CARAMEL SAUCE
1 tablespoon canola oil
1 tablespoon finely chopped garlic
2 tablespoons honey
1 teaspoon ancho chile powder
¼ cup vegetable or chicken stock
1 tablespoon fresh lemon juice
Salt and freshly ground pepper to taste

BROCCOLINI
1 tablespoon canola oil
½ pound broccolini, cut into bite-sized pieces
Salt and freshly ground pepper to taste

Makes 4 Servings

Caramelized CORN WITH PEPPERS

Dry-roasting corn brings out its sweetness and adds a nutty flavor. This colorful side dish is a marvelous complement to grilled meat, seafood, or chicken. ☀ SUMMER

HEAT A LARGE, HEAVY SKILLET over medium-high heat. When hot, add the corn kernels to the dry skillet and cook, stirring occasionally, until the kernels are light brown and begin to pop, about 5 minutes. Turn the kernels out into a bowl or onto a plate and set aside.

   In the same skillet, heat the oil. Sauté the green onion, red bell pepper, and green chile until slightly softened, about 3 to 5 minutes. Transfer the corn back to the skillet and add the lime juice and chile powder; stir together for another few minutes until corn is warmed through. Salt and pepper to taste and serve immediately.

2 cups corn kernels (if using frozen, thawed)
1 tablespoon corn oil
½ cup diced green onion
1 red bell pepper, stemmed, seeded, and diced
1 Anaheim or New Mexico green chile, stemmed, seeded, and diced
1 tablespoon fresh lime juice
1 teaspoon ancho chile powder (*see* NOTE)
Salt and freshly ground black pepper to taste

Makes 6 Servings

NOTE: *Ancho chile powder is available through mail order spice catalogs and specialty grocery stores. Or, you can make your own by puréeing a dried ancho chile in a spice grinder (see page 38).*

OPPOSITE: *Three Navajo sisters standing in front of "The Three Sisters" at Monument Valley, taken at dawn*

SAUTÉ OF TOMATOES, CORN, AND *Edamame*

Edamame, the Japanese name for fresh soybeans, can be found in the produce or frozen food department of most grocery stores. Cook them, either in the microwave or in boiling water, until tender before adding them to this colorful, healthy vegetable dish.

☀ SUMMER

HEAT OIL IN A LARGE NONSTICK SKILLET over medium-high heat. Add onion and sauté until golden, about 5 minutes. Add Southwest Spice Mix and garlic; stir for 1 minute. Add tomatoes with their juices; bring to a boil. Reduce heat and cook for 5 minutes, or until most of the juice has cooked away. Stir in edamame and corn. Cook until heated through and vegetables are tender, about 5 minutes. Season with salt and pepper. Sprinkle with cilantro and serve.

1 tablespoon olive oil
1 cup diced onion
2 teaspoons Southwest Spice Mix (see page 91)
2 cloves garlic, finely chopped
1 (14 ½-ounce) can tomatoes with chiles
2 cups shelled and cooked edamame beans
2 cups frozen corn kernels, thawed
Salt and black pepper to taste
2 tablespoons chopped fresh cilantro

Makes 6 to 8 Servings

Cowboy Beans

Chuck wagon cooks used to cook beans for days at a time and the cowboys always thought the beans were better on the third day than on the first. This version will also keep for days and, like those on the ranch, are even better reheated. ❁ SPRING

PUT THE BEANS, WATER, BEER, BACON, ONION, garlic, jalapeño, chile powder, salt, and pepper in a large, heavy pot. Bring to a boil, lower the heat, and simmer, uncovered, until the beans are tender, about 2 ½ to 3 hours. Stir beans every ½ hour, adding more hot water if necessary to keep them well covered, about 1 inch more water than beans. At the completion of the cooking time, the water should be just above the beans. If a thicker liquid is desired, remove ½ cup of the beans, mash them, and return them to the pot.

To serve, ladle a generous portion of beans onto each plate and garnish each portion with a sprinkling of cheese, diced tomatoes, and chopped cilantro.

1 pound dried pinto beans, picked through and rinsed
5 cups water
1 (12-ounce) bottle dark beer
4 slices bacon, cut into ½-inch pieces
1 cup diced white onion
4 cloves garlic, finely chopped
1 jalapeño chile, stemmed, seeded, and finely chopped
1 tablespoon chipotle chile powder
Salt and freshly ground pepper to taste

½ cup grated Cotija cheese
½ cup diced tomato
¼ cup chopped cilantro

Makes 6 Servings

Tomato and Cumin Rice

Cumin, cilantro, and the seed of the cilantro plant, coriander, spice up this zesty rice. A little heat is added by using canned tomatoes with green chiles, but if you prefer a milder version, just use unflavored tomatoes. ❁ SPRING

IN A HEAVY SAUCEPAN heat the butter over medium heat. Add the shallots and sauté until soft and translucent, about 3 minutes. Add the coriander and cumin and cook for 1 minute more. Add the rice and cook, stirring, until the rice takes on a nutty color and is well coated with the butter and spices, about 5 minutes. Add the chicken stock; bring to a boil. Add the tomatoes and their liquid; cover, lower the heat, and simmer until all the liquid is absorbed and rice is tender, about 25 minutes. Add the cilantro and season to taste with salt and pepper.

2 tablespoons butter
2 tablespoons finely chopped shallots
1 teaspoon ground coriander
1 teaspoon cumin, toasted and ground in a spice grinder (see page 38)
1 cup basmati rice
2 cups chicken stock
1 (14 ½-ounce) can diced tomatoes with green chiles
1 tablespoon chopped fresh cilantro
Salt and freshly ground pepper to taste

Makes 6 to 8 Servings

NOTE: *To make this a main dish, add 2 cups cooked shrimp or chicken about 5 minutes before rice is finished cooking.*

GREEN BEANS WiTH *Shallots* AND CHiLE OiL

Blanching the beans early in the day makes this a breeze to put on the table in less than 5 minutes. Quickly cooking the shallots and beans at the last minute in chili oil adds a blast of spice. ☼ SUMMER

BRiNG A LARGE POT OF WATER TO A BOiL over high heat; add beans and cook until just tender, about 5 minutes. Drain into a colander and rinse with cold water to stop the cooking. Set aside.

Heat a large skillet over medium heat; add canola oil, chile oil, and shallots and cook until shallots start to soften, about 2 minutes. Add the beans, toss with the shallots and oil, and cook until heated through, about 2 more minutes. Serve immediately.

1 pound green beans, trimmed
2 teaspoons canola oil
1 teaspoon chile oil (*see* NOTE)
¼ cup sliced shallots, separated into rings
Salt to taste

Makes 4 Servings

NOTE: *Chile oil is available in the Asian section of most grocery stores.*

POTATO *Casserole* WiTH MEXiCAN CHEESES

I serve this delicious potato dish often, because it uses no cream and just a small amount of cheese, yet it tastes as rich and creamy as the high-fat versions. Plus, it's quite easy since you don't have to layer the potatoes–just pour them into the baking dish. ❅ WiNTER

PREHEAT OVEN TO 350°F. Butter a 13 x 9-inch baking dish.

In a large skillet, melt the butter over medium heat. Add the onions, garlic, salt, and pepper. Cook until onions are soft, but not browned, about 5 to 10 minutes. Transfer to a large mixing bowl and add the potatoes and stock. Toss together and turn out into the prepared baking dish. Butter a piece of parchment or waxed paper and press the buttered side onto the surface of the potatoes. Bake until potatoes are tender, about 40 to 45 minutes.

Preheat oven to broil. Remove parchment paper and sprinkle cheeses evenly over the surface of the potatoes. Place the baking dish under the broiler and cook until golden brown, 3 to 5 minutes. Allow the potatoes to rest for 10 minutes before serving.

4 tablespoons unsalted butter
2 cups thinly sliced yellow onion
1 tablespoon finely chopped garlic
Salt and pepper to taste
3 pounds Russet potatoes, peeled and thinly sliced
1 cup chicken stock
½ cup grated Panela cheese (or substitute Gruyère)
¼ cup grated Cotija cheese
    (or substitute Parmesan)

Makes 8 to 10 Servings

Mustard and Cumin Glazed *Carrots*

The sweetness of the sugar, the bite of the mustard, and the earthy, nutty flavor of the cumin make this carrot dish one to remember. ❄ WINTER

WITH A VEGETABLE PEELER, peel the carrots. Using a mandoline or sharp knife, cut the carrots into thin diagonal slices. Bring about two quarts of water to a boil in a large saucepan; add the salt. Add the carrots and cook over medium heat until tender, about 5 to 7 minutes. Drain carrots in a colander and set aside.

In the same saucepan, heat the butter, mustard, orange juice, cumin, and brown sugar; cook over medium heat until syrupy, about 3 minutes. Add the carrots to the sauce and return the pan to medium heat. Simmer, stirring, until carrots are warmed through and well coated with the glaze, about 3 minutes. Divide among heated plates or put into a serving dish and sprinkle with chopped cilantro. Serve immediately.

2 pounds carrots
1 teaspoon salt
3 tablespoons butter
2 tablespoons Dijon mustard
2 tablespoons fresh orange juice
1 teaspoon cumin seed, toasted and ground (see page 38)
2 tablespoons brown sugar
2 tablespoons chopped fresh cilantro

Makes 4 Servings

Mashed Potatoes with Cheddar Cheese and *Poblano Chiles*

These potatoes have great texture and flavor because of the chiles and cheese. Experiment with other varieties of cheeses or chiles to create your own signature potatoes. 🌿 FALL

BRING A LARGE SAUCEPAN OF WATER to a boil over high heat. Add salt and potatoes and cook until tender, about 10 to 15 minutes. Drain potatoes in a colander.

Place a food mill over the empty pan in which potatoes were cooked (*see* NOTE). Pass potatoes through the mill, in batches, until all have been processed. Mix in the milk, butter, chiles, and cheese and stir until ingredients are well incorporated. Season to taste with salt and pepper and serve immediately.

NOTE: *Using a food mill will insure that your mashed potatoes will have a smooth, velvety texture every time.*

1 teaspoon salt
3 pounds Russet potatoes, peeled and cut into 1-inch pieces
½ cup milk, warmed
4 tablespoons unsalted butter, at room temperature
2 poblano chiles, roasted, seeded, and diced (see page 47)
1 cup grated Cheddar cheese
Salt and freshly ground pepper to taste

Makes 4 to 6 Servings

Roasted Baby Vegetables

This colorful mélange of little vegetables adds eye appeal to the plate as well as providing a healthy, low-fat side dish. If baby vegetables aren't available, cut larger ones into bite-sized pieces. ❄ WINTER

PREHEAT OVEN TO 450°F. Line a baking sheet with aluminum foil. In a large bowl, combine the vinegar, oil, herbs, and chile powder. Add vegetables and toss to coat. Spread them out on the prepared baking sheet and sprinkle them with salt and pepper. Roast in the hot oven until tender and lightly browned, about 25 minutes. Transfer to a serving plate and serve immediately.

¼ cup red wine vinegar
1 teaspoon extra virgin olive oil
1 teaspoon fresh thyme leaves
1 teaspoon finely chopped fresh rosemary
⅛ teaspoon ancho chile powder (or substitute cayenne pepper)
6 small pearl onions, peeled
6 baby zucchini, trimmed
6 baby summer squash
6 baby carrots, tops trimmed
1 red bell pepper, stemmed, seeded, and cut into 1 x 2-inch strips
Salt and freshly ground black pepper to taste

Makes 6 Servings

Butternut Squash with Blue Cheese and Walnuts

The saltiness and creaminess of blue cheese and the crunch of walnuts add so much texture and flavor to this dish that even non-squash lovers will be begging for more. I know because my father-in-law is one of those people! 🍃 FALL

CAREFULLY CUT THE BUTTERNUT SQUASH in half lengthwise using a large chef's knife or a cleaver. Remove the seeds. Place the squash, skin side up, in a glass baking dish that will fit in a microwave oven. Add the water to the bottom of the baking dish. Cover the dish with two layers of plastic wrap and poke a few holes in the wrap with a knife. Put the dish into the microwave and cook on high power until the squash is very tender, about 15 minutes. Allow to cool slightly and carefully remove the plastic wrap. With a large spoon, scrape the flesh of the squash into a serving bowl; discard the squash skin.

Preheat oven to 350°F. Bring a small pot with 2 cups of water to a boil; add walnuts and cook for 1 to 2 minutes. Strain and put walnuts on a baking sheet and toast in the oven until crisp and lightly browned, about 10 minutes. Remove from the oven and allow to cool.

Stir the walnuts and the blue cheese into the squash; salt and pepper to taste. Just before serving, reheat in the microwave on high power until squash is warmed through, about 3 minutes.

1 butternut squash, about 2 ½ pounds
¼ cup water
½ cup walnut pieces (about ¼-inch pieces)
½ cup crumbled blue cheese
Salt and freshly ground pepper to taste

Makes 6 Servings

CARAMELIZED ONION *Tart*

Cooking onions slowly for a long time brings out their natural sugar, making them deliciously sweet. Combined with a flaky crust and a creamy custard, they are absolutely irresistible. I like to serve this as a side dish with a simple meat or on its own for brunch, lunch, or a light supper. 🍂 FALL

TO PREPARE THE DOUGH, in a medium bowl, blend together the flour, salt, pepper, sugar, and butter with your fingertips, a fork, or a pastry blender until the mixture resembles coarse meal.

In a separate bowl, stir together the sour cream and water. Stir into dough with a fork until incorporated. Gather into a flat disc and, with a rolling pin, roll dough into a 9 x 3-inch rectangle and fold into thirds (like a letter) to form a 3-inch square. Turn dough so an open-ended side is nearest you, and then roll out dough into a 9 x 3-inch rectangle again, dusting work surface with flour as necessary. Fold into thirds as before and repeat rolling and folding 1 more time. Wrap the dough in plastic wrap and chill for at least 1 hour or up to 1 day.

Roll out pastry dough on a floured surface into a 13-inch round. Transfer to a 10-inch removable bottom quiche pan by rolling dough around rolling pin and unrolling it across pan. Press dough into pan and trim edges. Prick bottom of shell all over with a fork and chill until firm, at least 30 minutes.

Preheat oven to 375° F. Line pastry shell with aluminum foil and fill with pie weights or raw rice. Bake in middle of oven until sides are firm, about 20 minutes. Remove foil and weights and bake shell until golden, about 10 minutes more. Cool.

TO PREPARE THE FILLING, in a large sauté pan, melt the better over medium heat. Add the onions, sprinkle with sugar and salt to taste, and cook until lightly browned and caramelized, about 30 minutes. Cool. Spoon cooled onions into the bottom of the cooked tart shell.

Whisk together cream, eggs, and nutmeg. Season with salt and pepper. Pour evenly over the onions. Sprinkle cheese over the custard. Bake tart in the middle of oven until set, about 20 minutes. Serve warm or at room temperature.

BLACK PEPPER DOUGH

1 ¼ cups all-purpose flour

½ teaspoon salt

½ teaspoon freshly ground black pepper

⅛ teaspoon sugar

8 tablespoons (1 stick) unsalted butter, cut into small pieces

2 tablespoons sour cream

2 tablespoons ice water

FILLING

2 tablespoons unsalted butter

5 large yellow onions, peeled and thinly sliced

1 tablespoon sugar

Salt to taste

1 cup heavy cream

2 large eggs

½ teaspoon freshly grated nutmeg

Salt and black pepper to taste

1 cup finely grated Gruyère cheese

Makes 8 to 12 Servings

SOUTHWEST *Sauté* OF POTATOES, PEPPERS, AND ONIONS

Whether for breakfast or dinner, this rustic potato dish is sure to satisfy. Add more chiles, a different color bell pepper, or various types of onions to make variations. ❋ SPRING

HEAT A LARGE SKILLET over medium-high heat; add canola oil and butter. When hot, add the potato cubes and cook, stirring, until browned and almost tender, about 15 minutes. Add the green onion, chiles, garlic, and red pepper and continue cooking until all the vegetables are tender, another 10 minutes. Add the lime zest and salt and pepper to taste. Serve immediately.

2 tablespoons canola oil
2 tablespoons unsalted butter
2 pounds White Rose boiling potatoes, cut into ½-inch cubes
½ cup diced green onions
1 poblano chile, roasted, peeled, seeded, and diced (see page 47)
1 tablespoon finely chopped garlic
1 cup diced red bell pepper
1 teaspoon grated lime zest
Salt and freshly ground black pepper to taste

Makes 4 to 6 Servings

TOMATOES STUFFED WITH *Queso Fresco* AND CILANTRO

This tasty, colorful side dish is a delicious way to celebrate the first ripe tomatoes of summer. If you can't find Queso Fresco, use any mild, melting cheese. ☼ SUMMER

PREHEAT BROILER. With a sharp knife, scoop out the pulp from the top ¼ of each tomato. Set tomatoes aside.

In a small bowl, combine the Queso Fresco, red onion, cilantro, salt, and pepper. Fill each tomato with ¼ of the mixture. Place the tomatoes on a baking sheet and put about 6 inches under the broiler until the tomatoes are softened and the cheese is melted, about 4 to 5 minutes. Serve immediately.

4 medium, ripe tomatoes
½ cup grated Queso Fresco
1 tablespoon finely chopped red onion
1 tablespoon chopped fresh cilantro
Salt and freshly ground pepper to taste

Makes 4 Servings

Sweet Onion *Custard* with Salsa Fresca

Almost every state now grows their own sweet onions or imports them from their neighbors. Using yellow onions is a good substitute, but the custards may not be as mild. The salsa can be made with any kind of ripe tomato–yellow, red, cherry, or grape.

☀ SUMMER

TO PREPARE THE CUSTARD, preheat oven to 325°F. Brush the insides of 4 individual ½-cup ramekins with softened butter. Put the prepared ramekins in a baking dish.

In a medium skillet heat the olive oil over medium heat; add the onion and cook, stirring occasionally, until softened and translucent, but not browned, about 10 minutes. Add the cream, raise the heat, and bring to a boil. Remove from the heat and allow to cool slightly. Put the cream/onion mixture into a blender and purée until smooth. Add egg yolks and the whole egg and purée just until mixed. Salt and pepper to taste. Pour into the prepared ramekins. Fill the baking dish with enough hot water to come halfway up the sides of the ramekins; bake in the oven until no ripples form when you jiggle them back and forth, about 25 to 30 minutes.

TO PREPARE THE SALSA FRESCA, in a medium bowl, mix all the salsa ingredients together; allow to sit about 30 minutes so the flavors can blend.

To assemble, run a knife around the inside of each ramekin and unmold the custards onto plates. Spoon the salsa around each custard and serve immediately.

SWEET ONION CUSTARD
1 tablespoon butter, softened
1 tablespoon olive oil
1 large sweet onion, finely chopped
1 cup heavy cream
4 egg yolks
1 whole egg
Salt and freshly ground pepper to taste

SALSA FRESCA
½ cup diced tomatoes
2 tablespoons diced sweet or yellow onion
1 teaspoon finely chopped serrano chile
2 teaspoons olive oil
1 teaspoon fresh lime juice
Salt and freshly ground pepper to taste

Makes 4 Servings

Saguaro cactus, Saguaro National Park

Wild Rice and *Porcini* Pilaf

Wild rice is a wild grain that historically has been hand-harvested by Native Americans in Minnesota. Recently, however, it is being cultivated in other parts of our country and is less expensive. It is usually combined with another type of rice to lessen the expense and make the dish a little milder. The dried mushrooms add an intense flavor that enriches the taste of the rice. 🍂 FALL

SOAK THE MUSHROOMS in 1 cup of warm water to cover until softened, 20 to 30 minutes. Strain through a damp paper towel or cheesecloth, reserving the soaking liquid. Rinse the mushrooms well and coarsely chop them; set aside.

In a medium saucepan, heat the olive oil over medium-high heat. Add the onion, celery, sage, and thyme; sauté until onion is translucent, about 10 minutes. Add the wild and brown rice and the chopped mushrooms; cook, stirring, for about 30 seconds. Add the chicken stock and the reserved mushroom liquid; tightly cover the pan and simmer over low heat until the rice is soft and liquid is absorbed, about 40 minutes. Season to taste with salt and pepper.

½ ounce dried porcini mushrooms
2 tablespoons olive oil
1 cup finely chopped onion
½ cup chopped celery
2 teaspoons finely chopped fresh sage
1 teaspoon finely chopped fresh thyme
½ cup raw wild rice, rinsed
½ cup brown rice, rinsed
2 cups chicken stock
Salt and pepper to taste

Makes 6 to 8 Servings

Zucchini FRITTERS

This crunchy, healthy side dish can also be served as an appetizer by making the pancakes a smaller size and serving them with salsa. Try them as an accompaniment for an egg dish at your next brunch.

☼ SUMMER

PUT THE ZUCCHINI IN A LARGE COLANDER and sprinkle it with the lime juice and salt; allow to sit for 15 minutes. With your hands, squeeze any excess moisture from the zucchini and wrap it in paper towels; squeeze as dry as possible.

With a wooden spoon, beat the egg yolks in a medium bowl; stir in the flour, chile, red bell pepper, onion, and drained zucchini. In another bowl with an electric mixer or a whisk, beat the egg whites until stiff but not dry; gently fold into the zucchini mixture.

In a large nonstick skillet, heat the oil over medium-high heat. Drop the zucchini mixture by tablespoons into the hot oil. Cook, turning once, until browned and crisp on both sides, about 2 minutes per side. Serve immediately.

3 cups shredded zucchini (about 2 medium zucchini)
1 tablespoon lime juice
1 teaspoon salt
2 eggs, separated
¼ cup all-purpose flour
1 poblano chile, roasted, peeled, seeded, and diced (see page 47)
1 red bell pepper, roasted, peeled, seeded, and diced (see page 47)
2 tablespoons finely chopped onion
2 tablespoons corn oil

Makes 6 Servings

A soon-to-be-dry creek paints a silver sliver over a chasm pool of cross-bedded Kaibab sandstone in North Canyon, Marble Canyon

Breads

143

Blueberry Cornmeal Pancakes with Blueberry Syrup

A great brunch dish, these pancakes have great texture and flavor. The blueberry syrup is also delicious over ice cream if you have any left over. ❄ SPRING

TO PREPARE THE SYRUP, in a medium saucepan, cook the blueberries and maple syrup over medium heat until blueberries have burst, about 3 minutes. Strain syrup into a heatproof pitcher, pressing on the solids, and stir in the lemon juice. If making the syrup ahead of time, refrigerate, covered, and heat just before serving.

TO PREPARE THE PANCAKES, stir together the flour, cornmeal, baking powder, baking soda, salt, and brown sugar in a large bowl. Set aside.

In a medium bowl, whisk together the buttermilk, eggs, melted butter, and vanilla. Add to the dry ingredients and stir until just combined. Fold in the blueberries.

In a large nonstick skillet over medium heat, melt 1 tablespoon of the butter. Ladle mixture into pan in ¼ cup measures. When bubbles appear (about 2 minutes), flip pancakes over and cook until golden brown, another 1 or 2 minutes. Remove cooked pancakes and keep warm in a 250°F. oven. Repeat with remaining batter, adding additional butter as needed.

Place 2 pancakes on each plate and pass with the blueberry syrup.

BLUEBERRY SYRUP
2 cups fresh or frozen blueberries, thawed
1 cup pure maple syrup
1 tablespoon fresh lemon juice

BLUEBERRY CORNMEAL PANCAKES
1 cup flour
½ cup cornmeal
2 teaspoons baking powder
1 teaspoon baking soda
¼ teaspoon salt
2 tablespoons brown sugar
1 cup buttermilk
2 eggs
2 tablespoons melted butter
1 teaspoon vanilla
1 cup fresh or frozen blueberries, thawed
2 tablespoons butter

Makes 4 to 6 Servings

PAGES 142-143: *Bigtooth maple leaves on a mossy log, west fork of Oak Creek*

Vanilla

THE MOST LABOR-INTENSIVE AGRICULTURAL
PRODUCT in the world, vanilla, like chocolate and
coffee, grows only within twenty-five degrees of
the equator. Native to tropical America, vanilla
beans come from the pods of an orchid plant and
must be hand-cultivated, so they are very costly.
Once considered an aphrodisiac and so valuable
that they were reserved for royalty, the beans,
which take 9 months to develop on the vine, are
still extremely prized. In fact, to prevent theft,
workers sleep in the fields with guns the night
before harvesting.

Vanilla, the "nectar of the gods," is a magical
flavoring. It can be added to citrus to cut sharp-
ness, added to chocolate to boost its flavor, and
used in baked goods to soften and blend over-
powering flavors. It's even used to calm patients
undergoing chemotherapy and as aromatherapy
to soothe jangled nerves.

There are three varieties of vanilla beans:
Bourbon-Madagascar, Mexican, and Tahitian.
Bourbon vanilla gets its name from the Bourbon
kings of France when vanilla was brought to
Madagascar when it was under French rule.
Mexican beans have a smooth, rich flavor but are
scarcer because oil fields have replaced the areas
where the orchid once thrived. Tahitian vanilla is
intensely aromatic, though not as flavorful as the
other two types. But no matter which variety you
use, be sure and use pure vanilla in your cooking,
because imitation vanilla (vanillin) is made of coal
tar and paper pulp and leaves a bitter aftertaste.

Pumpkin Waffles with Cinnamon Syrup

Fun to serve for brunch, these waffles can be made a few weeks ahead of time, frozen, and reheated in the oven or a toaster. Or, the batter can be made ahead and kept, covered, in the refrigerator for up to 3 days. The cinnamon syrup can also be made ahead and kept in the refrigerator. 🍃 FALL

STIR TOGETHER THE FLOUR, baking powder, salt, sugar, cinnamon, and nutmeg in a medium bowl. In a separate bowl, whisk together the pumpkin, milk, egg yolks, and butter.

In another small bowl, beat the egg whites until stiff. Fold together the flour mixture and the pumpkin mixture; stir in ¼ of the beaten egg whites to lighten the batter. Gently fold in the remaining egg whites.

Preheat oven to 200°F. Heat a waffle maker and cook the waffles according to the manufacturer's instructions. Keep waffles warm in the oven while making the rest. Serve with butter and the prepared Cinnamon Syrup.

1 cup all-purpose flour
2 teaspoons baking powder
½ teaspoon salt
2 tablespoons sugar
¼ teaspoon ground cinnamon
⅛ teaspoon ground nutmeg
½ cup canned pumpkin
1 cup milk
2 eggs, separated
1 tablespoon butter, melted
Cinnamon Syrup (see page 174)

Makes 4 Servings

Golden-yellow maple leaves glow in the morning sun at south fork of Cave Creek, Coronado National Forest

CHEDDAR CORNMEAL *Biscuits*

Tangy Cheddar cheese and cornmeal give these biscuits a buttery flavor and a slightly crunchy texture. They're the perfect accompaniment to a bowl of soup or chili or alongside a summer salad. ☼ SUMMER

PREHEAT OVEN TO 400°F. Line a baking sheet with parchment paper.

In a large bowl, stir together the flour, cornmeal, baking soda, baking powder, and salt. Mix in the butter with your fingers or a fork until dough resembles coarse meal; stir in the Cheddar cheese. Add ⅓ cup of the buttermilk and stir with a fork until moistened, adding more milk by tablespoons if dry.

Pat the dough into a ½-inch-thick circle on a piece of waxed paper or on a floured surface. Cut the dough into 8 biscuits using a 2 ½-inch biscuit cutter. Form the remaining dough into a ½-inch circle and cut out 4 more biscuits. Transfer to the prepared baking sheet and bake in the center of the oven until lightly golden brown, about 12 minutes. Remove from the oven and cool.

1 cup all-purpose flour
½ cup yellow cornmeal
¼ teaspoon baking soda
1 teaspoon baking powder
½ teaspoon salt
4 tablespoons unsalted butter, cut into ½-inch size pieces
½ cup grated extra sharp Cheddar cheese
½ cup buttermilk

Makes 12 Biscuits

Chipotle CORNBREAD

The chipotle chiles add a smoky, slightly sweet heat to this moist cornbread–a heat that's not noticed until after a bite or two. For more impact, simply add another chipotle. ✺ SPRING

PREHEAT OVEN TO 375°F. Butter a 12 x 4-inch loaf pan, an 8-inch square pan, or a 9 x 5-inch loaf pan.

In a large bowl, whisk together the cornmeal, flour, sugar, baking soda, salt, baking powder, and cheese. In a medium bowl, whisk together the buttermilk, eggs, butter, and chipotle purée. Add the liquid mixture to the cornmeal mixture, stirring until just combined. Spoon into the prepared loaf pan and bake until a skewer comes out clean, 25 to 30 minutes. Cool slightly, remove from the pan, and allow to cool completely before serving.

1 cup yellow cornmeal
1 cup all-purpose flour
¼ cup sugar
1 teaspoon baking soda
1 teaspoon salt
2 teaspoons baking powder
1 cup (about 4 ounces) grated Monterey Jack cheese
1 cup buttermilk
3 large eggs
6 tablespoons unsalted butter, melted and cooled
3 chipotle chiles in adobo sauce, puréed and strained

Makes 1 Loaf

Skillet CORNBREAD

Green onions, cornmeal, and bacon add a wonderful texture to this rich, moist cornbread while the chiles add just the right amount of heat. Serve this cornbread warm for a hearty accompaniment to any meal.
☼ SUMMER

IN A WELL-SEASONED CAST IRON SKILLET or other ovenproof skillet with 2-inch high sides, cook the bacon over medium-high heat until crisp. Drain on paper towels and keep the fat in the skillet. Crumble bacon and set aside.

Preheat oven to 350°F. In a large bowl, mix together the cornmeal, flour, sugar, salt, baking powder, baking soda, cheese, poblano, green onion, and crumbled bacon. In another bowl, beat the eggs and whisk in the buttermilk. Add the liquid mixture to the dry and quickly mix them together.

To make the cornbread, reheat the skillet with the bacon fat and pour the mixture into it. The fat will be absorbed as the bread cooks. Bake until a skewer put in the center comes out clean and the bread pulls away from the sides of the pan, about 30 minutes. Allow the bread to cool in the skillet for 15 minutes and then cut into wedges, serving it warm from the skillet.

NOTE: *If you prefer to make corn sticks, heat the corn stick pans in the middle of the hot oven for 10 minutes. Remove the pans from the oven and put 1 tablespoon hot bacon fat into each of them, spreading the fat evenly among each mold. Divide the prepared batter among the molds, about 3 tablespoons each, and bake until a skewer comes out clean and tops are golden, about 20 minutes.*

6 slices bacon
2 cups yellow cornmeal
1 ½ cups all-purpose flour
½ cup sugar
½ teaspoon salt
1 teaspoon baking powder
1 teaspoon baking soda
1 cup extra sharp Cheddar cheese
1 poblano chile, roasted, seeded, peeled, and diced (see page 47)
¼ cup chopped green onions
3 large eggs
1 ½ cups buttermilk

Makes 1 (10-inch diameter) Loaf

Dried Cranberry, Orange, and Pecan Muffins with Orange Butter

Dried cranberries, pecans, and cornmeal give these moist muffins a lovely texture, and the orange glaze adds just the right hint of sweetness. Serve these at your Thanksgiving breakfast for a great prelude of what's to come. ❄ WINTER

PREHEAT OVEN TO 375° F. Butter or spray with vegetable oil twelve 2 ½-inch muffin cups.

TO PREPARE THE MUFFINS, in a medium bowl, stir together the flour, cornmeal, baking soda, and salt. In another medium bowl, whisk together the buttermilk, orange juice, orange zest, and egg. In the bowl of an electric mixture or with a hand mixer, beat together the butter and sugar until creamy. With mixer on low speed, mix in dry and liquid ingredients, alternately, starting and ending with the dry ingredients. Stir in pecans and cranberries. Divide batter among muffin cups and bake until muffins are golden brown and a skewer comes out clean, about 15 to 20 minutes. Remove from the pan and cool on a rack.

TO PREPARE THE GLAZE, in a small bowl, whisk together the confectioners' sugar, milk, and orange zest until smooth. Drizzle over cooled muffins and sprinkle with chopped pecans.

TO PREPARE THE ORANGE BUTTER, in a food processor or with an electric mixer, beat all of the butter ingredients together until smooth. Transfer to a decorative crock or bowl. Serve alongside the glazed muffins.

DRIED CRANBERRY, ORANGE, AND PECAN MUFFINS

1 ½ cups all-purpose flour
½ cup yellow cornmeal
1 teaspoon baking soda
¼ teaspoon salt
⅔ cup buttermilk
¼ cup fresh orange juice
1 teaspoon grated orange zest
1 egg
6 tablespoons unsalted butter
¾ cup granulated sugar
½ cup chopped toasted pecans (see page 38)
½ cup dried cranberries

ORANGE GLAZE

¾ cup confectioners' sugar
1 ½ tablespoons milk
1 teaspoon grated orange zest
¼ cup finely chopped toasted pecans (see page 38)

ORANGE BUTTER

1 stick (4 ounces) unsalted butter
½ teaspoon grated orange zest
1 ½ teaspoons fresh orange juice
¼ teaspoon salt

Makes 12 Muffins

Apple Pecan *Bread* with
Cinnamon Butter

Apples signify the arrival of fall in most parts of the country, including the Southwest. Apple cider, apple donuts, and apple pie celebrate this bountiful season. Here's an apple recipe you can make any time of the year, but it's especially good when the temperatures drop and it's cozy inside. 🍂 FALL

PREHEAT OVEN TO 350°F. Butter a 9 x 5-inch loaf pan.

TO PREPARE THE BREAD, in a large bowl with an electric mixer, cream together the butter and sugar until light and fluffy, about 3 to 5 minutes. Add the eggs, one at a time, and then the sour cream and vanilla.

In a separate bowl, sift together the flour, baking soda, salt, cinnamon, and nutmeg. Gradually add to the butter mixture until just combined. Stir in the orange zest, pecans, and apples. Spoon into the prepared loaf pan and bake until a skewer comes out clean, about 1 hour. Let cool in the pan for 15 minutes, transfer to a baking rack, and cool completely.

TO PREPARE THE CINNAMON BUTTER, using an electric mixer, beat all the butter ingredients in a medium bowl until smooth. Store, covered, if not using right away; bring to room temperature before serving. Serve in a decorative bowl alongside the warm bread.

APPLE PECAN BREAD

1 stick (½ cup) unsalted butter, at
    room temperature
1 cup sugar
2 eggs
¼ cup sour cream
1 teaspoon vanilla
2 cups all-purpose flour
1 teaspoon baking soda
½ teaspoon salt
¼ teaspoon cinnamon
¼ teaspoon nutmeg
1 teaspoon orange zest
½ cup chopped toasted pecans (see page 38)
1 cup peeled and diced Granny Smith apples

CINNAMON BUTTER

1 stick (½ cup) unsalted butter, at
    room temperature
½ cup confectioners' sugar
1 teaspoon cinnamon
1 teaspoon orange zest

Makes 1 Loaf

CORNBREAD *Pecan* STUFFING

Use this zesty stuffing for your turkey to add a Southwest touch to your Thanksgiving dinner. If using canned stock, do not add salt until everything has been combined; then adjust salt to taste. If you prefer a crusty stuffing, bake the casserole uncovered. 🌿 FALL

PREHEAT OVEN TO 375°F. Lightly butter an 8-inch square pan.

In a large skillet, over medium heat, cook the chorizo, breaking it up as it cooks, until browned, about 10 minutes. Add the red pepper, chile, and onion and sauté until vegetables are tender, about 5 minutes.

Put crumbled cornbread in a large bowl. Add oregano, parsley, pecans, and chorizo mixture. Stir in butter and just enough chicken stock to moisten bread well. Add salt and pepper to taste,

if desired. Spoon stuffing into prepared pan, cover with aluminum foil, and bake until heated through, about 30 minutes.

½ pound chorizo
1 red bell pepper, seeded and diced
1 Anaheim or New Mexico green chile, seeded and diced
1 cup diced white onion
4 cups cooked, crumbled cornbread
1 teaspoon dried Mexican oregano
1 tablespoon finely chopped parsley
½ cup toasted chopped pecans (see page 38)
¼ cup (2 ounces) unsalted butter, melted
¾ to 1 cup chicken stock
Salt and freshly ground pepper to taste

Makes 6 to 8 Servings

Cumin ROLLS

The dough for these rolls will keep for 5 days in the refrigerator. For variety, try different flavorings by using orange zest, poppy seeds, or sesame seeds instead of the cumin. ❄ WINTER

IN A SMALL BOWL, proof the yeast with warm water and 1 teaspoon of the sugar. Allow to sit until foamy, about 5 minutes.

In a large bowl, combine the milk, butter, remaining sugar, and salt; stir until butter is melted and sugar is dissolved. Add the yeast mixture, eggs, and 1 ½ cups of the flour. Beat until well mixed. Add enough of the remaining flour to make a stiff dough. Knead on a floured board until smooth and elastic, 5 to 10 minutes. Place dough in a lightly oiled bowl, turn to coat, cover with plastic wrap, and refrigerate overnight or up to 4 days.

Remove dough from the refrigerator and allow to come to room temperature. Preheat oven to 400°F. Lightly butter 24 muffin cups.

Pull off a piece of dough the size of a small egg. Dip the dough in melted butter, and then in the toasted cumin seeds. Stretch the dough into an 8-inch rope and tie into a knot. Place in a greased muffin cup. Repeat with remaining dough. Bake for 12 to 15 minutes, or until lightly browned. Serve warm.

1 (¼-ounce) package active dry yeast
¼ cup warm water (110° to 115°F.)
¼ cup sugar
1 cup milk, scalded and cooled to lukewarm
3 tablespoons unsalted butter at room temperature
1 teaspoon salt
2 eggs, beaten
3 to 3 ½ cups all-purpose flour
½ cup unsalted butter, melted
½ cup cumin seeds, toasted (see page 38)

Makes 2 Dozen Rolls

SOUTHWEST GRILLED *Pizza*

The crisp crust and scrumptious Southwest toppings on this pizza make it a favorite year-round, but it's particularly good in the summer when you don't want to heat up the kitchen and your grill is already nicely seasoned. ☼ SUMMER

TO PREPARE THE DOUGH, proof the yeast with the sugar in the ⅔ cup lukewarm water. Allow to sit until foamy, about 5 to 10 minutes. Put the yeast mixture in the bowl of a food processor with the olive oil, flour, and salt. Process the mixture until it comes together in a ball, adding more water if too dry and more flour if too wet. Remove the dough from the bowl and, on a floured surface, knead it until smooth and elastic, about 2 more minutes. Put the dough into a lightly oiled bowl, turn to coat, and cover the bowl with a clean kitchen towel. Put the bowl in a warm place to rise until double in bulk, about 1 hour. Punch down the dough and roll it out on a floured surface until it is as thin as possible and forms an approximate circle about 14 inches in diameter.

Preheat a barbecue grill to high heat. Lightly oil the grill. If using an uncooked chicken breast, salt and pepper it and put it on the coolest side of the grill. Cook until browned on one side; turn over and continue cooking until chicken is firm and cooked through, about 3 to 4 minutes per side. Remove chicken and cut it into small pieces.

Gently place the pizza dough on the hottest part of the grill. Cook until bottom is firm and grill marks appear. Use tongs to flip the crust over and move it to a cooler part of the grill.

Brush olive oil over the cooked side of the pizza dough and add toppings, starting with the salsa and then the cheese, bell pepper, chile, and black olives. Return the pizza to the hot part of the grill and cook until the cheese is melted, about 4 to 5 minutes. Remove the pizza with the back of a baking sheet and transfer it to a cutting board. Top it with the avocado slices and the lettuce. Cut into wedges and serve immediately.

DOUGH

1 (¼-ounce) package dry yeast
1 teaspoon sugar
⅔ cup water
2 tablespoons olive oil
2 to 2 ¼ cups all-purpose flour
1 teaspoon salt

1 boneless, skinless chicken breast half or 1 cup diced cooked chicken
Salt and pepper to taste
1 tablespoon olive oil
1 cup Yellow Tomato Salsa (see page 22) or salsa of your choice
1 ½ cups grated Asadero cheese
1 red bell pepper, roasted, peeled, seeded, and diced (see page 47)
1 poblano chile, roasted, peeled, seeded, and diced (see page 47)
¼ cup sliced black olives
1 avocado, peeled and cut into small cubes
1 cup shredded Romaine lettuce

Makes 1 (14-inch) Pizza

Desserts

Pumpkin GINGER LAYER CAKE

The fresh ginger in the cake and the crystallized ginger in the frosting add a lovely tang to this slightly spicy pumpkin cake. It's a nice change from the same old pumpkin pie for your Thanksgiving dessert.

🍃 FALL

PREHEAT OVEN TO 350°F. Butter 2 (9-inch) cake pans. Line the bottom of each pan with a buttered round of parchment paper.

TO PREPARE THE CAKE, sift the flour, baking powder, baking soda, salt, cinnamon, and ground ginger together over a piece of waxed paper. Set aside. In a medium bowl, stir together the pumpkin, milk, and fresh ginger. Set aside.

In the bowl of an electric mixer fitted with the paddle attachment, cream together the butter and the sugar until smooth, about 3 minutes. Mix in eggs, one at a time, scraping the bowl after each addition. Add ⅓ of the flour mixture on low speed, and then add ⅓ of the pumpkin mixture. Repeat 2 more times until all of the ingredients are combined. Spoon the cake batter into the buttered pans and bake in the middle of the oven until the cake starts to pull away from the sides of the pan and a wooden skewer inserted in the center comes out dry, about 35 to 40 minutes.

Remove from the oven and cool for 10 minutes on a wire rack; take the cakes out of the pans, and remove the parchment paper circles; cool completely.

TO PREPARE THE FROSTING, toss the crystallized ginger slices with about 1 tablespoon of the confectioners' sugar. Finely chop the ginger and set aside.

In the bowl of an electric mixer, cream together the softened cream cheese and the butter. Add the vanilla and ground ginger. Gradually add the remaining confectioners' sugar, adding milk or cream, if necessary, to make it the correct spreading consistency. Fold in the chopped crystallized ginger.

To assemble, slice each cake horizontally into 2 layers. Place one cake layer on a platter and spread with ½ cup of frosting. Repeat with 2 more layers. Top with remaining layer and spread top and sides with remaining frosting. Refrigerate until frosting is set, about 1 hour.

CAKE

4 cups Softasilk cake flour
4 teaspoons baking powder
1 teaspoon baking soda
½ teaspoon salt
1 teaspoon ground cinnamon
1 teaspoon ground ginger
1 (15-ounce) can pumpkin
1 cup milk
2 tablespoons minced fresh ginger
1 cup (2 sticks) unsalted butter, at room temperature
2 ½ cups brown sugar
4 eggs

FROSTING

3 large pieces crystallized ginger
1 pound confectioners' sugar
8 ounces cream cheese, at room temperature
½ cup (1 stick) butter, at room temperature
1 teaspoon vanilla
½ teaspoon ground ginger

Makes 16 Servings

Tres Leches CHOCOLATE CAKE

The tres leches (three milks) come from sweetened condensed milk, evaporated milk, and whole milk (I've substituted heavy cream for the whole milk). In this moist, rich cake, they are used to melt the chocolate in the filling and in the soaking syrup that permeates the chocolate cake. An authentic taste of Mexico!

✾ SPRING

TO PREPARE THE FILLING, put the chocolate in a large bowl. In a saucepan over medium heat bring the milks and cream to a boil. Pour the hot milk mixture over the chocolate and allow to stand for 1 minute; gently whisk until smooth. Stir in the rum. Cover the bowl with plastic wrap and refrigerate for at least 4 hours until mixture is chilled.

TO PREPARE THE CAKE, position the rack in the center of the oven and preheat to 350° F. Lightly butter the bottom and sides of a 9 x 2-inch round cake pan. Line the bottom of the pan with a circle of parchment or waxed paper. Dust the sides of the pan with flour and tap out the excess.

In a small bowl, stir together the flour, cocoa, 1 tablespoon of the sugar, baking powder, and salt. Sift the flour mixture onto a piece of waxed paper.

In the bowl of a heavy-duty electric mixer fitted with the wire whisk, beat the eggs and extra egg yolks at medium speed until frothy. Increase speed to high and add the remaining sugar in a steady stream. Continue beating until the egg mixture has tripled in volume and forms a thick ribbon when whisk is lifted, 5 to 7 minutes. Lower the speed to medium and beat in the butter and vanilla. Resift ⅓ of the flour mixture over the batter. Using a rubber spatula, fold the flour mixture into the batter. In two more additions, resift the remaining flour mixture over the batter and fold it in. Scrape the batter into the prepared pan and spread evenly. Bake the cake until the edge of the cake pulls away from the sides of the pan, 15 to 20 minutes. Run a knife around the edge of the cake; invert the cake onto a wire rack and remove the cake pan and the paper. Cool completely.

TO PREPARE THE SOAKING SYRUP, in a medium bowl, whisk together all of the syrup ingredients. Set aside or refrigerate if not using immediately.

To assemble, cut the cake horizontally into 2 layers. Place one of the layers in the bottom of a 9-inch round springform pan. Using a hand-held electric mixer set at medium speed, beat the chilled filling for 2 to 3 minutes until it begins to form soft peaks. The filling will continue to thicken as you spread it. Using a pastry brush, moisten the cake layer in the pan with half of the soaking syrup. Scrape half of the chocolate filling over the cake layer and spread it evenly. Place the second cake layer on top of the filling and brush it with the remaining syrup. Spread the remaining filling over the cake and cover the surface gently with plastic wrap. Refrigerate for at least 2 hours.

When ready to serve the cake, blow warm air from a hairdryer or press a hot towel around the edges of the springform pan. Release the clamp on the pan and gently remove the side of the pan and the plastic wrap from the cake. Smooth any rough surfaces. Decorate the cake with fresh raspberries, if desired.

FILLING
12 ounces bittersweet or semisweet chocolate, finely chopped
½ cup sweetened condensed milk
½ cup evaporated milk
1 cup heavy cream
1 tablespoon dark rum

CAKE
⅓ cup Softasilk cake flour
¼ cup sifted unsweetened cocoa
⅓ cup plus 1 tablespoon granulated sugar
¼ teaspoon baking powder
⅛ teaspoon salt
2 large eggs
2 large egg yolks
3 tablespoons unsalted butter, melted and cooled
1 tablespoon vanilla

SOAKING SYRUP
2 tablespoons evaporated milk
½ cup sweetened condensed milk
½ cup heavy cream
2 tablespoons dark rum

1 pint fresh raspberries

Makes 10 to 12 Servings

Plum, *Prickly Pear,* AND MESQUITE CRUMBLE

The fruit of the prickly pear is called a tuna, and the flesh is a gorgeous magenta color. It brightens this dish and pairs beautifully with the plums. The topping contains mesquite powder, or flour, which is made from pulverized pods of the mesquite tree. It is available at specialty and health food stores or from Native Seed Search. My choice of ice cream with this crumble would be cinnamon or butter pecan.

☼ SUMMER

IN A LARGE SAUCEPAN over medium-high heat, combine the water, sugar, cinnamon stick, and vanilla. Cook, stirring, until the sugar is dissolved, about 3 minutes. Stir in the plums and set aside.

Carefully remove the skins from the prickly pear tunas as they may still have some stickers in them. Put the peeled fruit in a food processor and purée. The mixture will not be completely smooth as the hard black seeds will still be present. Strain the mixture into the pan with the plums. Remove the cinnamon stick and the vanilla bean, if using, from the saucepan and discard. Spoon the fruit mixture into a 7 x 11-inch baking pan and set aside.

PREHEAT OVEN TO 350° F. TO PREPARE THE CRUMBLE, in a medium bowl, mix together the flours, oatmeal, sugar, cinnamon, and nutmeg. With a fork or your hands, work the butter into the mixture until it resembles coarse meal. Spoon onto the fruit mixture and bake until top is crisp and plums are softened, about 45 minutes. Cool for at least 30 minutes. Spoon into bowls or onto plates and top with your favorite ice cream, if desired.

½ cup water
½ cup sugar
1 cinnamon stick
1 teaspoon vanilla bean paste or 1 vanilla bean, split open
2 pounds plums (about 8 to 10), pitted and sliced
4 prickly pear tunas

CRUMBLE
½ cup flour
½ cup mesquite flour
1 cup quick-cooking oatmeal
⅓ cup packed brown sugar
¼ teaspoon ground cinnamon
⅛ teaspoon freshly ground nutmeg
8 tablespoons (1 stick) unsalted butter, cut into pieces and chilled

Makes 8 Servings

CHOCOLATE *Flan* WITH DULCE DE LECHE

A rich, velvety flan is paired with a subtle caramel sauce in this Mexican-inspired dessert. If you'd rather make one large flan, use an 8-inch round cake pan and bake it about 10 minutes longer. 🍃 FALL

PREHEAT OVEN TO 325°F. Butter 12 (4-ounce) ramekins and put them in a large baking dish.

TO PREPARE THE DULCE DE LECHE CREAM, in a large, heavy-bottomed saucepan, bring the milk to a boil. Reduce to a simmer and add sugar and baking soda. Simmer for 25 to 30 minutes, stirring frequently, until milk becomes thick and resembles a light caramel sauce. Remove from heat and cool completely. In the bowl of an electric mixer with the whisk attachment, beat heavy cream to soft peaks. Fold milk mixture into cream and refrigerate, covered, until ready to serve.

TO PREPARE THE CARAMEL, in a small, heavy-bottomed saucepan, combine the sugar and water. Cook over medium-high heat, stirring, just until sugar is dissolved. Increase heat to high and cook without stirring until mixture turns light brown. Remove from heat. Carefully pour hot caramel into ramekins, dividing it evenly. Set aside.

TO PREPARE THE FLAN, combine the chocolates in a large bowl and set aside. In a microwave, heat milk until almost boiling, about 2 minutes; add espresso powder and stir until dissolved. Pour mixture over the chocolate. Allow to sit for 1 minute. Whisk until chocolate is melted and mixture is smooth.

In another bowl, whisk together the eggs and sugar until well blended. Gradually whisk in the chocolate mixture, Crème de Cocoa, if desired, and vanilla. Divide mixture evenly among the ramekins.

Pour hot water into the baking dish so that it comes halfway up the sides of the ramekins. Bake flans in the water bath until centers are just set, about 35 to 45 minutes. Run a knife around the edges of the ramekins and turn them out immediately onto dessert plates. If they resist, dip them in very hot water for about 30 seconds. Serve with Dulce de Leche Cream on the side.

DULCE DE LECHE CREAM
2 cups whole milk
½ cup granulated sugar
⅛ teaspoon baking soda
1 cup heavy cream

CARAMEL
1 cup granulated sugar
¾ cup water

FLAN
5 ounces bittersweet chocolate, finely chopped
1 ½ ounces Mexican chocolate, such as Ibarra, finely chopped
1 ½ cups whole milk
2 teaspoons instant espresso powder
5 large eggs
⅔ cup granulated sugar
1 tablespoon Crème de Cocoa, (optional)
½ teaspoon vanilla

Makes 12 Servings

Pecan AND Chocolate Pie

We had a beautiful pecan tree at our former home, and it was a labor of love to shell all those nuts. But we celebrated by making this rich, decadent dessert, and it was always well worth it. Now, with fresh pecans available year round, you can make it anytime.
🍂 FALL

TO PREPARE THE PASTRY, put the butter, flour, sugar, and salt in the bowl of a food processor and pulse until mixture resembles a coarse meal. With the machine running, add just enough ice water to moisten the mixture. Do not over process. Remove the mixture from the bowl, turn out onto a board, and, with your hands, press the dough together, adding more water if necessary. Form into a disc, wrap in plastic wrap, and refrigerate for at least 2 hours or up to 3 days in the refrigerator.

Remove the dough from the refrigerator and with a rolling pin, roll out the dough into a 13-inch circle. Line a 9-inch pie pan with the dough and refrigerate for 2 hours or overnight.

Preheat oven to 350°F. Put pecan pieces on a baking sheet and toast in the preheated oven until pecans are toasted, 5 to 7 minutes. Lower heat to 325°F.

TO PREPARE THE FILLING, in a medium bowl, melt the chocolate and butter together in a microwave oven, about 1 minute on high power. Stir until well incorporated. Cool slightly.

In a large bowl, whisk together the eggs and brown sugar. Add the corn syrup, salt, and cooled chocolate mixture; whisk until mixture is smooth.

To assemble, sprinkle the pecan pieces over the bottom of the chilled pastry shell. Pour the filling over the pecans. Bake the pie until the filling is set and the crust is golden brown, 45 to 50 minutes. Cool completely before serving.

NOTE: *If not using the nuts right away, keep them in the freezer to keep them from turning rancid.*

Maple trees in their fall colors, Fry Canyon, Coconino National Forest

PASTRY
6 tablespoons cold unsalted butter, cut into 6 pieces
1 cup all-purpose flour
1 tablespoon sugar
½ teaspoon salt
3 to 4 tablespoons ice water
1 ½ cups pecan pieces (*see* NOTE)

FILLING
4 ounces bittersweet chocolate, cut into small pieces
2 tablespoons unsalted butter
3 eggs
½ cup firmly packed dark brown sugar
¾ cup light corn syrup
¼ teaspoon salt

Makes 8 Servings

FROZEN *Lime* PIE

Nothing is as refreshing after a spicy meal than something cold and tart, and this creamy pie is the perfect ending to a Southwest lunch or dinner. It's very easy to make and keeps well in the freezer, tightly wrapped, for up to 3 days. ❋ SPRING

TO PREPARE THE CRUST, preheat oven of 350° F. Butter a 9-inch pie plate. Put cookies in a food processor and pulse until they are the consistency of cornmeal. You should have about 2 cups of cookie crumbs. Melt the butter in a medium bowl in a microwave oven; add the cookie crumbs and mix well. Pat the mixture into the prepared pie plate and bake until lightly browned and firm, about 10 minutes. Cool.

TO PREPARE THE FILLING, put the heavy cream and lime curd into the bowl of an electric mixer with a whisk attachment. Whip together until soft peaks form. Add the lime zest and continue beating until stiff. Turn the mixture out into the cooled crust and put in the freezer. Freeze until firm, about 4 hours. (If keeping the pie in the freezer longer than 4 hours, wrap it in plastic wrap.) Just before serving, garnish the center of the pie with a twisted slice of lime.

CRUST
2 ½ cups gingerbread cookies (about 6 ounces)
4 tablespoons (½ stick) unsalted butter

FILLING
1 ½ cups heavy cream
½ cup lime curd (*see* NOTE)
2 tablespoons freshly grated lime zest
1 lime slice, cut down the center and twisted

Makes 8 to 10 Servings

NOTE: *Lime curd is available in specialty grocery stores in the same department as the jellies and jams. This same pie can be made by substituting the lime curd and zest with lemon curd and lemon zest.*

CRISPY *Lemon* AND HAZELNUT BARS

Many Arizona residents have lemon trees in their yards and are always looking for ways to use this healthful citrus fruit. The hazelnuts add a nice crunch and buttery contrast to the acidic lemon flavor.
✻ SPRING

TO PREPARE THE BARS, preheat oven to 325°F. Butter an 8 x 8-inch square baking pan. In the bowl of an electric mixer fitted with the paddle attachment, beat together the butter and the confectioner's sugar until light and fluffy, about 5 minutes. Add the eggs and beat until incorporated. Add the salt, lemon zest, and cream. Add the flour last, mixing until just combined. The mixture will be dry and somewhat crumbly. Pat it into the prepared pan and bake until lightly browned and the edges begin to pull away from the sides, 25 to 30 minutes. Keep warm while preparing the glaze.

TO PREPARE THE GLAZE, in a small bowl, stir together the confectioner's sugar and the lemon juice until smooth. Drizzle the mixture over the warm bars and spread evenly with a small spatula. Sprinkle with the toasted hazelnuts and cool thoroughly. Cut into bars.

NOTE: *To toast hazelnuts, also called filberts, place them on a baking pan and put them in a preheated 350°F. oven. Cook until they become a shade darker, about 10 to 15 minutes. Remove them from the oven and immediately wrap them in a clean kitchen towel. Gently roll them in the towel to remove their skins.*

BARS

1 stick (4 ounces) unsalted butter, at
    room temperature
½ cup plus 2 tablespoons confectioner's sugar
2 eggs
¼ teaspoon salt
2 teaspoons grated lemon zest
1 tablespoon heavy cream
1 ¾ cups all-purpose flour

GLAZE

1 cup confectioner's sugar
2 tablespoons fresh lemon juice

¼ cup toasted, skinned, and chopped hazelnuts
    (*see* NOTE)

Makes 24 Bars

OPPOSITE: *Golden light illuminates the sculpted walls and powdered sand of the Upper Antelope slot canyon in Page, Arizona*

GINGERBREAD-CRUSTED
Apple TART

This is not your ordinary apple pie—ginger, chile powder, and molasses flavor the crust; chiles enhance the apple filling; and toasted almonds and oatmeal furnish the crunchy topping. 🌿 FALL

TO PREPARE THE CRUST, put the flour, sugar, salt, ginger, chile powder, and cinnamon in the bowl of a food processor and pulse until combined. Add the molasses and butter and pulse until the mixture resembles coarse meal. Gradually add the cold water through the feed tube until the mixture starts to come together. Do not over process. Remove the mixture from the processor onto a lightly floured surface and bring it together with your hands, forming a flat disk about 6 inches in diameter. Wrap in plastic wrap and chill for at least 1 hour. Roll out into a 13-inch circle and transfer it to an 11-inch tart pan with a removable bottom. Chill while making the filling and topping.

Preheat oven to 375°F.

TO PREPARE THE FILLING, combine all filling ingredients in a large bowl. Mix well and set aside.

TO PREPARE THE TOPPING, put all topping ingredients, except the butter, in the bowl of a food processor; pulse until nuts are finely chopped. Add the butter and pulse until the butter is in pea-sized pieces.

Arrange filling in chilled tart shell and spoon topping over filling. Bake until crust and topping are browned and apples are tender, about 45 minutes. Allow to cool for 15 minutes; remove sides from the tart pan. Cool slightly and serve warm topped with whipped cream or cinnamon ice cream.

CRUST
1 ½ cups all-purpose flour
3 tablespoons sugar
¼ teaspoon salt
1 teaspoon ground ginger
1 teaspoon ancho chile powder
½ teaspoon cinnamon
1 tablespoon molasses
1 stick (8 tablespoons) unsalted butter, cut into
    1-inch pieces and chilled
4 to 5 tablespoons cold water

FILLING
4 Granny Smith apples, peeled, cored, and
    thinly sliced
1 tablespoon fresh lemon juice
¼ cup packed brown sugar
1 serrano chile, stemmed, seeded, and finely diced
¼ teaspoon cinnamon

TOPPING
½ cup packed brown sugar
½ cup whole toasted almonds
⅓ cup rolled oats
⅓ cup all-purpose flour
1 stick (8 tablespoons) unsalted butter, cut into
    1-inch pieces and chilled

Makes 12 Servings

RED, WHITE, AND BLUE *Tart*

Blueberries in a sour cream filling are baked into a rich crust and then topped with rings of raspberries. This perfect summer dessert is as good as it looks.

☀ SUMMER

TO PREPARE THE CRUST, put the flour, sugar, salt, lemon zest, and butter in the bowl of a food processor; pulse until the butter is in pea-sized pieces. In a small bowl, mix the lemon juice with the water; with the food processor running gradually add the liquid to the flour mixture. Process only until the mixture starts to come together. Turn the mixture out onto a board and bring it together with your hands to form a disk. Wrap in plastic wrap and refrigerate for at least 2 hours or overnight. On a floured board, roll the dough into a 14-inch circle. Transfer to a 10-inch tart pan with a removable bottom. Freeze for at least 30 minutes or until ready to bake the pie.

Preheat oven to 400°F. Remove the tart shell from the freezer and line it with foil; fill with dry rice or pie weights. Bake until sides are set, about 15 to 20 minutes. Remove foil and weights.

TO PREPARE THE FILLING, in a large bowl stir together the sour cream, sugar, egg, vanilla, cinnamon, and salt. Mix well; gently fold in the blueberries. Spoon into the partially baked crust and bake until filling is set, about 25 minutes. Cool.

Decorate the tart with 2 circles of raspberries around the edge. Remove side of tart pan and transfer to a platter. Serve warm.

View from Cremation Canyon at Grand Canyon National Park during monsoon season

CRUST

1 ¼ cups all-purpose flour

2 tablespoons sugar

¼ teaspoon salt

1 teaspoon grated lemon zest

8 tablespoons (1 stick) cold unsalted butter, cut into pieces

1 tablespoon fresh lemon juice

3 tablespoons ice water

FILLING

1 cup sour cream

½ cup sugar

1 egg, beaten with a fork

1 teaspoon vanilla extract

½ teaspoon cinnamon

¼ teaspoon salt

2 ½ cups fresh blueberries (about 12 ounces)

1 ½ cups fresh raspberries

Makes 12 Servings

DOUBLE *Chocolate*, ANCHO CHILE, AND ALMOND TART

This rich, sumptuous dessert replicates the delicious combination of flavors found in Mexican hot chocolate, and it is perfect for entertaining because it is made a day ahead of serving time. In Mexico, chocolate is usually ground with almonds, sugar, and a touch of cinnamon and then whipped into hot water to make a delicious drink. Ancho chiles have overtones of chocolate in their unique taste and adding them to this dessert enhances the intensity of the chocolate. ❄ WINTER

TO PREPARE THE CRUST, beat the butter, sugar, cinnamon, chile powder, and salt together with an electric mixer until creamy. Add the vanilla and cocoa and beat until the mixture forms a smooth paste, about 2 minutes. Add the flour and mix only until just combined. Turn the dough out onto a piece of plastic wrap; press it into an 8-inch disk. Wrap dough in plastic wrap and chill until firm, about 45 minutes.

Roll the dough out between pieces of plastic wrap into an 11-inch circle. Peel off the top piece of plastic wrap and invert the pastry into a 9-inch tart pan with a removable bottom. Press the pastry into the sides of the pan and peel away the other sheet of plastic wrap. Trim the dough to be even with the top of the pan and refrigerate until firm, at least 30 minutes or overnight.

Preheat oven to 375°F. Prick the bottom of the tart shell with a fork. Bake until the pastry is dry, about 12 to 14 minutes. Cool.

TO PREPARE THE ALMONDS, put the almonds on a baking sheet and toast in the preheated oven until lightly browned, about 10 minutes. Toss with sugar and cinnamon while still warm. Set aside.

TO PREPARE THE FILLING, put the ancho chile in a small bowl; cover with very hot water and let steep until soft, about 30 minutes. Remove from the water, discard seeds and stem, and put chile in a blender with 1 tablespoon of the water in which the chile was soaked. Blend until smooth; you should have about 1 tablespoon of purée. Strain and set aside.

Place the chocolate in a medium bowl. In a small saucepan, bring the cream to a simmer over medium heat. Pour the hot cream over the chocolate and let stand for 1 minute. Stir until chocolate is melted and the mixture is smooth. Stir in the ancho chile purée and the Amaretto.

To assemble, spread almonds on the bottom of the cooked tart shell. Pour the chocolate mixture over the almonds and spread to form a smooth layer. Refrigerate until chilled and set, about 3 to 5 hours. About 30 minutes before serving, remove the tart from the refrigerator and take off the sides of the pan. Cover the tart with a stenciled design or doily and sprinkle with cocoa powder.

CRUST
8 tablespoons (1 stick) unsalted butter, softened
½ cup sugar
¼ teaspoon cinnamon
¼ teaspoon ancho chile powder
⅛ teaspoon salt
½ teaspoon pure vanilla extract
6 tablespoons unsweetened cocoa powder
¾ cup all-purpose flour

ALMONDS
1 cup slivered almonds, chopped
2 teaspoons sugar
1 teaspoon cinnamon

FILLING
1 ancho chile
8 ounces bittersweet chocolate, chopped
1 cup heavy cream
1 tablespoon Amaretto

Makes 12 to 16 Servings

LEMON *Bizcochitos*

Bizcochitos are a favorite dessert in the Southwest during the holidays, and they are traditionally made with lard. This melt-in-your-mouth version is made with butter and lemon for a fresher, lighter taste.
❄ WINTER

SIFT TOGETHER THE FLOUR and baking powder over waxed paper. Set aside.

With an electric mixer, cream together the sugar and butter; add anise seed, eggs, lemon juice, and zest. Slowly stir in the flour mixture and mix until a soft dough forms. Shape dough into a disk, cover with plastic wrap, and refrigerate for at least 2 hours or until firm.

Preheat oven to 375°F. Lightly butter 2 baking sheets. Roll out dough on a floured board to ¼-inch thickness. Cut with southwestern-shaped cookie cutters (coyote, cactus, chile, etc.)

In a small bowl, mix the cinnamon and sugar together; sprinkle liberally over cookies. Transfer to prepared baking sheets and bake until lightly browned, about 10 minutes. Remove from cookie sheets to a cooling rack and cool completely before serving.

2 ½ cups all-purpose flour
1 teaspoon baking powder
1 ½ cups sugar
1 cup (2 sticks) unsalted butter
1 ½ teaspoons anise seed, crushed
2 eggs
2 teaspoons fresh lemon juice
½ teaspoon finely grated lemon zest
1 tablespoon ground cinnamon
1 tablespoon sugar

Makes about 2 Dozen Cookies

Mexican CHOCOLATE CHIP COOKIES

These cookies replicate the taste of Mexican chocolate, which comes in 3.3-ounce tablets that are boxed and used for making hot chocolate. In Oaxaca, chocolate venders grind the chocolate to the customer's specifications, depending how much sugar, ground almonds, and cinnamon are desired. ❀ SPRING

PREHEAT OVEN TO 350°F. Spray 2 baking sheets with nonstick cooking spray or line them with parchment paper. In the bowl of an electric mixer fitted with a paddle, beat the butter and sugar together until creamy, about 2 minutes. Add the egg and vanilla extract.

In a separate bowl, sift together the flour, cinnamon, baking powder, and salt; add to the butter mixture and mix just until blended. Stir in the chocolate chips and the almonds.

Drop dough by rounded tablespoons onto the prepared baking sheets, about 2 inches apart. Bake until browned on top but still soft, about 12 to 14 minutes. Cool and store in an airtight container.

½ cup (1 stick) unsalted butter
¾ cup packed brown sugar
1 large egg
1 teaspoon vanilla extract
1 ¼ cups all-purpose flour
1 teaspoon ground cinnamon
½ teaspoon baking powder
¼ teaspoon salt
1 (6-ounce) package semisweet chocolate chips
½ cup toasted slivered almonds

Makes 2 ½ to 3 Dozen Cookies

ALMOND BUTTER AND
RED PEPPER JELLY *Cookies*

These cookies evoke childhood memories of peanut butter and jelly and are sure to please all those young at heart. The almond butter is a little more delicate tasting than peanut butter and the red pepper jelly has just a hint of heat, which tempers its sweetness. ☀ SUMMER

PREHEAT OVEN TO 375° F. Line 2 baking sheets with parchment paper or a nonstick baking sheet. In the bowl of an electric mixer fitted with the paddle attachment, put the almond butter, butter, and brown sugar. Beat until well blended, about 2 minutes. Add the eggs, one at a time, and then the vanilla.

In a separate bowl, sift together the flour and baking soda; add to the butter mixture and mix just until blended, about 30 seconds. Form the dough into 1-inch balls and place them on the prepared baking sheets. With the handle of a wooden spoon, make a depression in the center of each ball. Bake the cookies until lightly browned and firm, 8 to 10 minutes. Remove from the oven and put cookies on a rack. While they are cooling, fill each depression with about 1 teaspoon of the jelly. Cool completely.

NOTE: *Almond butter is available at specialty food stores and health food stores or you can make your own by toasting almonds and grinding them in a food processor until paste-like.*

1 cup almond butter *(see NOTE)*
½ cup (1 stick) unsalted butter at
    room temperature
1 cup firmly packed light brown sugar
2 eggs
1 teaspoon vanilla
2 cups all-purpose flour
1 teaspoon baking soda
1 cup red pepper jelly

Makes about 5 ½ Dozen Cookies

CINNAMON SUGAR TORTILLA WEDGES WITH *Coffee* ICE CREAM AND MEXICAN *Chocolate* SAUCE

Mexican chocolate has a hint of cinnamon, so this chocolate sauce includes just of touch of it. Melting chocolate in coffee intensifies the cocoa flavor, resulting in a scrumptious underpinning for the cinnamon. ❊ SPRING

TO PREPARE THE CHOCOLATE SAUCE, combine the coffee and cream. In a medium saucepan, heat to boiling. Place the chocolate in a heatproof bowl and pour the hot coffee mixture over it. Allow to stand for at least 1 minute. Stir together until smooth; stir in cinnamon. Refrigerate if not using immediately.

TO PREPARE THE TORTILLA WEDGES, preheat oven to 400°F. In a medium bowl, combine the butter, sugar, and cinnamon with a fork until well mixed. With a spatula or table knife, spread each tortilla with some of the butter mixture.

Cut each tortilla into 8 wedges. Place wedges on 2 baking sheets, buttered side up and spaced equally apart. Bake tortillas, uncovered, until crisp, puffed, and golden, about 8 minutes. Remove from oven.

To assemble, put a scoop of coffee ice cream in the center of a stemmed glass and drizzle chocolate sauce over the top. Stand 4 tortilla crisps in each glass. Garnish with a fresh sprig of mint and serve immediately.

MEXICAN CHOCOLATE SAUCE

¼ cup strong, prepared coffee
½ cup heavy cream
8 ounces semisweet or bittersweet chocolate, finely chopped
¼ teaspoon ground cinnamon

TORTILLA WEDGES

8 tablespoons (1 stick) unsalted butter, at room temperature
3 tablespoons sugar
3 tablespoons ground cinnamon
4 (8-inch) flour tortillas

1 quart coffee ice cream
8 fresh mint sprigs

Makes 8 Servings

Blazing red ring of a barrel cactus, blossoms backed by prickly pear, Santa Rita Mountains, Coronado National Forest

GRILLED *Bananas* WITH BUTTER PECAN ICE CREAM AND MEXICAN *Chocolate* SAUCE

As long as the grill is hot from cooking the steaks, chicken, or any other main dish, why not make dessert on it, too? Just brush the grill well after cooking the meat and lightly oil it again before grilling the bananas. If you don't want to use the grill, you can make this dessert in a large nonstick skillet.
☼ SUMMER

LIGHT A GRILL TO MEDIUM-HIGH HEAT. Peel the bananas and slice them diagonally ½-inch thick. Put them on a plate and drizzle them with the honey; sprinkle with cinnamon. Grill the bananas until golden on one side, about 2 minutes. Turn over and cook the other sides, about 2 minutes more. Divide the bananas among 6 plates. Place a scoop of ice cream on top of the bananas and drizzle with chocolate sauce. Serve immediately.

3 large firm bananas
3 tablespoons honey
½ teaspoon cinnamon
1 pint Butter Pecan el Diablo Ice Cream
   (see page 176)
¾ cup Mexican Chocolate Sauce (see page 172)

Makes 6 Servings

Margarita SORBET

For either a great ending to a spicy meal or served as a late-afternoon refresher in the hot summer months, this sorbet is best made with a fine tequila. The best ones are made from 100 percent blue agave, the desert succulent that is pressure-cooked, and then fermented.
☼ SUMMER

DISSOLVE SUGAR AND WATER together in a small saucepan over medium heat. Remove from the heat and cool. Stir in lime juice, tequila, and Triple Sec or Grand Marnier. Refrigerate until well chilled. Process in an ice cream maker according to manufacturer's directions.

Place scoops of sorbet in margarita glasses and garnish the rim of each with a slice of lime. Serve immediately.

1 cup sugar
2 cups water
1 cup fresh lime juice
½ cup tequila
⅓ cup Triple Sec or Grand Marnier

6 to 8 lime slices

Makes 6 to 8 Servings

Peach and Cinnamon Crisp Sundaes

Unique and refreshing, this ambrosial ice cream confection is best at the height of the summer when peaches are perfectly ripe. The crunch adds a delightful texture and the cinnamon syrup is an unexpected surprise. ☼ SUMMER

TO PREPARE THE CINNAMON SYRUP, put all syrup ingredients in a small, heavy saucepan over medium heat. Bring to a boil, stirring occasionally, and cook until sugar is dissolved. Lower heat and simmer 15 minutes. Cool completely and remove cinnamon sticks. If not using immediately, store in a sealed container at room temperature until ready to use.

TO PREPARE THE CINNAMON CRUNCH, preheat oven to 350°F. Put cinnamon graham crackers in the bowl of a food processor and process until they are crumbs. Toss with melted butter and spread onto a baking sheet. Bake in the preheated oven, stirring occasionally, until golden and crunchy, 7 to 10 minutes. Cool and set aside.

TO PREPARE THE PEACHES, peel and slice the peaches; put into a large bowl. Toss with sugar, cinnamon, and lemon juice.

To assemble, put two scoops of ice cream in each of 4 bowls. Spoon peaches over ice cream. Drizzle cinnamon syrup over the peaches and ice cream, and then sprinkle cinnamon crunch over all. Decorate each sundae with a cinnamon stick.

CINNAMON SYRUP
½ cup water
¾ cup sugar
¼ cup dark corn syrup
2 cinnamon sticks, split lengthwise

CINNAMON CRUNCH
4 cinnamon graham crackers
¼ cup (½ stick) unsalted butter, melted

PEACHES
4 peaches, pitted
2 tablespoons sugar
½ teaspoon cinnamon
1 tablespoon lemon juice

1 pint cinnamon vanilla ice cream
4 cinnamon sticks

Makes 4 Servings

Peaches

ONE OF THE MOST TRAGIC PERIODS in Navajo
history was the time of the Long Walk. In 1864,
Kit Carson marched many of the Navajo people
to captivity, but before doing so, he destroyed the
Navajo flocks and crops, including their prized
peach orchards. When they later returned to their
lands, the people replanted the peaches in
Canyon de Chelly, where they quickly flourished.
Today, those peach trees are a symbol of the
strength and endurance of the Navajo Nation.

Butter Pecan EL DIABLO ICE CREAM

The sugar, butter, and cayenne-coated pecans add a delightful crunch and interest to the rich vanilla ice cream. If you don't have an ice-cream maker, you can take your favorite store-bought ice cream, soften it, stir in the rum and nuts, and then freeze it again until firm. Serve this spicy ice cream with tarts, cakes, or a rich chocolate or caramel sauce. 🌿 FALL

POUR THE HALF AND HALF and the cream in a heavy, medium saucepan. Bring the mixture to a boil over medium heat, stirring occasionally to make sure it does not boil over.

In a medium bowl, with an electric mixer, beat the egg yolks and sugar until the mixture is fluffy and pale in color, about 4 minutes. Add ¼ of the hot cream mixture to the eggs, and then pour the entire egg mixture back into the saucepan with the cream. Place the pan over low heat and stir constantly with a wooden spoon until the mixture thickens so that a line drawn on the back of the spoon does not fill in. Be careful not to let the mixture boil, or the egg yolks will curdle. Strain mixture through a fine sieve and cool in a bowl set over ice cubes. Stir in the rum.

Freeze the mixture in an ice cream machine according to the manufacturer's directions. When the mixture is almost frozen, stir in the caramelized pecans. Continue to freeze until hard. Serve alone or with your favorite dessert.

1 cup half and half cream
1 cup heavy cream
4 egg yolks
½ cup sugar
2 tablespoons dark rum

½ cup Caramelized Pecans (see page 66)

Makes 3 ½ Cups

A waterfall on the south fork of Cave Creek feeds a swirling pool of leaves, Cave Creek Canyon, Chiracahua Mountains, Coronado National Forest

Margarita and *Chile* Poached Pears with Pear and *Raspberry* Coulis

Poached pears are a refreshing, healthy ending to a meal. These are particularly flavorful because they are poached in ancho chiles, tequila, and lime juice.
❄ WINTER

REMOVE THE ZEST from 1 of the limes and place zest in a pot large enough to hold all the pear halves. Juice all of the limes (there should be approximately ½ cup lime juice) and add the juice to the cooking pot; add the Triple Sec, tequila, sugar, water, and ancho chile pieces. Bring the mixture to a boil over medium heat; add the pear halves and lower heat to a simmer; cook until pears are tender, about 30 minutes. Remove the pot from the heat and allow the pears to cool in the poaching liquid. If not using immediately, cover and refrigerate for up to 24 hours.

Remove the pears from the poaching liquid. Put 2 of the pear halves in a blender with ½ cup of the poaching liquid and the raspberries. Purée; if not sweet enough, add more sugar. If the sauce is too thick, add more of the poaching liquid and mix again. Strain the sauce through a mesh strainer.

Ladle a few tablespoons of sauce onto each of 8 dessert plates. If desired, use heavy cream to make a design in the sauce. Place a poached pear half, cut side down, onto the center of each plate and garnish with a sprig of fresh mint.

3 limes
¼ cup Triple Sec
¾ cup Tequila
¾ cup sugar
3 cups water
1 ancho chile, stemmed, seeded, and cut
   into pieces
5 pears, peeled, cored, and cut in half

1 (12-ounce) bag frozen raspberries, thawed
¼ cup heavy cream in a squeeze bottle, optional
8 sprigs fresh mint

Makes 8 Servings

Dulce De Leche and Chocolate *Mousse*

Dulce de leche is a caramelized, sweetened condensed milk and tastes like a rich caramel sauce. You can make your own by cooking milk, sugar, and baking soda together, but Latino markets now sell it in the can, which makes this dessert incredibly easy.
❄ WINTER

IN A HEAVY, MEDIUM SAUCEPAN, heat the milk and dulce de leche, stirring until well blended. Add the chocolate and whisk until chocolate is melted and mixture is smooth. Allow to cool.

In a medium bowl, beat the heavy cream with an electric mixer until it forms soft peaks. Gently

fold the heavy cream into the cooled chocolate mixture. Divide into 6 martini or decorative glass dishes and refrigerate until firm, about 4 hours. Garnish with whipped cream, if desired.

1 ½ cups whole milk
1 (13 ½-ounce) can dulce de leche
6 ounces bittersweet chocolate, finely chopped
1 cup heavy cream
Whipped cream, optional

Makes 4 to 6 Servings

PRICKLY PEAR AND PEPITA
Crème Brûlée

The flavor of prickly pear syrup is quite subtle in these silky custards and the piquant pepitas, which are pumpkin seeds, are a lovely surprise once you dip into them. The cinnamon- and chile-coated seeds add a delightful texture and an explosion of flavor.

🌿 FALL

PREHEAT OVEN TO 350°F. Butter 8 (½-cup) ramekins or soufflé dishes and place them in a shallow pan.

In the bowl of an electric mixture fitted with the whisk attachment, whisk together the egg yolks and sugar until the sugar is dissolved and the mixture is thick and pale yellow, about 5 minutes. Lower the speed and add the prickly pear syrup, vanilla, and heavy cream.

Put about 1 tablespoon of the Piquant Pepitas in each of the ramekins. Pour prickly pear mixture over the pepitas, dividing equally. Pour enough water into the shallow pan to come halfway up the sides of the ramekins. Bake custards until just set in the center, about 30 minutes. Remove ramekins from the water bath and cool completely. Cover and refrigerate for at least 6 hours or up to 2 days.

Preheat broiler. Put ramekins on a baking sheet. Sprinkle about 2 teaspoons sugar evenly over the surface of each custard. Broil until the sugar melts and turns dark brown, rotating baking sheet for even browning, about 2 minutes. Or, if you have a propane torch, melt the sugar with it instead of using the broiler. Place each ramekin on a dessert plate and serve.

NOTE: *Prickly pear syrup is available at specialty grocery stores or through mail order catalogs.*

9 egg yolks
½ cup sugar
¼ cup prickly pear syrup (*see* NOTE)
1 teaspoon vanilla
2 ½ cups heavy cream
½ cup Piquant Pepitas (see page 39)
¾ cup sugar

Makes 8 Servings

OPPOSITE: *Engelmann's prickly pear cactus with fruit, Saguaro National Park*

An Edible Cactus

THE MOST POPULAR EDIBLE CACTUS in the Southwest is the prickly pear, whose magenta red fruit, also called a tuna, grows on the ends of the pads of the plant. Both the fruit and the pads are used in Mexican and Southwest cooking and are very nutritious. Health food aficionados treasure them because they are high in protein, calcium, phosphorus, iron, and vitamins. The pectin in the pulp is believed to help reduce cholesterol, and the plant fibers help keep blood sugar levels steady. Two other interesting bits of trivia–first, Diego Rivera used cactus gel to preserve his paintings, and second, a recent study has found that an extract of prickly pear cactus can prevent a severe hangover!

When buying prickly pear fruit in the market, look for those that are slightly soft with a uniform dark red color. The rich, magenta flesh of the fruit is sweet and studded with edible, but very hard, black seeds that are usually discarded. To prepare the fruit, peel it with a sharp knife, purée the flesh in a food processor, and then strain out the seeds. The resulting liquid, which smells like a melon, is delicious in drinks, jellies, candies, sauces, and syrups.

The pads of the prickly pear, called nopales, are pale to dark green, fleshy, and used raw in salads or cooked and eaten as a vegetable. Fresh pads are preferred and are sold in the produce section of many Southwest grocery stores. Nopalitos, which are sliced or diced nopales, are also sold in the produce section, but you can also find them canned in water or pickled in jars in many supermarkets across the country. To prepare the fresh pad, you need to remove the needles and eyes with a vegetable peeler and then trim the edges with a sharp knife. Cut the pad into strips and use the strips raw, or put them into boiling water for a few minutes and then quickly plunge them into ice water to stop the cooking process. Similar to tart green beans, they're good in stews, chilis, or other baked dishes.

Tequila | SUNRISE MELON

The orange and red colors in this melon medley are reminiscent of an Arizona sunrise, and the marinade is the same as the drink immortalized by the Eagles in their song of the same name. It's a refreshing summer dessert or a great wake-up dish for brunch.

☼ SUMMER

IN A MEASURING CUP OR SMALL BOWL, combine the juice, tequila, orange zest, and grenadine. Put the watermelon and cantaloupe in a large bowl and pour marinade over all. Refrigerate, covered, for at least 1 hour or up to 24 hours. Just before serving, mix in the slivered mint leaves. Serve in stemmed glasses, each garnished with an orange slice and a sprig of fresh mint.

½ cup fresh orange juice
½ cup tequila
1 tablespoon orange zest
2 tablespoons grenadine
3 cups cubed watermelon
3 cups cubed cantaloupe
¼ cup slivered mint leaves
6 to 8 orange slices
6 to 8 sprigs fresh mint

Makes 6 to 8 Servings

CHOCOLATE BANANA Bread Pudding
WITH BANANA CARAMEL SAUCE

The chocolate banana bread is a fabulous addition to breakfast, brunch, or tea, but when made into bread pudding, it's even more decadent. The small amount of chile powder added gives the bread a richer, more complex taste without really adding any heat. Any leftover sauce can be used over ice cream. ❀ SPRING

TO PREPARE THE BANANA BREAD, preheat oven to 350°F. Lightly grease the bottom and sides of a 9 x 5-inch loaf pan. In the bowl of an electric mixer fitted with the paddle, beat together the butter and sugar until light and fluffy, about 2 minutes. Beat in eggs, adding them 1 at a time. Add bananas and vanilla.

Sift together the flour, soda, chile powder, and cocoa onto a piece of waxed paper. Add about ⅓ of the flour mixture to the banana mixture and mix well. To the banana mixture, add ½ of the buttermilk, and then another ⅓ of the flour mixture; repeat until all of the banana mixture, buttermilk, and flour mixture are mixed well. Add chopped chocolate and mix until just combined. Turn into the prepared pan and bake until a skewer comes out clean, about 1 hour. Cool and unmold. Cut chocolate banana bread into 1-inch cubes and set aside (*see* NOTE).

TO PREPARE THE BREAD PUDDING, preheat oven to 325°F. Butter the bottom and sides of a 9 x 13-inch baking pan. Evenly spread the banana bread cubes in the bottom of the pan. In the bowl of an electric mixer fitted with the whip attachment, whisk the egg yolks, whole eggs, and sugar at medium speed until pale yellow in color, about 3 to 5 minutes. Reduce the speed to low and add the half and half and vanilla. Whisk until thoroughly combined. Pour the egg mixture over the bread cubes and press down with the back of a spatula until the bread is evenly coated. Cover the pan with aluminum foil and bake until the custard is set, about 1 hour. Cool slightly, cut into squares, and transfer to plates.

TO PREPARE THE CARAMEL SAUCE, in a medium, heavy saucepan, combine the sugar and water and cook over medium-high heat, stirring gently, until the sugar dissolves. Increase the heat to high and cook, not stirring at all, until the mixture turns dark amber in color, about 10 minutes. Standing back (the mixture will splatter), carefully and gradually add the cream, and then the bananas. Continue cooking until the cream is well incorporated and the bananas are broken up. Ladle warm sauce over each serving of bread pudding and serve immediately.

NOTE: *The Chocolate Banana Bread can be served one day, and then the leftovers can be used for the bread pudding the next. If you have half a loaf left, only make half of the egg/cream mixture in the bread pudding part of the recipe and use an 8 x 8-inch square pan for baking.*

CHOCOLATE BANANA BREAD
½ cup (1 stick) unsalted butter, at
   room temperature
1 cup sugar
2 large eggs
3 ripe bananas, mashed with a fork
1 teaspoon vanilla
1 ¼ cups all-purpose flour
1 teaspoon baking soda
1 teaspoon ancho chile powder
¼ cup good quality cocoa
½ cup buttermilk
6 ounces bittersweet chocolate, finely chopped

BREAD PUDDING
4 large egg yolks
3 large eggs
½ cup sugar
1 pint half and half cream
1 teaspoon vanilla

BANANA CARAMEL SAUCE
1 cup sugar
2 tablespoons water
2 cups heavy cream
2 ripe bananas, peeled and sliced

Makes 12 Servings

ACKNOWLEDGEMENTS

I WANT TO THANK MY HUSBAND, TERRY, for his help tasting and evaluating the recipes in this book and for his constant support the last 38 years. I also wish to extend my gratitude to the special women who tested the recipes: Linda Hopkins, Kim Howard, Monica Goddard, Sue Green, and Judy Niver.

RESOURCES

ALBUQUERQUE TORTILLA COMPANY
AND CHILE PRODUCTS
1507 W. Hatcher
Phoenix, AZ 85021
(602) 371-9766
Frozen Hatch chiles, chile sauces, fresh tortillas

BUENO FOODS
2001 Fourth Street SW
Albuquerque, NM 87102
(800) 952-4453
www.buenofoods.com
Blue cornmeal, fresh New Mexico green chiles
(in season only), frozen New Mexico green chiles,
pure chile powders, red chile puree, chile ristras

DESERT PRODUCE
4102-1 E. Baseline
Phoenix, AZ 85040
(602) 437-0840
Fresh Hatch chiles, dried chiles, chile ristras,
desert jellies, Southwest decorations

GUADALUPE FARMERS MARKET
9210 Avenida Del Yaqui
Guadalupe, AZ 85283
(480) 730-1945
Fresh chiles, dried chiles, desert produce

MELISSA'S SPECIALTY FOODS WORLD
VARIETY PRODUCE, INC.
P. O. Box 21127
Los Angeles, CA 90021
(800) 588-0151
www.melissas.com
Achiote (annatto seeds), corn husks, cumin
seeds, dried chiles, dried beans, epazote, pepitas,
pepper jelly, posole, salsas

NATIVE SEEDS/SEARCH
526 N. Fourth Avenue
Tucson, AZ 85705
(520) 622-5561
www.nativeseeds.org
Blue cornmeal, dried beans, heirloom seeds,
mesquite flour, posole

PENZEY'S, LTD.
3310 N. Hayden Road
Scottsdale, AZ 85251
(480) 990-7709
(800) 741-7787
www.penzeys.com
Achiote (annatto seeds), cardamom seeds, chili
powders, cumin seeds, dried chiles, epazote,
ground chile powders, saffron, vanilla beans

SANTA FE SCHOOL OF COOKING
116 W. San Francisco Street
Santa Fe, NM 87501
(800) 982-4688
www.santafeschoolofcooking.com
Chile roasting grills, chile powders, chiles, salsas,
posole, masa harina, corn husks, blue corn
meal, tortilla press, Mexican chocolate,
Southwest pottery

OPPOSITE: *Sand dunes at sunset
with Sangre de Christo
Mountains in background,
snakeweed and rabbitbrush in
foreground, Great Sand Dunes
National Park and Preserve*

INDEX

Page numbers in italics refer to menus.

Achiote Butter-Basted Turkey with Ancho Gravy, *12*, 88
Almond Butter and Red Pepper Jelly Cookies, 170
Almonds, Spiced, *2*, 39
Anaheim chiles. *See* green chiles
ancho chiles, 48
    Chicken Mole, *13*, 86
    Corn Soup with Poblano Chiles, 48
    Double Chocolate, Ancho Chile, and Almond
        Tart, 168
    -Dressing, *4*, 63
    -Gravy, *12*, 88
    Margarita and Chile Poached Pears with Pear and
        Raspberry Coulis, *2*, 177
    Marinated Pork Tenderloin with Avocado Sauce, 104
    Pickled Ancho Chiles Stuffed with Vegetable
        Medley, 125
    powder, 129
    Sangrita Crab Cocktail, *9*, 30
    -Sauce, 100
    -Sauce, Sun-Dried Tomato and, 110
    See also poblano chiles
appetizers, 15–39
apples
    -Pecan Bread with Cinnamon Butter, *10*, 152
    Salad, Smoked Trout, Pecan and, 75
    -Tart, Gingerbread-Crusted, *12*, 166
Après Ski menu, *4*
Apricot Chicken, 83
Artichoke Quesadillas, *5*, 18
Asadero cheese, 19
avocados
    Bacon, Avocado, and Raspberry Quesadillas with
        Chipotle Sauce, *4*, 20
    Black Bean Salad with Vinaigrette Dressing, 62
    Corn and Avocado Salsa, 103
    -Cream, *7*, 16
    -Dressing, *5*, 70
    Grilled Shrimp Salad, *7*, 74
    Hand-Mixed Guacamole, 22, 113
    Layered Avocado, Sour Cream, and Red Bell
        Pepper Mold, *13*, 24
    Marinated Shrimp with Rainbow Vegetables, 35
    -Mousse, *3*, 42
    -Sauce, 104
    Southwest Club Wraps, *8*, 89
    Tomatillo Sauce, 118
    Tostaditas of Guacamole and Shrimp, 31

bacon
    -Avocado, and Raspberry Quesadillas with
        Chipotle Sauce, *4*, 20
    Skillet Cornbread, 149
    Southwest Club Wraps, *8*, 89
Baked Chiles Rellenos, 123
Banana Caramel Sauce, *5*, 182
Bananas, Grilled, with Butter Pecan Ice Cream and
        Mexican Chocolate Sauce, *7*, 173
Barbara's Southwest Spice Mix, 91
Basil Cream, *10*, 49
beans
    Baked Chiles Rellenos, 123
    Beef and Black Bean Chili, *4*, 58
    Black Bean Salad with Vinaigrette Dressing, 62
    Black Bean Soup with Lime Cream, *11*, 44
    Cowboy Beans, 132
    Gratin of the Three Sisters, 126
    Green Beans with Shallots and Chile Oil, *12*, 133
    Huevos Rancheros Verdes with Black Beans, 118
    Sauté of Tomatoes, Corn, and Edamame, *11*, 130
    Southwest Hummus, *13*, 23
    White Bean Dip with Cumin Tortilla Chips, *13*, 21

You'll-Never-Miss-the-Meat Chili, *2*, 46
beef
    and Black Bean Chili, *4*, 58
    Marinated and Stuffed Filet Mignons with Merlot
        Habanero Sauce, 98
    Marinated Flank Steak with Ancho Chile Sauce, 100
    Marinated Steak Salad with Tomatillo Dressing
        and Cotija Cheese, 72
Beurre Blanc, 114
Biscuits, Cheddar Cornmeal, *4*, 147
Bizcochitos, Lemon, *13*, 169
black beans
    Beef and Black Bean Chili, *4*, 58
    Huevos Rancheros Verdes with Black Beans, 118
    -Salad with Vinaigrette Dressing, 62
    -Soup with Lime Cream, *11*, 44
Black Pepper Dough, 136
Bloody Mary Soup with Avocado Mousse, *3*, 42
blueberries
    -Cornmeal Pancakes with Blueberry Syrup, *6*, 144
    Red, White and Blue Tart, 167
    -Syrup, *6*, 144
Boneless Leg of Lamb with Potatoes and Jalapeños, 102
breads, 143–155
    Apple Pecan Bread with Cinnamon Butter, *10*, 152
    Blueberry Cornmeal Pancakes with Blueberry
        Syrup, *6*, 144
    Cheddar Cornmeal Biscuits, *4*, 147
    Chipotle Cornbread, *5*, 147
    Chocolate Banana Bread, 182
    Cornbread Pecan Stuffing, *12*, 154
    Corn Pancakes, *9*, 27
    Cumin Rolls, 154
    Dried Cranberry, Orange, and Pecan Muffins with
        Orange Butter, 150
    panko crumbs, 65, 106
    -Pudding, 182
    Pumpkin Waffles with Cinnamon Syrup, 146
    Skillet Cornbread, *7*, 149
    Southwest Caesar Salad, 76
    Southwest Grilled Pizza, 154
Broccolini with Chile-Honey Caramel Sauce, 129
Buffalo Tenderloin with Porcini Butter, *11*, 101
Butternut Squash with Blue Cheese and Walnuts,
    12, 135
Butter Pecan el Diablo Ice Cream, 176

Caesar Salad, 76
cakes
    Pumpkin Ginger Layer Cake, 158
    Tres Leches Chocolate Cake, 159
calabacitas, 125
capsaicin, 47
caramel, 162
Caramelized Corn with Peppers and Cotija, 129
Caramelized Onion Tart, 136
carrots
    Mustard and Cumin Glazed Carrots, 134
    Roasted Baby Vegetables, 135
chayote squash
    Cream of Chayote Soup, 53
    Grilled Shrimp Salad, *7*, 74
    Marinated Shrimp with Rainbow Vegetables, 35
    Stuffed Chayote Squash, 122
Cheddar Cornmeal Biscuits, *4*, 147
cheese, 19
    Baked Chiles Rellenos, 123
    Butternut Squash with Blue Cheese and Walnuts, 135
    Caramelized Corn with Peppers and Cotija, 129
    Caramelized Onion Tart, 136
    Cheddar Cornmeal Biscuits, 147
    Chicken, Green Chile, and Tortilla Lasagna, 81
    Chicken and Green Chile Enchiladas, 82

Cotija and Cherry Tomato Salad, *8*, 72
Cotija-Crusted Halibut with Tomatillo Salsa, 106
Goat Cheese and Shrimp Stuffed Poblanos with
        Red Bell Pepper Sauce, 32
Goat Cheese Crisps with Smoked Salmon and
        Roasted Peppers, 18
Gratin of the Three Sisters, 126
Greens with Ancho Dressing, Blue Cheese, and
        Toasted Pecans, *4*, 63
Huevos Rancheros Verdes with Black Beans, 118
Individual Serrano Soufflés on Greens with Pears
        and Piñon Nuts, *10*, 65
Marinated Steak Salad with Tomatillo Dressing
        and Cotija Cheese, 72
Mashed Potatoes with Cheddar Cheese and
        Poblano Chiles, *11*, 134
Potato Casserole with Mexican Cheeses, 133
Queso Fresco, 19
Queso Quesadilla, 19
Skillet Cornbread, 149
Sonoran Pasta, 84
Southwest Corn Pudding, 123
Tomatoes Stuffed with Queso Fresco and Cilantro,
    7, 138
chicken
    Apricot Chicken, 83
    -Breasts with Red Bell Peppers and Poblano Sauce, 80
    -Chipotle Nachos with Avocado Cream, *7*, 16
    -Fajita Salad, *5*, 70
    Green Chile and Tortilla Lasagna, 81
    and Green Chile Enchiladas, 82
    -Mole, *13*, 86
    Posole with Chicken and Tomatillos, 56
    Southwest Grilled Pizza, 154
    See also ostrich; quail; turkey
Chile-Honey Caramel Sauce, 129
Chile-Honey Glaze, 94
Chile Oil, *12*, 133
chiles
    handling, 47
    powder, 91, 129
    roasting, 47
    See also specific name, e.g. ancho chiles
Chiles Rellenos, Baked, 123
chilis
    Beef and Black Bean Chili, *4*, 58
    You'll-Never-Miss-the-Meat Chili, *2*, 46
Chilled Red Bell Pepper Soup with Basil Cream, *10*, 49
Chilled Tomatillo and Cucumber Soup, *8*, 54
chipotle chiles
    Apricot Chicken, 83
    Chicken Chipotle Nachos with Avocado Cream, *7*, 16
    Chicken Mole, *13*, 86
    -Cornbread, *5*, 147
    -cream, 111
    Creamy Crab on Corn Pancakes, *9*, 27
    -Glazed Shrimp, *13*, 112
    Posole with Chicken and Tomatillos, 56
    -Sauce, *4*, 20, 116
    -Sauce with Raspberries, *4*, 20
    Smoked Trout, Apple, and Pecan Salad, 75
    Southwest Caesar Salad, 76
    Southwest Club Wraps, *8*, 89
    Southwest Turkey Burgers, 91
    Tomatillo Dressing, 72
    Tri-Color Potato Salad, *8*, 77
chocolate, 87
    -Banana Bread Pudding with Banana Caramel
        Sauce, *5*, 182
    Chicken Mole, *13*, 86
    Double Chocolate, Ancho Chile, and Almond Tart,
        13, 168
    Dulce de Leche and Chocolate Mousse, *3*, 177

-Flan with Dulce de Leche, *10*, 162
Mexican Chocolate Chip Cookies, 169
Mexican Chocolate Sauce, *7*, 172–73
Pecan and Chocolate Pie, *4*, 163
Tres Leches Chocolate Cake, 159
cilantro, 73
Cilantro and Pecan Pesto on Goat Cheese Toasts, *11*, 36
Cinnamon Sugar Tortilla Wedges with Coffee Ice
    Cream and Mexican Chocolate Sauce, 172
Cinnamon Syrup, 174
cookies
    Almond Butter and Red Pepper Jelly Cookies, 170
    Lemon Bizcochitos, 169
    Mexican Chocolate Chip Cookies, 169
corn, 57
    and Avocado Salsa, 103
    Caramelized Corn with Peppers and Cotija, 129
    Gratin of the Three Sisters, 126
    Grits with Attitude, *6*, 122
    -Pancakes, *9*, 27
    Pickled Ancho Chiles Stuffed with Vegetable
        Medley, 125
    -Pudding, 123
    -Sauce, Creamy, 92
    Sauté of Tomatoes, Corn, and Edamame, *11*, 130
    Sonoran Pasta, 84
    -Soup with Poblano Chiles, 48
    -sticks, 149
    You'll-Never-Miss-the-Meat Chili, *2*, 46
    See also hominy
cornbread
    Chipotle Cornbread, *5*, 147
    -Pecan Stuffing, *12*, 154
    Skillet Cornbread, *7*, 149
cornhusks, *9*, 107
Cornmeal Crusted Orange Roughy with Mango
    Salsa, 109
Cotija, 19
    Caramelized Corn with Peppers and Cotija, 129
    and Cherry Tomato Salad, *8*, 72
    -Crusted Halibut with Tomatillo Salsa, 106
    Marinated Steak Salad with Tomatillo Dressing
        and Cotija Cheese, 72
Cowboy Beans, 132
Crab on Corn Pancakes, Creamy, *9*, 27
Cranberry Relish, *12*, 89
Cream of Chayote Soup, *13*, 53
Creamy Corn Sauce, 92
Crispy Lemon and Hazelnut Bars, 165
crudités, 21
Cumin Rolls, 154
Cumin Tortilla Chips, *13*, 21

desserts, 157–183
dips and spreads, 21
    Cinnamon Butter, 152
    Hand-Mixed Guacamole, 22
    Orange Butter, 150
    Porcini Butter, *11*, 101
    Southwest Hummus, 23
    White Bean Dip with Cumin Tortilla Chips,
        13, 21
    See also dressings; sauces and salsas
Double Chocolate, Ancho Chile, and Almond Tart,
    13, 168
dressings
    Ancho Dressing, *4*, 63
    Avocado Dressing, *5*, 70
    Tomatillo Dressing, 72
    Vinaigrette Dressing, 62
    See also dips and spreads; sauces and salsas
Dried Cranberry, Orange, and Pecan Muffins with
    Orange Butter, 150

Duck Breasts with Hot Orange Sauce, *3*, 93
Dulce de Leche, *10*, 162
Dulce de Leche and Chocolate Mousse, *3*, 177

eggs
    Caramelized Onion Tart, 136
    Huevos Rancheros Verdes with Black Beans, 118
    Individual Serrano Soufflés on Greens with Pears
        and Piñon Nuts, *10*, 65
    Sweet Onion Custard with Salsa Fresca, 139
    Tri-Color Potato Salad, *8*, 77
Enchiladas, Chicken and Green Chile, 82
entrées, 79-119

fajitas
    Chicken Fajita Salad, *5*, 70
    Shrimp Fajitas, 113
Father's Day Barbecue menu, 7
Fiesta Fruit Salad, *6*, 77
fish. *See* seafood
Fish in Cornhusks with Orange-Tomato Salsa,
    9, 107
Fish Tacos, 111
Fourth of July Picnic menu, *8*
Frozen Lime Pie, *6*, 164
fruit
    Apple Pecan Bread with Cinnamon Butter, 152
    Banana Caramel Sauce, *5*, 182
    Blueberry Cornmeal Pancakes with Blueberry
        Syrup, *6*, 144
    Chipotle Sauce with Raspberries, *4*, 20
    Dried Cranberry, Orange, and Pecan Muffins with
        Orange Butter, 150
    Fiesta Fruit Salad, *6*, 77
    Frozen Lime Pie, 164
    Gingerbread-Crusted Apple Tart, 166
    Grilled Bananas with Butter Pecan Ice Cream with
        Mexican Chocolate Sauce, *7*, 173
    Individual Serrano Soufflés on Greens with Pears
        and Piñon Nuts, *10*, 65
    Jicama, Orange, and Noplitos Salad, *2*, 69
    Margarita and Chile Poached Pears with Pear and
        Raspberry Coulis, *2*, 177
    Peaches and Cinnamon Crisp Sundaes, 174
    Plum, Prickly Pear, and Mesquite Crumble, 161
    prickly pear, 179
    Prickly Pear and Pepita Crème Brulée, 178
    Red, White and Blue Tart, 167
    Smoked Trout, Apple, and Pecan Salad, 75
    Tequila Sunrise Melon, 180

Gingerbread-Crusted Apple Tart, *12*, 166
Goat Cheese and Shrimp Stuffed Poblanos with Red
    Bell Pepper Sauce, 32
Goat Cheese Crisps with Smoked Salmon and
    Roasted Peppers, 18
Gratin of the Three Sisters, 126
Gravy, Ancho, *12*, 88
Green Beans with Shallots and Chile Oil, *12*, 133
green chiles
    Beef and Black Bean Chili, 58
    Caramelized Corn with Cotija and, 129
    Cornbread Pecan Stuffing, *12*, 154
    Enchiladas, Chicken and, 82
    Grilled Shrimp Salad, *7*, 74
    Lasagna, Chicken, Tortilla. and, 81
    Marinated Shrimp with Rainbow Vegetables, 35
    Shrimp Fajitas, 113
    Shrimp Tortilla Soup, *5*, 59
    -Soup, 55
    Southwest Corn Pudding, 123
    Tomato, Hominy, and Chile Soup, 54
    Tomato and Cumin Rice, 132

You'll-Never-Miss-the-Meat Chili, *2*, 46
Greens with Ancho Dressing, Blue Cheese, and
    Toasted Pecans, *4*, 63
Grilled Bananas with Butter Pecan Ice Cream and
    Mexican Chocolate Sauce, *7*, 173
Grilled Pizza, Southwest, 154
Grilled Pork Chops with Corn and Avocado Salsa, 103
Grilled Portabello Mushroom and Roasted Red Bell
    Pepper Sandwiches, 116
Grilled Shrimp Salad, *7*, 74
Grits with Attitude, *6*, 122
guacamole
    Hand-Mixed Guacamole, 22, 113
    Southwest Club Wraps, *8*, 89
    Tostaditas of Guacamole and Shrimp, 31
guajillo chiles
    Chicken Mole, *13*, 86
    Creamy Guajillo Sauce, 105

habanero chiles
    Duck Breasts with Hot Orange Sauce, *3*, 93
    Merlot Habanero Sauce, 98
Hand-Mixed Guacamole, 22, 113
Hearthside Dinner menu, *11*
Holiday Open House menu, *13*
hominy, 57
    Posole with Chicken and Tomatillos, 56
    Tomato, Hominy, and Chile Soup, 54
Hot Orange Sauce, *3*
Huevos Rancheros Verdes with Black Beans, 118
Hummus, Southwest, *13*, 23

Ice Cream, Butter Pecan el Diablo, 176
Individual Serrano Soufflés on Greens with Pears and
    Piñon Nuts, *10*, 65

jalapeño chiles
    Bloody Mary Soup with Avocado Mousse, *3*, 42
    Boneless Leg of Lamb with Potatoes and
        Jalapeños, 102
    Corn and Avocado Salsa, 103
    Cotija and Cherry Tomato Salad, *8*, 72
    Cowboy Beans, 132
    Creamy Corn Sauce, 92
    Enchilada Sauce, 82
    Grilled Pork Chops with Corn and Avocado
        Salsa, 103
    jelly, 114
    Mango Salsa, 109
    -Orange Glazed Scallops with Beurre Blanc, 114
    Roasted, and Southwest Hummus on Pita Bread, 23
    Tomatillo Salsa, 106
    Tostaditas of Guacamole and Shrimp, 31
jicama
    -Orange and Nopalitos Salad, *2*, 69
    Santa Fe Slaw with Caramelized Pecans, *9*, 66

Lamb, Boneless Leg of, with Potatoes and Jalapeños, 102
Lamb Chops, Spicy, *7*, 97
Lasagna, Chicken, Green Chile, and Tortilla, 81
Layered Avocado, Sour Cream, and Red Bell Pepper
    Mold, *13*, 24
Legend of the Three Sisters, 127
Lemon and Hazelnut Bars, Crispy, 165
Lemon Bizcochitos, *13*, 169
lime
    -Cream, *11*, 44
    -curd, 164
    Frozen Lime Pie, *6*, 164
    Margarita and Chile Poached Pears with Pear and
        Raspberry Coulis, *2*, 177
    Margarita Sorbet, 173
    -oil, 62

INDEX

Mango Salsa, 109
Margarita and Chile Poached Pears with Pear and
    Raspberry Coulis, 2, 177
Margarita Sorbet, 173
Marinated and Stuffed Filet Mignons with Merlot
    Habanero Sauce, 98
Marinated Flank Steak with Ancho Chile Sauce, 100
Marinated Pork Tenderloin with Avocado Sauce, 104
Marinated Shrimp with Rainbow Vegetables, 6, 35
Marinated Steak Salad with Tomatillo Dressing and
    Cotija Cheese, 72
masa harina, 57
Mashed Potatoes with Cheddar Cheese and Poblano
    Chiles, 11, 134
Medallions of Pork Tenderloin with Creamy Guajillo
    Sauce, 105
menus, 2–13
Merlot Habanero Sauce, 98
mesquite powder, 161
Mexican cheese, 19
Mexican chocolate, 87
Mexican Chocolate Chip Cookies, 169
Mexican Chocolate Sauce, 7, 172–73
Mexican crema, 123
Mother's Day Brunch menu, 6
mushrooms
    Grilled Portabello Mushroom and Roasted Red
        Bell Pepper Sandwiches, 116
    Porcini Butter, 101
    Wild Mushroom Toasts, 13, 37
    Wild Rice and Porcini Pilaf, 92, 140
Mustard and Cumin Glazed Carrots, 134

Nachos, Chicken Chipotle with Avocado Cream,
    7, 16
New Mexico green chiles. *See* green chiles
New Year's celebration menu, 2
nopales, 69, 179
nuts
    Apple Pecan Bread with Cinnamon Butter, 152
    Butternut Squash with Blue Cheese and Walnuts, 135
    Cornbread Pecan Stuffing, 154
    Cranberry Relish, 12, 89
    Crispy Lemon and Hazelnut Bars, 165
    Dried Cranberry, Orange, and Pecan Muffins with
        Orange Butter, 150
    Greens with Ancho Dressing, Blue Cheese, and
        Toasted Pecans, 4, 63
    Individual Serrano Soufflés on Greens with Pears
        and Piñon Nuts, 10, 65
    Marinated and Stuffed Filet Mignons with Merlot
        Habanero Sauce, 98
    Pecan and Chocolate Pie, 4, 163
    Pecan Crusted Salmon with Sun-Dried Tomato
        and Ancho Chile Sauce, 110
    Santa Fe Slaw with Caramelized Pecans, 9, 66
    Smoked Trout, Apple, and Pecan Salad, 75
    Spiced Almonds, 2, 39

onions
    Caramelized Onion Tart, 136
    Southwest Sauté of Potatoes, Peppers, and
        Onions, 138
    Sweet Onion Custard with Salsa Fresca, 139
Orange Butter, 150
Orange Glaze, 150
Orange Roughy with Mango Salsa, 109
Orange-Tomato Salsa, 9, 107
ostrich farming, 96
Ostrich Kebabs with Chile-Honey Glaze, 94
Oyster Shooters, 9, 31

pancakes and waffles
    Blueberry Cornmeal Pancakes with Blueberry
        Syrup, 6, 144
    Corn Pancakes, 9, 27
    Pumpkin Waffles with Cinnamon Syrup, 146
Panela cheese, 19
panko crumbs, 65, 106
Pasta, Sonoran, 5, 84
Peach and Cinnamon Crisp Sundaes, 9, 174
peaches, 175
Pear and Raspberry Coulis, 2, 177
Pears, Margarita and Chile Poached, with Pear and
    Raspberry Coulis, 2, 177
Pecan and Chocolate Pie, 4, 163
Pecan Crusted Salmon with Sun-Dried Tomato and
    Ancho Chile Sauce, 110
peppers, bell
    Black Bean Salad with Vinaigrette Dressing, 62
    Bloody Mary Soup with Avocado Mousse, 42
    Caramelized Corn with Peppers and Cotija, 129
    Chicken Breasts with Red Bell Peppers and
        Poblano Sauce, 80
    Chicken Fajita Salad, 70
    Chilled Red Bell Pepper Soup with Basil Cream, 49
    Cranberry Relish, 12, 89
    Goat Cheese Crisps with Smoked Salmon and
        Roasted Peppers, 18
    Grilled Portabello Mushroom and Roasted Red
        Bell Pepper Sandwiches, 116
    Layered Avocado, Sour Cream, and Red Bell
        Pepper Mold, 24
    Marinated Shrimp with Rainbow Vegetables, 35
    Red Bell Pepper Sauce, 31, 32
    Roasted Baby Vegetables, 135
    Sonoran Pasta, 84
    Southwest Sauté of Potatoes, Peppers, and
        Onions, 138
    Tri-Color Potato Salad, 8, 77
    Yellow Gazpacho with Red Gazpacho Sorbet, 50
Pesto, Cilantro and Pecan, on Goat Cheese Toasts,
    11, 36
Pickled Ancho Chiles Stuffed with Vegetable
    Medley, 125
piñon nuts, 65
Piquant Pepitas, 13, 39
Pizza, Southwest Grilled, 154
Plum, Prickly Pear, and Mesquite Crumble, 161
poblano chiles
    Artichoke Quesadillas, 5, 18
    Chicken Fajita Salad, 70
    Chilled Tomatillo and Cucumber Soup, 8, 54
    Corn Soup with Poblano Chilis, 48
    Cranberry Relish, 12, 89
    Goat Cheese and Shrimp Stuffed Poblanos with
        Red Bell Pepper Sauce, 32
    Grits with Attitude, 6, 122
    Mashed Potatoes with Cheddar Cheese and
        Poblano Chiles, 11, 134
    -Sauce, 80
    Scallop Seviche, 28
    Skillet Cornbread, 7, 149
    and Smoked Salmon Toasts, 3, 36
    Sonoran Pasta, 5, 84
    Southwest Grilled Pizza, 154
    Southwest Sauté of Potatoes, Peppers, and
        Onions, 138
    Zucchini Fritters, 141
    See also ancho chiles
Porcini Butter, 11, 101
pork
    Cornbread Pecan Stuffing, 154
    Grilled Pork Chops with Corn and Avocado
        Salsa, 103

Marinated Pork Tenderloin with Avocado Sauce, 104
Medallions of Pork Tenderloin with Creamy
    Guajillo Sauce, 105
Pulled Pork, 13, 102
Portabello Mushroom and Roasted Red Bell Pepper
    Sandwiches, 116
Posole with Chicken and Tomatillos, 56
potatoes
    Boneless Leg of Lamb with Potatoes and
        Jalapeños, 102
    Mashed Potatoes with Cheddar Cheese and
        Poblano Chiles, 11, 134
    Potato Casserole with Mexican Cheeses, 133
    Southwest Sauté of Potatoes, Peppers, and
        Onions, 138
    Tri-Color Potato Salad, 8, 77
prickly pears
    nopales, 69, 179
    and Pepita Crème Brulée, 12, 178
    -syrup, 178
    -tunas, 161, 179
Pulled Pork, 13, 102
pumpkin
    -Ginger Layer Cake, 11, 158
    and Ginger Soup with Toasted Pepitas, 12, 45
    Piquant Pepitas, 13, 39
    -Waffles with Cinnamon Syrup, 146

Quail Stuffed with Wild Rice on a Creamy Corn
    Sauce, 92
quesadillas
    Artichoke Quesadillas, 5, 18
    Bacon, Avocado, and Raspberry Quesadillas with
        Chipotle Sauce, 4, 20
Queso Freso, 19
Queso Quesadilla, 19

raspberries
    Bacon, Avocado, and Raspberry Quesadillas with
        Chipotle Sauce, 4, 20
    Chipotle Sauce with Raspberries, 4, 20
    Margarita and Chile Poached Pears with Pear and
        Raspberry Coulis, 2, 177
    Red, White and Blue Tart, 167
resources, 185
rice
    Tomato and Cumin Rice, 132
    Wild Rice and Porcini Pilaf, 92, 140
Roasted Baby Vegetables, 135
roasted chiles, 47
Roasted Jalapeños and Southwest Hummus on Pita
    Bread, 13, 23

salads, 61–77
    See also dressings
Salsa Fresca, 111, 139
sandwiches
    Grilled Portabello Mushroom and Roasted Red
        Bell Pepper Sandwiches, 116
    Southwest Club Wraps, 8, 89
Sangrita Crab Cocktail, 9, 30
Santa Fe Slaw with Caramelized Pecans, 9, 66
sauces and salsas
    Ancho Chile Sauce, 100
    Avocado Cream, 7, 16
    Avocado Mousse, 3, 42
    Avocado Sauce, 104
    Banana Caramel Sauce, 5, 182
    Basil Cream, 10, 49
    Beurre Blanc, 114
    Chile-Honey Caramel Sauce, 129
    Chile-Honey Glaze, 94
    chipotle cream, 111

Chipotle Sauce, *4*, 20
Chipotle Sauce with Raspberries, *4*, 20
Corn and Avocado Salsa, 103
Cranberry Relish, *12*, 89
Creamy Corn Sauce, 92
Creamy Guajillo Sauce, 105
Dulce de Leche, *10*, 162
Enchilada Sauce, 82
Jalapeño-Orange Glaze, 114
Lime Cream, *11*, 44
Mango Salsa, 109
Merlot Habanero Sauce, 98
Mexican Chocolate Sauce, 172–73
Orange Glaze, 150
Orange-Tomato Salsa, *9*, 107
Pear and Raspberry Coulis, *2*, 177
Poblano Sauce, 80
Red Bell Pepper Sauce, 31, 32
Salsa Fresca, 111, 139
Sun-Dried Tomato and Ancho Chile Sauce, 110
Tomatillo Salsa, 106
Tomatillo Sauce, 118
Yellow Tomato Salsa, 22, 154
    See also dips and spreads; dressings
Sauté of Tomatoes, Corn, and Edamame, *11*, 130
Scallop Seviche, 28
seafood
    Chipotle-Glazed Shrimp, *13*, 112
    Cornmeal Crusted Orange Roughy with Mango
        Salsa, 109
    Cotija-Crusted Halibut with Tomatillo Salsa, 106
    Creamy Crab on Corn Pancakes, *9*, 27
    Fish in Cornhusks with Orange-Tomato Salsa, *9*, 107
    Fish Tacos, 111
    Goat Cheese and Shrimp Stuffed Poblanos with
        Red Bell Pepper Sauce, 32
    Goat Cheese Crisps with Smoked Salmon and
        Roasted Peppers, 18
    Grilled Shrimp Salad, *7*, 74
    Jalapeño-Orange Glazed Scallops with Beurre
        Blanc, 114
    Marinated Shrimp with Rainbow Vegetables, *6*, 35
    Oyster Shooters, *9*, 31
    Pecan Crusted Salmon with Sun-Dried Tomato
        and Ancho Chile Sauce, 110
    Poblano Chile and Smoked Salmon Toasts, 36
    Sangrita Crab Cocktail, *9*, 30
    Scallop Seviche, 28
    Shrimp Fajitas, 113
    Shrimp Tortilla Soup, *5*, 59
    Smoked Trout, Apple, and Pecan Salad, 75
    Tostaditas of Guacamole and Shrimp, 31
Seafood Extravaganza menu, *9*
serrano chiles
    Avocado Dressing, 70
    Baked Chiles Rellenos, 123
    Cream of Chayote Soup, *13*, 53
    Gingerbread-Crusted Apple Tart, *12*, 166
    Gratin of the Three Sisters, 126
    Hand-Mixed Guacamole, 22, 113
    Huevos Rancheros Verdes with Black Beans, 118
    Individual Serrano Soufflés on Greens with Pears
        and Piñon Nuts, *10*, 65
    Marinated Shrimp with Rainbow Vegetables, 35
    Ostrich Kebabs with Chile-Honey Glaze, 94
    Red Bell Pepper Sauce, 31
    Salsa Fresca, 111, 139
    Scallop Seviche, 28
    White Bean Dip with Cumin Tortilla Chips, *13*, 21
    Yellow Tomato Salsa, 22, 154
    You'll-Never-Miss-the-Meat Chili, *2*, 46
shrimp
    Chipotle-Glazed Shrimp, 112

-Fajitas, 113
Goat Cheese and Shrimp Stuffed Poblanos with
    Red Bell Pepper Sauce, 32
Grilled Shrimp Salad, *7*, 74
Marinated Shrimp with Rainbow Vegetables, *6*, 35
-Tortilla Soup, *5*, 59
Tostaditas of Guacamole and Shrimp, 31
    See also seafood
Skillet Cornbread, *7*, 149
Smoked Trout, Apple, and Pecan Salad, 75
Sonoran Pasta, *5*, 84
Sorbet, Red Gazpacho, 50
soups, 41–59
Southwest Caesar Salad, 76
Southwest Club Wraps, *8*, 89
Southwest Corn Pudding, 123
Southwest Grilled Pizza, 154
Southwest Hummus, *13*, 23
Southwest Sauté of Potatoes, Peppers, and Onions, 138
Southwest Spice Mix, 91
Southwest Turkey Burgers, 91
Spiced Almonds, *2*, 39
Spice-Rubbed Buffalo Tenderloin with Porcini Butter,
    11, 101
Spicy Lamb Chops, *7*, 97
spreads. *See* dips and spreads
Spring Buffet menu, *5*
squash
    Butternut Squash with Blue Cheese and Walnuts, 135
    Cream of Chayote Soup, 53
    Gratin of the Three Sisters, 126
    Grilled Shrimp Salad, *7*, 74
    Marinated Shrimp with Rainbow Vegetables, 35
    Pickled Ancho Chiles Stuffed with Vegetable
        Medley, 125
    Roasted Baby Vegetables, 135
    Stuffed Chayote Squash, *3*, 122
    Zucchini Fritters, 141
steak. *See* beef
Stuffing, Cornbread Pecan, *12*
Sun-Dried Tomato and Ancho Chile Sauce, 110
Sweet Onion Custard with Salsa Fresca, 139
syrups
    Blueberry Syrup, *6*, 144
    Cinnamon Syrup, 146, 174
    prickly pear, 178

tamales, 57
tarts
    Caramelized Onion Tart, 136
    Double Chocolate, Ancho Chile, and Almond
        Tart, 168
    Gingerbread-Crusted Apple Tart, *12*, 166
    Red, White and Blue Tart, 167
Tennis Luncheon menu, *10*
Tequila Sunrise Melon, 180
Thanksgiving menu, *11*
Three Sisters, 126, 127
tomatillos
    Beef and Black Bean Chili, 58
    Chicken, Green Chile, and Tortilla Lasagna, 81
    Chilled Tomatillo and Cucumber Soup, *8*, 54
    -Dressing, 72
    Enchilada Sauce, 82
    Green Chile Soup, 55
    Posole with Chicken and Tomatillos, 56
    -Salsa, 106
    -Sauce, 118
tomatoes
    Bloody Mary Soup with Avocado Mousse, 42
    Chicken Fajita Salad, 70
    Cotija and Cherry Tomato Salad, *8*, 72
    and Cumin Rice, 132

-Hominy, and Chile Soup, 54
Marinated Shrimp with Rainbow Vegetables, 35
Marinated Steak Salad with Tomatillo Dressing
    and Cotija Cheese, 72
Orange-Tomato Salsa, *9*, 107
Salsa Fresca, 111
Sauté of Tomatoes, Corn, and Edamame, *11*, 130
Shrimp Tortilla Soup, *5*, 59
Sonoran Pasta, 84
-Stuffed with Queso Fresco and Cilantro, *7*, 138
Sun-Dried Tomato and Ancho Chile Sauce, 110
Yellow Gazpacho with Red Gazpacho Sorbet, 50
Yellow Tomato Salsa, 22
You'll-Never-Miss-the-Meat Chili, *2*, 46
tortillas
    Chicken, Green Chile, and Tortilla Lasagna, 81
    Chicken Chipotle Nachos with Avocado Cream, *7*, 16
    Cinnamon Sugar Tortilla Wedges with Coffee Ice
        Cream and Mexican Chocolate Sauce, 172
    Cumin Tortilla Chips, *13*, 21
    Fish Tacos, 111
    Goat Cheese Crisps with Smoked Salmon and
        Roasted Peppers, 18
    Huevos Rancheros Verdes with Black Beans, 118
    masa harina, 57
    Shrimp Fajitas, 113
    Shrimp Tortilla Soup, *5*, 59
    Southwest Club Wraps, *8*, 89
Tostaditas of Guacamole and Shrimp, 31
Tres Leches Chocolate Cake, 159
Tri-Color Potato Salad, *8*, 77
turkey
    Achiote Butter-Basted Turkey with Ancho Gravy,
        12, 88
    Southwest Club Wraps, *8*, 89
    Southwest Turkey Burgers, 91

Valentine's Day menu, *3*
vanilla, 145
vegetables, 121–141
Vinaigrette Dressing, 62

Waffles, Pumpkin, with Cinnamon Syrup, 146
White Bean Dip with Cumin Tortilla Chips, *13*, 21
Wild Mushroom Toasts, *13*, 37
Wild Rice and Porcini Pilaf, 92, 140
Wraps, Southwest Club, *8*, 89

Yellow Gazpacho with Red Gazpacho Sorbet, 50
Yellow Tomato Salsa, 22, 154
You'll-Never-Miss-the-Meat Chili, *2*, 46

Zucchini Fritters, 141

ABOUT THE AUTHOR

 BARBARA POOL FENZL, CCP (Certified Culinary Professional) is a major figure on the American culinary stage. She is the owner of Les Gourmettes Cooking School in Phoenix, established in 1983, and a renowned cooking teacher in both the United States and the Périgord region of France. She is the host of the PBS series "Savor the Southwest," five-time host of Phoenix public television's annual pledge drives "KAET Cooks," and is a regular guest on other Phoenix television programs. She has authored two books–*Southwest the Beautiful Cookbook* and *Savor the Southwest*–was the food editor of *Southwest Passages* and *Phoenix Home and Garden* magazines, and is a frequent contributor to *Bon Appétit* magazine and other national publications.

A leader in the food community, Barbara is past president of the International Association of Culinary Professionals, benefactor and past board member of the American Institute of Wine and Food, past president of the Arizona Chapter of Les Dames d'Escoffier, and a past member of the James Beard Foundation Restaurant Awards Committee. She has been inducted into the Arizona Culinary Hall of Fame, received the Greater Phoenix Chef's Association Humanitarian of the Year award, and was named a Master of the Southwest by *Phoenix Home and Garden* magazine. She has studied cooking at the Cordon Bleu (London), Ecole LeNotre, and Luberon College. She and her husband, Terry, have lived in Phoenix, Arizona, for more than 36 years.